Secrets of the
SNOW GLOBES

January 29, 2016

Dianne Novak

Secrets of the
SNOW GLOBES

THE SEARCH FOR THE BUCCANEER'S BOUNTY

DIANNE NOVAK

TATE PUBLISHING
AND ENTERPRISES, LLC

Published by Tate Publishing & Enterprises, LLC
127 E. Trade Center Terrace | Mustang, Oklahoma 73064 USA
1.888.361.9473 | www.tatepublishing.com

Tate Publishing is committed to excellence in the publishing industry. The company reflects the philosophy established by the founders, based on Psalm 68:11,
"The Lord gave the word and great was the company of those who published it."

Book design copyright © 2014 by Tate Publishing, LLC. All rights reserved.
Cover design by Junriel Boquecosa
Interior design by Jake Muelle
Photographer's credit—Archibald Studios in Andover, Minnesota.

Published in the United States of America
ISBN: 978-1-62994-524-8
1. Fiction / Action & Adventure
2. Fiction / Fantasy / General
14.01.29

DEDICATION

To the glory of God, as in all things.
For my husband, Tony, who helps keep the kid in me alive.

CHAPTER 1

The sun poured its golden heat over Jake's head, sparking bright glints in his curly blond hair. He looked up; bright blue eyes squeezed shut, letting the sunlight shine directly on his face as he pulled the last of the scraggly weeds from the flower garden. He looked at the piece of living trash in his hand.

"No! Oh crud!" He held one of Mom's prized hot pink petunias, not a dirty old weed. He'd been so careful, wanting to show he was old enough to be trusted with Mom's favorite gardens. Summer in the big Kincaid yard was sunny, colorful, and smelled great. One garden was filled with tall lupines and bell-shaped columbines to attract butterflies and hummingbirds. The garden bed outside the back door grew fragrant herbs for Mom's restaurant. And there were patches of petunias, daisies, and day lilies wherever there was sunshine.

Mom normally took care of the gardens herself. But this summer, Mom had a chance to work with a famous Chicago chef who was visiting in Minnesota for the season. It was a really big deal for her. And it meant she was working full time until the school year started again. Jake wanted to show everyone that he was grown up enough to take care of Mom's gardens. But now this—he'd taken his eye off his work for just one second, and he'd ruined everything.

Jake dropped to his knees, quickly trying to press the roots back into the rich, dark soil. He scrabbled a deeper hole into the small mound of dirt where the flower had been growing. He pushed the plant in and patted the earth gently over it. The petunia drooped but stayed in the ground. His stocky body shaking a little, he jumped to his feet and ran to pull the hose over, wanting to give the little flower a good solid drink, praying it would survive.

He pushed the backpack he carried everywhere with him farther away from the flowers. He didn't want all his important stuff to get wet by accident. He turned on the water—not wide open because he'd learned the hard way that too much water was just as bad for flowers as not enough. He turned back to the garden, hoping the flower was still standing, that it hadn't fallen over and died.

"What are you doing?!" The hose jerked in his hand as the water was suddenly shut off. He turned to see his sister, Becca, cranking the faucet. She flipped her long, thick, dark-brown braid back over her shoulder, a stuck-up gesture Jake knew only too well. "Are you trying to make a mess?"

"I'm watering the flowers," he said crossly. "Turn that back on."

Becca stalked over to him, her dark brown eyes flashing angrily at his tone. "What are you trying to do? Drown them?" She spoke to him like he was a five-year-old. She always had to act like the boss of everyone.

"I'm taking care of Mom's gardens. I just weeded, and now I'm going to water." Jake stomped back to the faucet to turn the water back on, hoping Becca would follow him and not look at the sad, limp flower. "I know what I'm doing."

"There's a better way to do this." Becca made a move as though she would turn the faucet off again, but Jake stood firmly in front of it.

"I know what I'm doing," he insisted again.

"You can't use the hose that way," Becca said, making a grab for it. "You have to put the sprayer head on it."

Jake pulled the running hose out of her reach. "I know that. I was just running water to … clean off the hose connection." In fact, he'd forgotten about the sprayer head, but he wasn't about to say that to Becca. "Go away. I'll finish this job myself."

Becca made another quick grab at the hose. "I just want it done right for Mom. Give me the hose, and I'll show you."

"No!" Jake jerked the hose and water splashed across their feet. "Leave me alone!"

"Stop it!" Becca jumped back from the water. "You're soaking my shoes."

"Oh, they're not soaked." He flicked the hose toward her feet again. "Yet."

"Knock it off!" Becca made a quick move toward the faucet. "Just turn it off!"

Jake held the running hose up further, like a shield, to keep her away from the faucet handle. Becca made a sharp move to one side. He turned toward her, and she quickly jumped the other way and reached in for the spigot. Jake jerked back toward her, and water splashed over her feet again. Becca shrieked and grabbed his arm, trying to hold the stream of water away from her. He yelled and clutched at her hand.

Then they were both grabbing at each other and at the hose, and water was spraying everywhere. Cold water drenched their hair and dripped down their necks, and their screams and shouts got louder. The more they struggled, the more water flew around them. Suddenly, they heard a window slide open, and their dad's voice rang out. "What is going on?"

No one meant for it to happen. But the fighters turned as though pulled by a cord toward the sound, the hose tight between their hands, water spritzing forcefully through their fingers. Water squirted through the screen and straight into Dad's face.

CHAPTER 2

With one motion, as though it had suddenly become electrified, Becca and Jake dropped the hose. But it was too late. They stood, stunned, waiting for Dad's explosion.

When the water hit his face, Dad jumped back from the screened window. But now he was back, water dripping off the end of his nose. "In the house. Now." His voice was quiet, scary quiet. Becca stepped over to the faucet and twisted it closed. Jake grabbed his backpack, and Becca followed him into the house.

Dad met them at the back door and silently pointed them to the living room. They both kicked off their wet tennis shoes inside the door. They didn't want to make things worse by tracking wet grass across the floor. Becca risked a quick glance at Dad's face and was sorry she did. He did not look at all happy. Not at all. They walked wordlessly into the living room.

Becca and Jake sat side by side on the couch, their eyes fixed on the carpet. Dad didn't say anything. Becca scuffed her bare toes across the rug fibers. Dad didn't say anything. Jake shifted his backpack off his shoulders. Dad still didn't say anything.

Just when Becca thought she might burst, Dad said, "I thought this was going to work out." He didn't sound angry. No, it was worse. He sounded … disappointed. Becca looked up and saw the expression on his face. Yeah. Disappointed.

"Dad, I'm sorry," she said, though she didn't really feel too sorry. "I was just trying to show him how to do it right."

"I was doing it right," Jake said. "I know how to take care of the gardens."

"But you didn't have the sprayer on—"

"I was going to put it on after—"

"That's it." Dad's voice cut through their bickering. "Enough. This has got to stop." Dad paced in front of them. "School just ended. We have a whole summer vacation to get through. Your mom really deserves this chance to work with Chef Morgan. But she'll go back to part-time, if she thinks you two can't handle this."

Becca shifted uncomfortably, and Jake stared at his toes.

"We thought you kids were old enough. At eight and ten—"

"Almost nine," Jake protested.

Dad's look was cold. "Eight. And barely ten. I made special arrangements to work from home so I could be here for emergencies—big stuff, not nonsense like this. Do you get that?" Dad waited for a response.

"Yes, sir."

"Yeah, Daddy."

"If you kids can't make this work, we're going to have to hire a *baby*sitter—and I stress the word 'baby' here. You'd hate that, wouldn't you?" Again, he wanted an answer.

"We would."

"Oh man, yeah."

"So do I need to start looking for a sitter?"

"No, sir."

"Please don't, Dad."

Dad stopped pacing and took a deep breath. "Okay. So here's the new plan. You will get along at all times, in all things. There will be no yelling, shoving, hitting, kicking, or whining. No more bossing your brother around, Becca. And, Jake, you can't just go off like a bomb every time someone wants to help you."

"Yes, sir."

"I know, Dad. Sorry."

Dad sighed deeply. "You two need to get along. And I think I know a good way to promote teamwork." He thought for a moment. "Yep, you've got a new job. You're going to clean out the shed. Together."

"That thing's empty," Jake protested.

"Not the new one. The old shed."

Becca started. "The old shed? I've never been in there. Don't you always tell us it's too dangerous?"

Dad smiled. Becca decided it wasn't an altogether nice smile. "But aren't you two trying to prove to me you're old enough to take care of some things around here? It's time we start making use of that new shed—and that means cleaning out the old one."

Jake looked at Becca. "That old wreck of shed? Really?"

Becca shrugged. "I guess he's serious."

"I'm serious, all right. And I don't want to hear of a single problem, even a little disagreement. Work together to get the job done." Dad pushed his damp hair back off his forehead. "And no more hoses for today."

CHAPTER 3

D andelion fluff and dust drifted up around Becca and Jake as
they shuffled through the yard toward the old ramshackle
shed. Cicadas buzzed overhead, droning lazily, in rhythm with
the kids' pace across the grass. Summer in Ramsey, an outlying
suburb of Minneapolis, was starting off beautifully. The semirural
town, and the large lot of the Kincaid house, was a great place to
spend a warm early summer day. Jake stopped, squatting to see
the progress a colony of brown ants was making on their latest
anthill. He looked closely, watching the ants rush into the hole,
their mandibles empty, and hurry back out carrying a grain of
sand. He began to settle into a seated position until Becca's sharp
voice cut into his daydream.

"Jake, come on. We gotta do this." She stood before the door
of the old shed, wrinkling her nose as she looked at the peeling
paint and crumbling wood. The new metal shed stood in the far
corner of the yard, gleaming brightly in the sunshine as though
waiting eagerly to be filled up and made useful. The hand-built,
aging wooden shed sagged away from the new building. It looked
ready to be torn down, waiting patiently to be done with it all.

Jake dragged himself and his backpack up to Becca's side, his
shoulders slumping like the shed. "Clean out *all* of it?" he whined.
Becca gently slapped his arm with the back of her hand. "Right,

no whining …" Jake allowed his pack to slip off his shoulders, and took a step toward the shed. "So where do we start?"

Becca pulled on the door handle. The door groaned but did not budge. She grabbed on with both hands and yanked again. A moan, a slight screech, and the door moved an inch. The shed was not quite ready to give up after all. Jake took hold with Becca, and they both leaned back, straining to move the door. With a loud squeal and cracking sound, the door suddenly let loose, and Becca and Jake flew back, falling to their seats, facing the dark, musty interior of the shed.

The door wobbled on its hinges, looking as though it had opened for the last time. A few dust particles drifted lazily out of the doorway, glinting briefly in the sun before blowing gently away into the air. Sunlight picked out a few details just inside the door, showing cobwebs, a few scrunched boxes, and a light cord swaying slightly in the breeze.

"Looks … kinda dirty," Becca said, her sunburned nose wrinkling with mild disgust. "Sorta buggy, maybe."

Jake jumped up. "Yeah, cool." He charged through the doorway and pulled the light cord, shedding the skimpy light of the uncovered sixty-watt lightbulb over the scene. He swept his arms around his head, looking like a crazy person to Becca. "Wooh, webs!" He laughed as he wiped his hand over his face. "Bet there's spiders!"

"Don't sound so happy." Becca got up off the grass, carefully brushing off the back of her khaki shorts. "I could do without them." She walked to the door and peered carefully inside.

"Look at all this stuff, Becca. We've got loads to look through. Like a treasure hunt." Jake's eyes gleamed as he thought of all the potential swag they could find. "Just like a pirate treasure hunt!"

"Maybe we should get a broom …"

"Why? It's just dust." Even as he spoke, however, he started back toward the house. "What else?"

"Nothing—I'll put out this tarp so we can set stuff on it. Oh, wait, drag the trash can back with you." Becca pulled the old canvas sheet off a stack of boxes, as Jake accelerated toward the house, in a hurry to dig into adventure.

CHAPTER 4

Becca pushed her way behind another pile of boxes that rocked dangerously as she passed. The tall stack blocked the feeble light from the single bulb that hung in the middle of the shed, throwing her into deep shadows. Jake looked up from the box he'd been checking and suddenly found himself alone. "Becca?" he called uncertainly. "Where'd you go?" With no response, Jake shifted nervously toward the door and sunlight. "No fooling around, huh, Becca …" A scraping sound from Becca's dark corner was enough to send Jake sprinting out into the yard. He ran, looking back over his shoulder and barreled straight into a young redheaded, freckle-faced girl who was peering into the shed. They fell heavily to the ground, both grunting loudly.

"Geez, Jake!" the redhead hollered. "What the heck?"

"Something … in the shed …" Jake panted, looking fearfully back at the old shed.

"Looks like lots of stuff in the shed," she responded. "But it's just boxes and junk …"

Jake looked at her with disgust. "Uh, duh, I know that. But there's something else …"

Becca appeared out of the shadows and poked her head around the doorjamb. "What's all the noise? Hey, Paige, when did you get here?" Paige McGuire was Becca's best friend and had been since she and her mom moved into the neighborhood three years ago. It was Becca and Paige's plan to spend every single day of summer vacation together.

"Just in time to get whaled on by your baby brother." Paige picked herself up off the ground. "He was kinda spooked by cardboard boxes."

"Was not!" He turned angrily from Paige to Becca. "And where were you? Suddenly I was in there alone."

Becca held up her hands in a quieting gesture. "Sorry, sorry—I just dug in behind a stack of boxes. I didn't hear you. Don't blow a gasket." She looked meaningfully toward the open den window at the corner of the house. "Dad won't like the yelling."

Jake stopped short, just as he was taking his next breath for an angry remark. He too glanced at the house then let out his breath with a big sigh. "Right. Got it. Just don't hide like that, when we're in the dark."

Paige watched them with interest. "Well, this is something new, isn't it? Becca and Jake, stopping their own fight before it begins." She laughed. "Marcus had better get here quick to see history in the making." Marcus Bowman was the final member of this friendship foursome. He lived two blocks away, with his parents and baby brother and sister. "So why the truce?" Paige asked.

"Had a little problem with a hose this morning," Becca said sheepishly. "Dad threatened to get a babysitter if we couldn't get along. We're proving we can work together with this." Becca grinned and waved at the old shed. "There's actually some kind of interesting stuff in here. Want to help?"

Paige wrinkled her freckled nose as she stepped closer to look into the dark. "Mostly it looks dirty. How can there be anything interesting under all that dust and cobwebs? And I'm not sure I should help you with your punishment. Your dad might think that's cheating."

Jake got off the grass and walked back into the shed. "Well, at least we wouldn't lose you behind a stack of boxes. We'd hear you talking and talking …" He still stung from her claim that he was afraid of cardboard boxes.

Becca whacked his arm. "Jake, don't be mean."

Paige just laughed. "No, it's fair. I teased him, he gets pay back. And I do tend to talk when I'm in situations that make me nervous." She cocked her head to one side. "And when I'm feeling happy." She thought a little more. "And when I'm awake …" Her bubbly giggle rang out as she laughed at herself.

"What ho, friends!" A voice called from near the fence that surrounded the Kincaid yard.

"Marcus!" Jake called happily. Marcus grinned as he stepped through the gate and sauntered across the backyard.

"What's happening, my fellow travelers?" Jake liked the way Marcus talked, even if it was kind of unusual. Marcus was brilliant—everybody said so. And he studied all kinds of things, even more than he had to for school. Outwardly, he was the least like the others—older (he was eleven), very serious, African American. But Marcus and Becca had been friends since they were babies. And Marcus treated Jake like a friend, even though he was almost three years older. He never made him feel like a dumb kid. That meant the world to Jake.

"We're exploring," Jake shouted, suddenly excited to tell his friend about their task. "Just in our shed, but there's lots of stuff to find."

Marcus rubbed his hands together. "A treasure hunt, is it? Sounds promising. Hey, Paige, Becca. Looking good." He brushed a cobweb off Becca's sleeve. "Looks like you've been working hard."

"They've been naughty," Paige teased. "But I guess they could use our help."

"Let's have a plan," Becca said. "We should get organized."

Jake rolled his eyes, and Paige gave him a quick grin. Marcus just said, "Of course, a plan. Statistically, we'll go through more items if we each take a quadrant of the shed. However, if we work as two teams, we can work more efficiently to move larger objects."

Becca shook her head. "Or we can just bring each item out into the sun so we can really see what's in it. It's all got to come out eventually."

"And then we all get to see everything and work together," Paige said. "I like that."

"Then that's the plan!" Jake called as he ran back into the shed. "Let's get dusty!"

CHAPTER 5

The four friends dug through boxes and bags, dragging it all into the daylight. On the lawn, they separated everything into piles—obvious trash into the garbage can, items that were definite keepers over by the new shed, and a stack of items on the tarp, because they needed discussion. Some of the stuff was maybe not trash, but it wasn't clear if they should keep it either. Old rakes with just a few teeth broken off, boxes of tangled Christmas lights that Becca and Jake had never seen used, oily pieces of machinery—lawnmower? Bike? Car? Marcus knew some of them, but there were many parts that just looked dirty and useless. They ended up making a pile of things for Mr. Kincaid to check.

Almost every box was crushed or broken in some way. Jake thought they should just throw all these items out. At one point, he tried to throw out a battered box that turned out to hold the Easter decorations Mom put up every year. After that, Paige worked right next to him to make sure he didn't toss a hidden treasure. "You can't judge a good thing by its beat-up box," she scolded him.

They were making pretty good progress, having dug through about a quarter of the contents of the shed, when Becca found the box. It was tucked on a shelf, hidden under a couple of layers of empty shoe boxes. Becca swept the lighter cardboard aside and stared. The box was perfect, not a mark or crunch anywhere. In the dimness, it almost seemed to glow slightly. She reached up to touch it gingerly. She jerked her hand back as she felt a slight tingle. What was in this unmarked box?

She reached back up and this time kept her fingers on the heavyweight cardboard. The tingle was really quite a pleasant feeling, warming her hand. She reached up with her other hand to try and lift the container off the shelf. But it was too heavy for her to take down on her own. "Hey, Marcus, give me a hand, can you?"

Marcus came over and reached up to take one end. "Whoa! What is that?"

Becca took the other end. "I have no idea. I can't see any writing on the box. Let's get it down where we can really look at it."

"It may be electrical—not safe to hold for too long."

"No, it's fine. Can't you feel it? The warmth … kind of cozy, really."

Marcus almost chuckled but choked it back when he realized she was right. The box did seem welcoming somehow. "Let's see what this is." They lifted together and brought it carefully out into the sunshine.

Once it was out where they could really see the box, Becca saw that there was, in fact, some writing on it. There was only one word written across the top. Perfect, beautifully formed cursive writing—and it said "Becca." A box she had never seen, buried deep in the old shed, and it had her name on it.

Marcus and Becca knelt beside the box. The cardboard seemed ordinary enough—except that it was in perfect condition. How long had it been sitting in that filthy shed? But there wasn't a speck of dirt on it. Becca still felt that slight energy coming off it, though there was no sound or anything to indicate what could be causing it.

Becca's name had been written perfectly across the edges of the box flaps then taped over with crystal clear packing tape. Even that seemed almost impossible. No skips or misalignments in any of the beautifully flowing lines.

Paige and Jake hauled a couple of boxes out of the shed and saw Marcus and Becca sitting on the grass. "Hey, lazies. We're working here!" Paige said.

"You must see this," Marcus replied. "It's something really remarkable."

"It's got Becca's name on it," Jake said, dropping his box and reaching for theirs.

"Don't!" Becca cried. "It's ... just ... don't."

Jake pulled back his hand as he felt the slight electrical charge. "What *is* this?"

Paige sat beside Becca, holding her hand out cautiously toward the box. "That's odd. So what's in it?"

"I have no idea."

"But, Becca, it's got your name on it, and it's obviously brand new. Who put it in here?"

"No clue."

"A birthday present?"

"For ten months from now?"

Marcus put his head to one side, regarding the box. "It's really not that new," he observed. "The quality of this cardboard—its weight, the way the flaps fit, the corner construction. I was studying the invention of containers and how they have evolved over the years—"

"You're studying cardboard," Becca stated, disbelieving.

"Well, kind of a sidetrack. I'd gotten interested in shipping originally and shipping containers—"

"Never mind, got it, got it. So you don't think this cardboard is new. We'll just take that as a given."

"I'm just saying that I don't think, despite most appearances, that this box was put in here recently. You can see the dust on the shelf is undisturbed. The wall behind where it sat is lighter than the wall above it. So the box has been protecting that wall from the dirt and grime that has gathered over the years. And this cursive style is very old-fashioned. Very few people, even adults, write in this way any longer." Marcus looked seriously at the others. "This box has been waiting here for Becca for quite some time."

Becca shivered. Waiting for her. That sounded so ... certain. Scary but exciting. "I guess ... I should ... should I open it?"

CHAPTER 6

Paige shoved Becca's arm. "Of course you should open it! What a goofy question. Get on with it!"

Jake gave his enthusiastic agreement. "Yes! Let's get this thing open!"

Marcus took out his small pocket knife. "Let's approach this carefully. We don't know what's in there, so we must proceed with caution." He handed Becca the knife. "Slit through the tape with this. Not too deep, so you don't hit whatever's inside."

Becca took the knife from him and took a deep breath. She put knife to tape and pressed gently. As she dragged the blade across, the tape seemed to split as easily as a zipper. The flaps popped up slightly. Becca handed the knife back to Marcus, then paused with her hands on the box top. "Here goes." She squeezed her eyes shut tight, a little nervous about what she'd find then pulled the box open. She squinted one eye open, then both. "Oh."

All that showed was a layer of cardboard, with a white envelope taped precisely in the center. Again, that beautiful handwriting showed her name—"Becca."

"So do we open the envelope or lift off the cardboard?"

"Cardboard!" the three others cried in unison.

Becca nodded then slid her fingers between the box sides and the edges of the cardboard layer. She lifted it straight up and set it carefully to one side. With that thick layer of protection removed, they all saw the tops of shining, rounded glass globes. Eight of them across the top, and the box was deep enough to hold at least two layers. More than a dozen round clear orbs, that held … what?

They all peered down into box, eyeing the contents of the globes. Was that the top of a castle? And that one looked like a horse, perhaps. One looked like a very old-fashioned car. What could these be?

"Snow globes!" Marcus exclaimed. "I think we're looking at snow globes."

"Who would give me a box of snow globes?" Becca said. "Where did they come from? Who wrote my name on the box?" She couldn't imagine why anyone would have a box full of globes, as pretty as they might be. Globes filled with water, surrounding a miniature scene of some kind. And little plastic snowflakes and glitter that would float around when the globe was shaken up.

"And your name is on the envelope," Marcus reminded them. He lifted the envelope carefully off the cardboard, releasing it from the small circle of tape that held it in place. He handed it to Becca. "There must be something in here."

Becca turned it over, feeling the thickness of the cream-colored paper. She slid her finger carefully under the flap, testing to see if she could lift it carefully open. The flap lifted easily, yielding to her slightest pressure, as though just waiting for her touch. She slid the single sheet of elegant writing paper out and unfolded it. "It's from Aunt Elizabeth!" she exclaimed. But she died a long time ago."

"Aunt Elizabeth!" Jake said disbelievingly. "She's been dead practically since I was a baby!"

"You weren't a baby—you were three. And I was about five."

Jake made a face at his sister. "Well, nearly a baby. What I'm trying to say is that she couldn't have just put it here."

"No, she couldn't," Becca said. Looking at Paige, she added, "She's actually my mom's aunt—our great-aunt. She told the best stories—told me a new one every time I saw her."

"I remember her," Marcus said. "I met her a few times. She always said you were the daughter she never had."

Becca laughed. "That's right—she did! Mom told her she could take me home a few times too."

Marcus said "And Aunt Elizabeth would say—" and here he imitated the voice of an elderly person—"Oh, Shannon, your daughter is destined for great adventures. She's got a right to be a bit high-spirited.' That made your mom laugh."

Jake said, "High-spirited. Yeah, that's what I'd call it." Becca punched him in the arm good-naturedly.

Paige said, "She sounds wonderful. I wish I could have met her. If that's how she felt about you, Becca, I can see why she'd leave you such a great gift."

"I loved her so much. I've always been sad that I didn't get to have more time with her." Becca skimmed the note. "It says here she got the snow globes from her aunt. She says Mom didn't need adventure, that I'd learn from these journeys." She looked up from the letter. "There's that word again—adventure. What did she mean by that, do you suppose?"

Jake pulled at Becca's arm impatiently. "We can think about that later. Come on, let's look at one. Pleeeeease …" Jake was practically twitching, he was so excited to see a globe.

"All right, all right. Just calm down." Becca touched the top of one of the globes tentatively. "Which one? There are so many …"

Paige encouraged her. "Just pick what you feel. Any one will be gorgeous, I just know it. Go on, pick one."

Becca tucked the letter back in the envelope and the envelope in the back pocket of her shorts. She lightly stroked the tops of the globes. Why did this decision seem so difficult? It's just a snow globe—but it felt as though her choice would totally change their lives. Becca took a deep breath and decided.

CHAPTER 7

Becca let her breath out as she carefully lifted the left corner snow globe out of the carton. Its clear glass sparkled like a diamond in the sunshine. How long had it been in the old shed? There wasn't a speck of dust on it. She ran her fingers gently over the glass. The sphere felt cool against her skin, giving her fingertips a slight tingly sensation. The globe dazzled, magnifying the bright sunlight pouring down on them.

The glass ball sat atop a carved wooden base, dark and sleek. It felt almost silky in her hand as she balanced its weight carefully. She lifted it up so all of them could see into the interior scene.

Inside the globe, in its own small universe, a sailing ship rode the waves. It appeared to be a large vessel, with three masts, flying all its sails. The rigging lines that held the canvas were taut as though straining forward in a full wind. The waves that supported this carved schooner were deep blue, sparkling beneath the light layer of artificial snow that covered the bottom of the globe.

Entranced by the detailed work of the globe, they felt a change in the air around them. It grew damp, and Becca could taste salt on her lips. Was that a seagull's cry she heard? The rush of waves? She tore her gaze away from the snow globe and looked at the others to see if they felt and heard these same things.

Marcus was licking his lips as though he did taste something unusual. Jake was peering around as though searching for the source of a distant noise. Paige wiped at her face as though wiping a fine mist away. What was happening to them?

Marcus finally broke the spell. "Do you … can you feel that?" As he spoke, they felt a change again and were simply in a summertime Minnesota backyard, warm and dry. A cicada buzzed, but no birds cried. "What was that?"

Becca set the snow globe carefully on the grass at the center of their little circle. "Was it the … ocean? Near where this ship is?" She immediately shrugged and dipped her head, to fend off their expected sarcastic remarks.

Marcus lifted the globe, looking closely at the vessel inside. "That's what it felt like," he said slowly. "This looks like a three-masted barque. Two longboats hanging port and starboard."

Paige pushed Marcus's arm. "What are you talking about? Like you know sailboats."

Marcus looked at her with infinite patience. "A ship, Paige. A fine vessel like this is always a ship. I did a lot of reading about it last summer. Interesting stuff. Sailing ships and pirates in the Caribbean and Bahamas."

"Like Captain Sparrow?" Jake asked.

"No, like the real thing, Jake. Those movies are just make-believe. Real pirates sailed the southern seas in barques and schooners and galleons. They captured merchant ships and attacked gold transports and—"

Becca interrupted, "We don't have time for the full lesson right now, Marcus. Maybe later. How come we heard and felt what we did?"

"I don't know," Marcus said as he peered at the ship from all sides. "Look, you can see the ship's name. There, along the prow. She's called *Bethany*." Sure enough, small lettering showed along the front of the ship, just below the delicate railing that ran along the deck. "And look at this!" He pointed to the top of the main mast in the center of the ship.

There, at the very tip of the mast, was a small bloodred flag. Square in the center, in miniature but clearly visible, was a skull and crossbones. "Pirates!" Jake whispered.

"I thought pirate flags are black," Paige said.

"Some were, but some were red. Black for death. Red for battle," Marcus said. "They even had hourglasses to show their victims that time was running out. Spears and cutlasses—broad swords that is. Bleeding hearts, blazing cannonballs. Lots of different images."

"*Bethany* doesn't sound like a pirate's name."

"Sometimes they stole merchant ships and used them. They didn't change the name because they could fool other ships into thinking they were safe. Take down the pirate flag and it still looked like a merchant ship."

Paige reached for the globe. "May I?" She took the globe carefully and turned it gently upside down. Light white flakes danced down from the bottom then flitted about the globe as Paige righted it again. "It really is a snow globe."

"Of course, silly," Jake said. "What did you think?"

Paige shook her head wonderingly. "Not sure. It feels like more than just a plain old snow globe. But I can't explain it any more than that."

Marcus took the globe carefully. "I know what you mean. It feels like something important here, but there is nothing in the look of this item to warrant that feeling. I'm not accustomed to not being able to explain such a strong impression."

Jake held out his hands. "Can I hold it for a minute? I'll be super careful, I promise." Marcus smiled and handed the globe to the youngest of their foursome. Jake held it as though it was a baby in a firm but gentle grip and nestled close to his chest to help support the weight. "It feels funny, but in a good way.

Becca, Aunt Elizabeth gave them to you. Did she ever talk to you about them?"

Becca patted Jake's back, and he handed the globe carefully to her. "I don't remember her mentioning them. She just told stories. Adventures. But she was a great storyteller. It always sounded like she'd been there. An old Western cattle drive. A princess finding her true love. They were beautiful stories." She looked at the tiny perfect ship under glass. "Did she tell me about sailing once? I think maybe …" Becca shook the globe lightly, stirring up the snow. "And they all seemed to start with a poem. She'd take me in her lap, tell me a poem, and then launch into these great stories."

Paige took the globe back, peering closely at it, examining the base, the glass, every inch. "What makes this so special?" She looked at the bottom then peered closer. "Hey, is there a little hinge here?" She handed it back to Becca.

"There is! So there must be a little door. But how does it open? I can't quite see."

Jake reached over and unzipped a pocket on his backpack. "I've got a magnifying glass." After he pulled the glass from the pocket, he automatically slipped the pack straps over his shoulders. The backpack was as much a part of his clothes each day as his jeans and T-shirt were. He never could quite explain why he felt the need to have his pack so close to him all the time. It was filled with bits and pieces, things he found during his day, as well as important purchases he made with his allowance. No one even gave it much thought anymore because they were so used to seeing it on his back.

"Perfect!" Becca took the glass and held it close to the base of the snow globe. "It is a little door." She squinted at it for a moment then set aside the glass. "If I just twist this …" As she said this, a small door opened in her hand. "There's something in here!"

CHAPTER 8

Becca showed them all the small door she had just opened in the base of the snow globe. "There's definitely something in here."

"What is it?" Paige asked.

"Looks like some paper." Becca carefully pulled at the tightly folded paper and teased it out into the sunshine. She handed the globe to Paige and unfolded the note carefully, pressing it flat against the grass.

"Well, read it!" Paige exclaimed. "I'm gonna die of curiosity."

Becca laughed at Paige's typical exaggeration. "Okay, okay. It's a poem, I think."

> Weigh anchor, ye lubbers and unfurl the mainsail.
> Brace up your heartstrings; put your courage to the test.
> Hands to your cutlass and look sharp at the gunwale,
> Prick up your ears now and hear the tale of your quest.
>
> Tis booty you're after, a buccaneer's bounty.
> A treasure's been lost and your home is behind you.
> Show yourself fearless; worry not for your safety.
> Accomplish your task and your history renew.

Becca looked up from the page she'd just read. "What?!"

Marcus said, "It's pirate language. The kind of things a pirate might say. Read it again."

Becca did. As she read it again, Paige absently turned the globe upside down, then upright again. The artificial snow swirled in the liquid and the globe sparked sharply in the sunlight.

A slight breeze kicked up in what had been still summer air. Jake raised his face, relishing the sudden coolness on his skin. He said, wonderingly, "It feels like fall." He got to his feet and tried to catch a small tuft of cotton that the wind had picked up. "I thought the cottonwoods were done shedding." The large trees that edged the back of the Kincaids' yard released white fluffy seeds each year in the early summer.

"They are done," Marcus said. "Where is this coming from?" All the children stood, Becca still clutching the poem, as the breeze grew stronger and more cotton filled the air.

The wind ruffled their hair, and Paige actually shivered slightly. "It's seventy-eight degrees today—how come the wind feels so chilly?" She shivered again as the puff of breeze turned into a stronger gust.

Becca lifted her hand as the air began to fill more and more with white puffs blown on the wind. She grabbed at them, trying to catch a sample. "Look, this isn't right …"

Marcus was trying to catch the cotton as well. "No, it's … look, it's not cotton." The children all looked around, peering at the thickening white surrounding them. "It's … it's snowflakes!"

Paige shook her head, as much to deny the statement as to get the hair out of her eyes. "It's June! It doesn't snow in June, even here in Minnesota!" The wind continued to build, growing stronger, and the snowflakes swirled around them. They huddled together, protecting their faces from the sharpening wind. "But it's a blizzard!"

The wind built and began to howl softly. The snow thickened, and soon they could see nothing but white—blinding white light filled with sharp cold stings as the flakes whipped against them. The swirling white and the rising howl began to confuse the children as they grabbed each other by the hands, trying to stay upright.

"What's happening?!" Becca cried, shouting above the turmoil.

"Don't know—hang on!" Marcus yelled as the wind began to shake them, pushing them off their feet to tumble to the ground. They rolled together, clinging, as the wind tried to pluck them away from each other. The lawn seemed to pitch, rising up, then down, then spinning faster and faster. They felt as though they were tossed into the air, then thumped to the grass again. Their world tilted and stung, spun and howled, faster, louder, going on and on with no letup until the snow swirled them into unconsciousness, no longer aware of the sound and the movement and the fear surrounding them.

CHAPTER 9

The first thing Becca felt as she came to her senses was the heat. Thick and warm, the air pressed against her skin, feeling more like a blanket than something she should breathe. Minnesota in the summer—humid, hot, quiet with only the occasional cicada hum to break the peace. But something was different. She lay on the ground, eyes closed, her senses trying to reorder themselves.

There'd been snow, swirling wind, freezing blasts. Now heat, sunshine, a breeze that smelled of ... lake? An ocean? Beneath her hand, Becca felt neither snow drifts nor crisp green grass. Sand, soft, sugar sand. A beach? How did she get from a Minnesota summer day in her backyard, to a blizzard, to a sandy beach? Slowly, almost against her will, her eyelids fluttered, then opened slightly.

Brilliant sunshine, blue sky, a few white wispy clouds. Nothing strange there. She carefully rolled her head to the left, blinking to clear her vision. As her eyes adjusted from the glaring sun, she saw a short stretch of sand that led into a ... a forest? But it wasn't the pine or oak woods Becca was used to seeing just beyond her backyard. These were pines, but they looked very different than the white pines and spruces of home. Tall, spindly trunks with tufted branches only near the top. They were surrounded by undergrowth like Becca had never seen. Ferns that appeared to be as tall as she was, white and blue flowers the size of small plates, grasses as thick as her finger. Confused, Becca turned to the other side, trying to make sense of her surroundings.

But this was no help because she was confronted only with Jake's face, quiet and peaceful as though asleep, about two feet from her own. As she watched, unsure if he was alive or not, his eyelids fluttered and opened. Focus took a moment to return, then he saw her and his eyes lit up as he recognized her. At least he was with her. They could manage anything together. But what exactly did they have to manage here?

"Jake, you okay?" she asked.

He considered, wiggling his toes, moving his head slightly to lift his mouth from the sand. "Yeah, I think. You?"

In response, Becca slowly sat up, shaking her head lightly, looking at her hands, arms, legs, and feet. She realized she was still clutching the poem. "Yeah, okay." Then her gaze focused beyond Jake, her eyes widening. He pushed himself up off the sand and turned to follow Becca's shocked stare.

Before them stretched yards and yards of white, delicate sand—empty and pristine, no footprints or towels or pop cans. A perfect beach, sliding right into a deep blue-green body of water, larger than Jake had ever seen. The sun sparkled off the tips of white-capped waves, leaping playfully from the surface of the water. Gentle waves lapped against the shore, rhythmically whooshing over the tops of each other. Water as far as Jake could see—no boats, no land, no anything but waves and waves. Could this be an ocean? Jake had never seen one except in pictures. But it looked different than Lake Superior—the biggest body of water he'd ever seen in person. Even its smell had a tang he'd never detected in any of the Minnesota lakes and rivers he knew.

Behind them, closer to the forest, Marcus grunted softly as he pushed into a sitting position. He reached over and gently touched Paige, who still lay motionless in the sand.

Paige groaned and rolled over slowly. She opened her eyes, squinted against the brilliant sunshine, then clutched a fistful of sand. "What is this? Where's the grass? How …" She sat up, letting the sand trickle out through her fingers. "Where'd all this sand come from?" She looked around, saw her friends' faces were as confused as her own. "What is going on here?"

Becca shrugged, Marcus looked thoughtful, and Jake jumped up, pointing to the water. "That's the ocean, I think. A real ocean! How did that get in our backyard?"

Becca looked at the paper in her hand. "What happened to the snow globe? I've only got the poem." She decided to fold the poem carefully and put it into her back pocket.

Marcus brushed at the sand near his foot, digging the globe out of the beach. He lifted it, and it glinted brightly, almost winking back at them as they gazed at it.

"It was the snow globe," Becca said. Marcus just nodded.

"What is that supposed to mean?" Paige demanded. "What could a snow globe do?"

Marcus nodded again. "That must be it. I don't know how, but the snow globe transported us somehow."

Becca said, "I don't think it was just touching it. I think it had to be from reading the poem. And we tipped it over to start the snow."

"Beach and ocean does not necessarily mean pirates," Paige objected.

Jake pointed out into the ocean. "No, but I think that means pirates."

They all looked and saw, just rounding the curve of land to their left, a sailing ship. At the top of the tallest mast, they could see a black flag waving in the wind, a white skull and crossbones emblazoned on the dark background.

"That means pirates," Marcus agreed. "And I believe we must be on an island. Look at the curve, the angle the ship is coming. It's rounding a fairly narrow point of land."

Becca shook her head in amazement. "You would know that. Can you tell where they are headed?"

"I believe they may be tacking into this natural harbor. They may intend to land here."

Paige laughed. "That big ship is not landing on this beach!"

"No, that isn't what landing means. But they'll drop anchor in the harbor and row onto the island in longboats. They'll land the small boats hanging off the sides of the ship."

"Well, I don't want to be on this beach when they land here!" Paige jumped to her feet then swayed slightly. "Whoa, I am still not over that wild ride."

Becca braced up her friend, giving her an arm for support. "You're right, Paige. We should find someplace to hide."

"The trees!" Jake hitched his backpack further up onto his shoulders. "There'll be someplace to hide in there."

"Hold on, Jake." Marcus pulled at the pack. "Let's put the globe inside here. Easier to carry, protected."

Becca winced. "Jake, you have to be really careful with that."

Jake rolled his eyes. "Uh, duh." He waited while Marcus settled the globe and zipped up the pack. "Now come on. That ship is still coming!"

They all hurried off the beach and away from their exposed position.

"Why would they be landing here?" Paige panted as she ran slowly in the soft sand. "Did they see us? Are they coming after us?"

"Unlikely. They are still far enough off to not have a good view of our position on the beach."

"They must need to get water, or maybe food," Becca said. "That's why we've got to keep an eye on them, so they don't find us by accident. Jake! Wait! Don't go into the woods without us!"

Jake stopped short at the verge of the weedy grass that showed the transition from the beach to the woods. "Come on, you guys! Hurry up, that ship is getting bigger by the minute!"

The three older children caught up to Jake, and they all turned to see the ship, sailing closer to land than they would have thought possible. They could see men climbing up the ropes tied to the masts. Others were working on a long rowboat tied to the side of the vessel. The kids all turned and ran into the forest.

CHAPTER 10

They crashed through the underbrush, making for the trees. Light flashed, sun shining through branches, alternating with shadows as they moved deeper into the forest. They couldn't afford to be seen by the pirates, not when they didn't know what the pirates planned to do on this island. But they didn't dare to lose sight of them completely either. Becca, at the back of their short line, looked over her shoulder again and again, tall grasses whipping against her shoulders and cheeks. Had the longboats landed yet? Could they be seen from the beach? How far did they have to run into the forest to be out of sight?

"Becca, come on!" Marcus pulled on her hand. "Stop looking over your shoulder! You're slowing down." She took one last glance and saw that, indeed, the first boat was nearly to the beach. She looked forward and put everything she had into running for the deep shade.

They ran until they could no longer see the beach and then ran a bit further. Finally, Paige collapsed at the base of a large pine tree, panting heavily. "I can't," she wheezed. "I can't go ... on ..."

Jake fell beside her, and Marcus and Becca joined them. They all gasped and huffed, trying to catch their breath, lost from the run and the fear they'd felt at the sight of the pirate flag flying from the tall mast of the ship. Even as winded as she was, Paige asked, "Are we far enough in? Are we hidden?"

"We should be fine," Marcus said. "Unless their intent is to come into the woods."

Paige bolted upright. "Do you think they might? We gotta go!"

Marcus laid a hand on her arm. "Hold on. We won't do any good wearing ourselves out for no reason." He held a finger to his lips, listening to the breeze rustle the branches above them. But they heard no voices, no branches breaking, no heavy footfalls. "We'd hear them, I think. I believe we're all right for the moment."

The four friends lay back against the earth cooled by the shade provided by the pines and their breathing quickly returning to normal. Marcus said, "We should crawl back toward the beach so we can keep an eye on what's happening."

Becca shook her head. "Wait, hold on. We don't even really know what to watch for. We can't just charge ahead if we don't know where we're at, what's happening to us."

Jake snorted. "Becca, we got pirates here! They won't just sit in the sand and wait while you make a plan." He started to crawl back the way they had come. "Commando!"

Becca slapped at his ankle and missed. "Jake!" she hissed. "Stop it! Don't act like such a child!"

Marcus began to crawl after him. "He's right—we've got to go. We need more information before we can formulate any kind of meaningful strategy. Come on—quiet now!"

As the four children crept back toward the beach, shouts and angry exclamations drew their attention, though the voices did not seem to be coming from anywhere in the woods. Marcus stopped Jake with a tap on the ankle then crawled up next to him. He carefully pushed back a leaf of a large, white-petaled lily plant so they could peer cautiously at the activity on the beach. Paige and Becca crawled up next to them to see.

The once-empty beach now swarmed with men, who had clearly just climbed out of large rowboats at the water's edge. Several were pulling the boats up the sand, anchoring them against the waves that continually broke on the shoreline. Becca noted a jumble of clothing styles, nothing like uniforms. Some wore long pants, with red checkered shirts. Others had short red or blue vests over shorter pants that ended at midcalf. A few wore scarves around their necks or bright sashes at their waists. Kerchiefs were knotted over long hair, and she even saw some ponytails.

One man, however, didn't climb from the boat and had to be pulled out. His hands were tied behind his back, and he was clearly a prisoner of the pirates. A scar-faced, scowling pirate yanked the prisoner out and threw him, face-first, into the sand. The captive rolled over, lifting his face from the sand, and struggled to his feet.

One last longboat slid onto the beach, and most of the men rushed over toward it. In the bow of the boat sat a man who was clearly someone of importance. He sat perfectly still, watching, while the other men worked to pull the boat out of the surf. He wore a satiny white shirt, open at the neck, with sleeves that billowed in the breeze. Several gold chains hanging from his neck glinted in the sun. His pants were a light tan, fitting tightly from his waist to below the knee, where they disappeared into the tops of leather boots. In his right earlobe, a polished golden ring dangled. His dark black hair curled down to his shoulders, and a thick mustache and goatee framed his hard, mean-looking expression. He carried a short, flexible whip, which he flicked idly as he waited for the rest of the men to secure the longboat.

As the children watched, one of the men hauling on the bow of the longboat slipped and splashed heavily into the surf. Water sprayed high, splashing nearby fellow sailors—and the man sitting in the bow. "You scurvy laggard!" the man cried and rose to his feet. He lifted his short whip high and swung it down on the fallen man's shoulder. The crew shouted encouragement as the man in the boat lashed at the sailor in the water.

It was the perfect distraction for the bound prisoner. He broke away from his captors and began running toward the forest where the children were hiding.

CHAPTER 11

The prisoner ran quietly, desperately, trying to put as much distance between himself and the pirates before they noticed him. He made it about halfway from the shore to the tree line before the scar-faced man saw that he was gone. "Jennings!" the pirate roared and gave chase. Soon, most of the men were running after the man called Jennings, waving broad swords and wooden clubs, shouting threats. The sand slowed his pace, but it also kept his followers from moving too swiftly as well, so he kept his advantage. Paige flinched at the rage and evil intent she could see on the pirates' faces even at this distance. As the bound man came closer, she could see the real fear in his expression. He clearly believed he was running for his life. "We have to help him," she whispered urgently, starting to stand up from her crouch.

"Wait!" Marcus grabbed her arm. "We can't just jump out. Let me think …" Becca clutched her hand in silent appeal. Paige realized that four kids had no chance in a direct fight with fifty armed men and squatted back down.

Suddenly, just when it looked like he might make the tree line, the bound man tripped, and his feet flew out from under him. He fell flat on his face in the sand, and the pack of mad men was on him. Jake nearly cried out, then clapped his hands over his ears as he heard the clubs hitting the man's torso and his grunts of pain.

Just when the children were sure the man would be killed before their very eyes, a shout came from behind the mob.

"Hold fast!" a deep voice roared. "The man who kills him is the man who dies in the next instant." The angry shouts continued, but the mob stopped beating the man in the sand. He moaned and rolled over so his face was clear of the dune where he was lying.

The children looked away from the mob and saw that the man from the bow of the longboat was striding up the beach, waving his sword as though ready to make good on his threat. "Avast now! Belay that noise!" The unruly group quieted, though angry murmurs and exclamations still broke out from time to time. "Back off, ye picaroons, or I'll have your heads. Mr. Otis Jennings and I needs have words, and I'll thank ye not to blow him down afore we do that."

The dark-haired man stopped by the bound man's side, sneering down his nose at him. "Otis Jennings," he growled. "Ye bilge-rat, are ye ready to die?"

"Captain Cocklyn, ye'll not be the one to scupper me," Otis said quietly. "Ye're a smarter man than that."

Cocklyn laughed wildly. "Matey, ye're the one with flattery. But ye're right—I need you alive for now. But there's much my cutlass can do without bleeding you dry." He laid the tip of his sword against Otis's cheek and twitched it slightly. A drop of blood immediately glistened on the helpless man's skin. "Now, laddy buck. Tell us where the booty is laid."

"Let me woold 'im, Captain," Scar-face snarled. "He'll speak soon enough." Jake didn't know what "woolding" was, but he didn't like the sound of it.

"Marcus, we gotta help him," he whispered.

"I know, give me a moment ..."

"Mayhaps 'tis what Otis needs for encouragement," the captain said thoughtfully. "Have your rope ready, Hargest?"

"Aye, sir!" The scarred sailor pulled a knotted length of rope from his pocket and pulled Otis up to his knees. "Hold 'im steady now, mates." Several others gathered around and held Otis in place as Hargest tied the rope around Otis's head just above his eyebrows. "Break me a stick, will you?"

"Jake—have you still got those firecrackers in your backpack?" Marcus asked urgently as they watched the terrible scene before them.

"Firecrackers?!" Becca squeaked. "Jake, what are you doing with firecrackers? Dad'll kill you!"

Jake dropped his head in embarrassment. "Don't tell him! I was just holding them for Tommy. Honest!" He was digging into his pack and pulled out a large packet of Black Cat firecrackers. "He took them off his big brother …" He handed them off to Marcus along with a small box of safety matches which he always carried in the secret depths of his backpack.

"Don't worry about it," Marcus said. "They'll be gone before we see your dad again. Becca, let him be. We've got to help Otis Jennings now."

One of the pirates had stepped into the underbrush and come back with a stout stick for the scarred pirate. He took it and stuck it between the rope and Otis' skull. He turned it once and the rope twisted, making the knots dig into Otis' brow. He took the first turn quietly, but sweat broke out on his forehead. The pirates yelled roughly, cheering on the snarling torturer.

"Gather up all the rocks you can find," Marcus directed the others. "Fill your pockets." He backed away from the beach before standing and testing a low-hanging branch on a nearby tree to see if it would take his weight. It did, and he scrambled up into its branches. "Come up as soon as your pockets are full."

On the beach, Hargest twisted the stick once again, pulling the rope tighter. Otis grunted involuntarily as the pressure increased. "Otis, me bucko, won't you tell me what I need to know?" The captain spoke sweetly into Otis Jennings's ear. "Surely ye'd like to keep your eyeballs in your skull now, wouldn't you?"

Paige shuddered upon hearing his words as she climbed up into the tree, making room for Becca. "Marcus, what are we doing? We have to hurry, they're hurting him!" All the kids were now in the tree, braced and ready to throw their rocks.

"When I let off the firecrackers, throw your rocks," he hissed to his friends. "As hard as you can. Hit them, and they'll think they're being shot at. Ready?"

As the kids prepared their attack, Hargest had tightened his torture rope even further. Small drops of blood were appearing on Otis's head and began to drip down his face. "Come on, Otis," Captain Cocklyn said impatiently. "I'll let Hargest finish his work, I will. You don't need your eyes to speak—and maybe you'll be more inclined to talk in the dark."

Suddenly, a large bang sounded out. It was quickly followed by more explosions and a volley of stinging shot. Becca and Jake had both targeted Hargest and nailed him solidly in the side of his head and neck. He dropped the stick, bellowing, and his hand flew to his cutlass. The band of pirates scattered, shouting and trying to see where the attack came from. Above the height of the men, however, the children were out of their line of sight.

Otis reacted in an instant as the pirates scattered. He leapt to his feet and ran hard to cross the twenty-five yards left to the tree line. The kids redoubled their efforts, increasing the confusion among the pirates. Marcus lit the firecrackers and threw them out of the woods at the feet of the sailors. Jake, Becca, and Paige continued to pelt the pirates with rocks, aiming carefully for the best reaction. They heard Otis pass beneath them, crash further into the woods, and then silence.

The pirates suddenly seemed to realize they'd lost their prisoner and started toward the woods themselves. The captain, recovering himself most quickly, roared out an order. "Avast! Hold your places!" The pirates turned, startled by this order, when their prey still had to be so close. The kids held their breaths, waiting to hear his next words.

"We don't know who we're up against here, men," he shouted. "I'll not lose my crew to a thoughtless battle plan. Back to the ship!" The pirates called out their surprise, angry to lose their chance at treasure.

"Blimey, Captain, what're ye thinking?" Hargest yelled, his face and neck still stinging from Becca and Jake's accurate shots. "We have this bilge rat!"

Captain Cocklyn looked at him derisively. "I'll not lose my booty to that weak rat, fear not. But we've more advantage at sea. We'll sail around this island 'til we find these blighters, take their ship, and maroon them here. A couple of weeks without food or fresh water, and Otis will talk. Or he'll lose his eyes for certain."

The pirates grumbled but seemed to see the captain's wisdom. With angry looks back over their shoulders, they left the woods and headed down the beach for their rowboats. In a surprisingly short time, the kids watched the pirate crew rowing back to their ship.

CHAPTER 12

When the children were certain that all the pirates were returning to the ship, they climbed down from the tree. Marcus handed the matches back to Jake, who tucked them safely back into his backpack. "Where do you suppose Otis went?" Paige asked.

"He ran right under our tree. We'll find him—he can't have gotten too far." Marcus led the way deeper into the woods, looking at the underbrush for signs of Otis's passage. Broken twigs, crushed grass, and scuffed dirt showed where he had crashed through the woods in his desperate flight.

"Otis?" Paige called. "Otis, we can help you ..." She was very worried about the blood she'd seen on his face, the tightness of the ropes around his wrists and forehead. "Otis, don't be afraid!"

"Afraid?!" a gruff voice called from just ahead and to the right of them. "Afraid of you lot when I was just facing down the bloodthirsty *Dark Falcon* crew?" A rustle in the bushes, then they saw Otis stand upright, swaying slightly with the sudden movement. The woolding rope still dug into his skin, drops of blood still glistening freshly. "Kids! Just a few wee children. This is my rescue party?"

Marcus reached his side and went to work loosening the knots that held his wrists tightly behind him. "Yes, sir, just us."

"We couldn't watch them kill you," Paige interjected, reaching up to remove the stick from the woolding rope. "Or … or …"

"Pop your eyes out," Jake finished. "That would be too gross."

Becca tugged at the woolding rope, loosening and then pulling it from Otis's head. He flinched as it pulled from the fresh wounds then rubbed his wrists as Marcus freed them. "Much obliged. I appreciate your aid." The man they saw before them was a short, older man with a grizzled beard and ice-blue eyes. He wore a red-checkered shirt and khaki cropped pants that were tucked into the tops of soft-soled, buckskin boots. His skin was the color of a walnut shell, deeply tanned from years in the Caribbean sun. He had the gray hair and wrinkled skin that reminded Becca of her grandfather, but he moved athletically, like her dad did on the softball field.

"Now who are you and where are your folks? Am I out of one fire and into another?" Otis looked around suspiciously, as though expecting to be recaptured by whomever these children belonged to.

"I'm Paige. This is Marcus, Becca, and Jake. It's just us—no one else with us."

"How come you to be on this island, then? Young'uns like you didn't come here alone."

Marcus held up a hand, warning the others against telling the full story of their arrival on the island. "We're … uh, we're castaways, sir. Shipwrecked with our ship's crew and complement lost. Marooned now, like you."

Otis laughed heartily. "Och, pay no attention to that Cocklyn's boasts. They'll not be marooning Otis Jennings against his own wishes. And if you children will crew for me, you'll be off this cursed rock before too many hours pass by."

Marcus looked unconvinced. "But surely there are no ships around, except for the *Dark Falcon*, as you call it."

Otis laid a finger alongside his nose and winked. "There's more to sailing this fine sea than having a great huge ship. So what do you say? Will you throw in your lot with me, or shall I send a rescue party for you when I reach my destination?"

Becca laid a hand on Marcus's arm, interrupting as he opened his mouth to speak. "We thank you for your offer, Mr. Jennings. But we have a couple of questions to ask before we agree to anything."

Otis looked her over shrewdly. "Here's the gal who knows her business, I'll wager. Fair enough. Never sign onto a crew without knowing all the facts. Come on, let's head for my vessel. It's a bit of a hike. You can ask your questions once we're there." He pulled a kerchief from his pocket and wiped his face, smearing the blood drops so he had a fierce, embattled look about him. He turned and began pushing deeper into the forest. "This way, maties."

Marcus glanced at the lush undergrowth that Otis Jennings was pushing through, then back over his shoulder at the others. He shrugged. "Let's see what he's got." He turned and pushed onto the path behind the former prisoner, the others following closely.

Just a few yards from the beach, their world seemed to change dramatically once again. The palm tree branches were nearly woven together, shading the path from the bright tropical sun. The temperature dropped noticeably, the breeze filtered by the close undergrowth. The screening plant life muffled the rush of the ocean waves, so suddenly they could hear birds and insects, chirping and buzzing around them. Paige, at the end of their little parade line, looked back and was astonished that she could no longer see the sand and ocean. Branches and grasses closed in behind her, blocking any view of the wide open space that was the beach. They could have been on an entirely different island—or deep in a mainland jungle. She sighed in relief. If she couldn't see the beach, the pirates at sea couldn't see her. Now she could focus on the next step of their strange journey.

Ahead of the kids, Jennings unexpectedly broke into song—a joyful tune, though they couldn't understand the words. "French, I think," said Becca. "He sounds happy."

Otis heard her and broke into a laugh. "Happy!? Of course, I'm happy! I'm alive, the sea awaits, and I know where I'm sailing. Come on, young lubbers, I'll teach you the joy of the sailing life!"

He turned forward again, pushing ahead more quickly, taking up his merry song once more.

"Tortured, abandoned on an island in the middle of the ocean ... and he talks of joy in a sailor's life." Becca snorted. "I'm not sure I see it."

Jake offered quietly, "Well, we are still alive. That makes me pretty happy."

Marcus laughed. "You're right, Jake. We are alive—so this is a pretty good day! Hey, we better move. I can't see Mr. Jennings anymore."

Marcus picked up their pace, moving closer to the pirate as he continued to push through the undergrowth. They walked along easily in his wake, enjoying the gentle wind in their faces, taking in the sights and sounds of a tropical land they had never visited before. Otis continued his singing, switching from French to English to Spanish and back again. His rhythms became a cadence for their strides, helping them to keep pace easily with the taller, longer-legged man. From time to time, they would see or hear and point out to one another an unusually colored blossom or a unique birdcall, followed by a bright flash of iridescent feathers. After they'd marched along in this peaceful way for about half an hour, Jennings suddenly picked up speed and ran out of sight.

"What's going on?" Becca asked. "Marcus, where did he go?" They stopped short and bunched together, confused. Then they heard the pirate's shout ahead of them. "Where are ye all, mates? Shake a leg—come and see our salvation!" The children ran toward his voice, anxious to see what Otis was so excited about. They rounded a curve and found him standing in front of a large patch of shrubs and grasses. "Here she be, lads and lasses!" He gestured at the foliage.

"Um ... there what be, Otis?" Paige said. All the children could see was bushes, grass, and leaves. How did Otis think that would save them?

CHAPTER 13

The children continued to peer at the vegetation. "What are we looking at?" Paige asked again.

"Ah, girl, blind as a bat, are you? Our ship! Our way off this godforsaken patch of dirt." The children moved closer, peering into the bushes. There, tucked into the center, they saw wood planking, curving away into shadows.

"It must not be very big," ventured Jake, eyeing the size of the patch Otis pointed to.

"Big enough, young master, big enough." Otis began pulling away the branches to reveal the prize that waited beneath. "Give a hand here then, or do you expect me to do all the work?" Everyone moved up and began dragging grasses, branches, and sticks out of the pile. Slowly but surely, they uncovered an oversized, ruddered canoe.

"A canoe?" Becca shook her head. "This is our salvation? We have to be on the ocean, not on some lake."

"Don't you take that tone with old Captain Jennings, miss," Otis cautioned. "Who's spent his whole life on the seas, you or me?" He rapped his knuckles against the thick wooden planking. "This is no toy boat we've got here. She'll get us where we need to go and in fine order too." He peered out at the surrounding jungle. "Looks quiet enough." He pointed out through a gap where they could see they had come across the small island through to the beach on the other side. "Go on, poke your head out there and see if we're clear," he said, giving Marcus a nudge. Marcus did as he was told, carefully parting the bushes he stood behind and looking up and down the vast stretch of sand. There was not another soul in sight, on land or sea.

"We're clear, sir."

"Good enough, then. Let's find ourselves a good spot to bed down tonight." Jennings led them out into a clearing at the verge of the sand. The wind freshened, and the smell of warm beach and salt water wafted to them.

"But wait a minute," Paige asked. "Where did this canoe come from? How did you know it was here? And what do you mean we can take it out on the ocean?"

Otis barked a short laugh. "This lass has more questions than a magistrate. And I reckon is a darn sight more set on getting her answers." He puffed out his chest proudly. "Never let it be said, little lady, that Otis Jennings doesn't know how to watch his own back. I been to this island dozens of times, and it was the work of a moment to contrive to get Cocklyn and his scurvy crew to bring me here. Once here, I knew I'd escape 'em."

Jake gasped. "You knew we'd be here? How?"

Otis laughed again. "No me hearty, I knew nothing about you. But I knew a chance would present itself for me because one always does. And that's why I left me canoe here against just such a predicament." Otis patted the bow of the overturned boat. "She's in fine shape, saving a bit of cleanup. Then we'll be off this desert strand and meet back up with my crew."

"Going back to those … those creeps?!" Becca protested. "We will not!"

Otis shook his head. "No, no, ye dafty. That lot isn't my crew. My crew is a good lot—and privateers, not wicked buccaneers, like these."

Paige opened her mouth to ask another question, but Marcus jumped in first. "Mr. Jennings, is this vessel truly ocean worthy? It seems small."

"Worthy it is, and it'll take us just fine to the next island but one. My crew is careening our own good barque, the *Bethany*, there. They'll be waiting for me."

Becca said slowly, "But not for us ..."

Marcus whispered, "Sssh, we'll talk later, figure out what's going on before we worry about that."

Otis grinned. "Ah, dearest, they'll take four small 'uns like you for my sake. They're not such a hard bunch they'd leave you marooned here on this worthless piece of sand." He stepped away from the canoe, turning toward the beach. "Right then. Let's see about making camp and finding a spot of dinner. We'll be needing a fire, so why don't you spread out and find me some kindling. I'll be right back here when you're done." Otis walked out of the shadows and into the sunlight, never looking back at his newfound companions.

As soon as he seemed far enough to be out of earshot, Paige said, in a stage whisper, "What's going on? What happened to Minnesota? This is not your backyard. This is all wrong." Her voice grew louder and louder until her last word was nearly a shout.

Becca shook her arm gently. "It's all right, Paige. We'll figure this out. Calm down."

Marcus glanced over his shoulder toward the beach. "Let's back up a little further into the woods. We do need to talk, and I don't want Otis to overhear us until we do have a better grasp of what's happened." They shifted away from the canoe and sat down further back into the shade.

"How did this happen?" Becca wondered. "Could it have been ... did the snow globe do this?"

Jake nodded vigorously. "It was snowing, remember? And that ship—it looked kind of like the one inside. Not exactly ..."

Marcus agreed. "Not exactly, but you've got the style right. I believe they are both barques. As unlikely as it seems, I think we must go with the working theory that somehow, the snow globe transported us to another time and place. One in which pirates sailed the open seas."

"Marcus, how do you know about pirates and barques and open seas?" Paige wrinkled her brow. "You always know the strangest things."

"My last summer's reading included some books on pirates and the seventeenth century. Some recreational reading. But it's fascinating, really. Their practices, why they rampaged …"

"And I'm sure your information will be helpful," Becca said. "But right now, we need to talk this through. If the snow globe sent us here, how do we get back?"

"'Tis booty you're after, a buccaneer's bounty," Marcus quoted. "Accomplish your task and your history renew."

"What? What are you saying?"

"It's the poem, Paige." Becca closed her eyes, trying to remember. "Prick up your ears now and … something …"

"Hear your request," Jake said.

"No, not quite…Hear the tale of your quest." Marcus pulled Jake closer to him by his backpack. "Let's see the globe."

Jake swung his pack off his shoulders and unzipped it. "Right here." He handed the shining globe carefully to Marcus while Becca pulled the poem out of her back pocket and read it again.

> Weigh anchor, ye lubbers and unfurl the mainsail.
> Brace up your heartstrings; put your courage to the test.
> Hands to your cutlass and look sharp at the gunwale,
> Prick up your ears now and hear the tale of your quest.

> 'Tis booty you're after, a buccaneer's bounty.
> A treasure's been lost and your home is behind you.

Show yourself fearless; worry not for your safety.
Accomplish your task and your history renew.

"It appears we have an assignment," Marcus said. "But I wish I knew more about how it all works."

Becca frowned for a moment at the globe then slapped a hand to her back pocket again. "The letter from Aunt Elizabeth!" She pulled it out triumphantly. "Maybe she tells us something." Unfolding the envelope and sliding the letter out, she began to read.

My dearest Becca,

I am so sorry I could not hold on to be able to tell you about these wondrous snow globes in person. I so wanted to explain it all, face-to-face. But I must tell you what I can in this letter, as it is all you'll ever know of the history of these snow globes. I did try to tell you some of what these globes can mean, as much as you could understand at such a young age. Do you remember my stories? Those stories were, in fact, adventures I lived through—and adventures you can now have for yourself. It's your turn to find the magic—your very own magic.

My aunt gave me these globes many, many years before you—or even your mother—was born. She told me she had received them from her great aunt, and she from an aunt or great aunt before her. It has been lost through generations how many Mulvaney aunts have passed these globes on to their nieces. In time, it will be your turn to decide if your niece (or perhaps grandniece) should have her own adventures.

Your mother never was one who craved adventure beyond her own backyard. But even at your young age, I can tell that you will learn much—and enjoy much— from these journeys. Each globe will take you on your very own escapade, each with its own goal. I don't know where they came from, or how their magic works. But I do know they will offer you opportunities you would never have otherwise. Trust me—you can accomplish these quests. I did, as did my aunt before me. Follow the poem, use your wits. You will learn lessons you would never have an opportunity to if you'd just stayed safe in your own yard. Pursue your magic, my darling Becca—you'll find wonder no one has ever experienced. Press on, my darling!

With deepest love,
Your Great-Aunt Elizabeth

They sat in silence, taking in the enormity of the gift Aunt Elizabeth had left. Adventure beyond anything their own homes could offer. Adventure—and the danger that goes along with it. They had no choice now but to press on, to go forward, as Aunt Elizabeth said.

"Otis has a hidden treasure," Becca said. "But he called himself a privateer."

"Pirates, buccaneers, privateers—there's not much difference," Marcus said. "I believe a privateer will fulfill the buccaneer requirement."

"This means our plan should be to stay with Otis Jennings. Help him find his treasure." But Becca shook her head even as she said it.

Paige shuddered. "I'm not sure about this …"

Jake patted Paige's arm. "It's okay, Paige. We'll be together. And we're having a great adventure!"

"Together … I guess that's what really matters, isn't it? We have to stick together."

"All right." Marcus stood and brushed dirt from the back of his shorts. "Our strategy—stay with Otis, help him find his treasure."

"Until we see a different way to go," Becca cautioned. "And we'd better keep the snow globe a secret." Marcus nodded, sliding it back into Jake's backpack. Becca tucked Aunt Elizabeth's letter and the poem into an interior pocket as well. "We don't know how the adults here might react." The globe winked brightly as Marcus zipped the pack shut.

"Good idea," Marcus said. "We'd better gather up some kindling and get back to the beach. Jake and I will try off this way."

"Wait, wait, wait," Paige said. "There's still so much I don't understand. Where are we? When are we, for that matter? Why doesn't Otis seem to notice how different our clothes are? What if we're wrong about this quest thing?'

Marcus smiled. "I think we're just going to have to take the quest on faith for now. It's the only thing that begins to tie together the facts we have before us. As for where and when, I can help with that. We must be in the Caribbean Sea somewhere—between the southernmost tip of Florida and the northern coast of South America. There are a lot of islands in this area—Cuba, the Bahamas, Haiti, and many smaller ones. And since we're dealing with pirates, we're likely in the seventeenth century, somewhere in the 1630's to 1650's."

"1650!" Jake exclaimed. "Like in the year 1650? That can't be real. The calendar doesn't go back that far."

Becca laughed. "Of course it does, Jake. You know Jesus was born about 2,000 years before us. This is only like ... 400 years before us." Her smile faded and they all stood silently for a moment, trying to grasp the fact that they were now living in history.

Paige finally said "I think I might be able to answer my own question about Otis not noticing our clothes. Magic."

"Magic?" Marcus said, unconvinced.

"Yes magic, Mr. Science," Paige said. "You're able to believe a magical blizzard blew us hundreds of years from our home, not to mention thousands of miles. But you don't think magic might be the explanation for our clothes? I think magic is making him see us in clothes that fit this time."

Jake pulled his tee shirt away from his chest. "I still see Superman's S on my shirt."

Paige nodded and said "So do I. But I think, if we could see with Otis' eyes, we'd see something different." She looked around. "I wonder if we had a mirror, if we could see it."

Becca pulled at Jake's backpack. "You must have one in here."

"What? No!" Jake pulled away from her. "Why would I carry a mirror? I'm not some girl."

Marcus said, "Sometimes guys use mirrors too, buddy. But I have an idea. I saw a small stream flowing out onto the beach, that shouldn't be too far from here. If the water's clear and the sun's at the right angle, we can see a reflection." He headed off to the west, seeking the creek he'd seen. Within a couple of minutes, he pulled up short. "Here it is! And there's a little pool that should be perfect."

They all knelt on the bank of the pool and leaned out over the still, clear water. They all gasped. Paige had been right. Their clothes did look different from what they saw when they looked directly at each other.

Both Marcus and Jake wore shirts with long, loose sleeves—Marcus in blue and Jake in a pale yellow. They both wore pants of lightweight wool and, when Jake stood, he could see the brown pant legs ended just below his knees. Marcus also saw that his gray pants were knee breeches. They were both bare-legged. Jake held his foot out over the pool and they could see he wore soft-skinned moccasins, as did Marcus.

The girls were surprised to see they no longer wore shorts and cotton shirts. They both wore long-sleeved white shirts, which were covered by tight-fitting sleeveless shirts that looked like tank tops. Becca wore a deep red bodice and Paige's was a bright kelly green. When they stood, still gazing into the pool, they both saw skirts that flowed softly from their waists to just above their ankles. Paige's skirt was a medium brown color and Becca swirled her smoky blue skirt around her legs.

"I can't feel the skirt," she said. "I can see it, but I can't feel it."

"Magic," said Paige, lifting her skirt to see neat brown leather shoes on her white-stockinged feet. "Absolute magic."

"You were right, Paige," Marcus admitted. "I wonder what other magic might be in store for us?"

Becca spun away from the pond after a last look. "We'd better not count on magic, though. We don't know how—or even if—it will help us anymore. So we'd better get that kindling Otis is expecting."

CHAPTER 14

The breeze rustled through the tops of the trees, but this far from the beach, it barely moved the leaves of the bushes surrounding the boys. As they sought small sticks and twigs for tinder, beads of sweat developed on their foreheads and trickled down their faces. The underbrush offered a wide variety of vegetation—bushes, flowers, tall grasses—but dried wood suitable for starting a fire was less abundant. They ranged further and further into the forest.

Jake felt the back of his shirt dampen beneath his backpack, but even so, he did not remove the pack. He'd been hot before—and his backpack was all he had of home, now that they were here ... wherever *here* was. As he reached for another dry twig, he felt his eyes sting with unshed tears. He swiped his arm across his face. He was not going to be the baby here. No crying—be tough. He scrubbed at his eyes, pushing back his fears.

Marcus called to him from a short distance away. "Got a pile of deadwood here, Jake. All we need!" Jake followed the sound of his voice, pushing past a large orchid to the small clearing where Marcus stood. There, a tree had fallen months ago and lay drying. "Hey, bud, we can load up and show the girls up but good." Marcus looked at Jake's face and knew—absolutely knew—how close to breaking down his young friend was. He turned back to the tree and began breaking branches off it. "So pretty weird day, don't you think? I know I feel like I'm on the edge of insanity."

Jake set down his armload of small twigs and began working on one of the branches. He kept his eyes carefully averted from Marcus. "Yeah ... kinda ... kinda a lot happening."

Marcus laughed. "Oh, that is an understatement! I'm glad you're here with me, bro. I'm not sure I could keep it together without your help." He spoke quietly, eyes on his work.

"Come on, Marcus. Don't try and feed me that."

"Seriously, pal." Marcus finally looked Jake in the eye. "The girls are great, but they have their own language, you know. They know how to boost each other up. But it's different for us guys, isn't it?" He reached over and punched Jake's arm. "Guys ... we handle our fear differently. You get that."

"You're afraid ... ?"

"Sure, it wouldn't be logical to *not* be afraid. Pirates, marooned, time travel—we're all scared, Jake. But we've got each other to make it through." Marcus shrugged. "You make me feel stronger, that's all."

Jake turned away for a minute. "I thought maybe I was the only one scared. I mean Paige is freaked out, but she's always kind of that way. You and Becca seem so ..." He shrugged.

"No way, Jake. Don't ever think you're the only one. This is a frightening situation, but we're in this together. We'll figure it out together." Marcus bent back to the task of breaking up the dry wood. "Come on, let's get back and get our fire started."

As the children came back to the beach from opposite directions, with their arms filled with branches in the forest, they saw Otis crouching quietly in the shallows of the bay, staring intently at the water. They dropped their firewood in a stack just outside the tree line and went across the sand toward the shore. Suddenly, Otis's hands flashed, stabbing into the water. Splashing and spraying water, he turned and flipped a live fish onto the sand, out of the reach of the waves. The fish flipped and twisted, flashing silvery in the sun low on the horizon. Otis laughed happily. "A few more like that, and we'll eat like kings tonight."

Paige wrinkled her nose. "Fish? I don't think I like fish."

"Well, get yerselves busy and go find yerself some o' those giant roaches then," Otis advised as he settled back into his crouch. "They're pretty meaty."

Paige shrieked and clapped her hand over her mouth. "Oh, no way! Are you trying to make me throw up?"

Otis concentrated on the water in front of him, ignoring Paige's outburst. Marcus said quietly, "I'm sure he's quite serious, Paige. There's not much to be had for dinner on this deserted island, and I'd guess he's offering you the best choice he knows."

Another jab at the water, more splashing, and another fish landed on the beach. "Head a bit further back into the woods there, back where them ferns are as high as you. You might find a satinleaf tree or two. Their fruit makes good eating."

Paige liked the sound of that. "What's it look like?"

"Fruit's dark red, bigger'n a berry. Marcus, how do you and Jake think you'd do starting a fire? Let the girls hunt the fruit. We need some nice coals to do justice to this fish."

"We're on it!" All the kids started back toward the woods. Marcus put a hand on Becca's arm. "Keep an ear open. I don't think the pirates will land again since their advantage is on the sea. But just be cautious."

"We'll watch out. You too—we still don't know what Otis is all about."

The girls pushed back into the woods, while Jake and Marcus prepared a spot for their fire. Becca checked back over her shoulder for a last glimpse of her little brother before the foliage closed in on them.

Paige took Becca's hand and gave it a squeeze. "Jake's fine. Marcus isn't going to let anything happen to him."

"Oh, I know Marcus loves Jake like a brother and will always watch out for him. I'm just a little worried about Jakie. He's gotten so quiet—he must be really scared."

Paige pushed a branch aside as they passed. "Truth be told, I'm kind of scared myself. I don't know if I really believe this whole snow globe thing. What if we're guessing wrong? What if Otis doesn't lead us to the right quest? What if we can't find the treasure? Are we stuck—"

Becca stopped and put her hands on Paige's shoulders. "Paige. Stop. Oh my gosh, you'll make yourself sick with all those questions."

Paige hung her head. "But that's what I'm thinking."

"I know. Me too. But we just have to go along for now, learn all we can, and then we can make a better plan. You know I'll get the information we need out of Otis tonight. Trust me on that." She gave her friend a quick hug. Paige put her arms around Becca and held tightly. The girls leaned on one another for a moment, drawing strength from being close. "Don't let the fear get to you, Paige. Press on, just like Aunt Elizabeth said."

CHAPTER 15

Jake leaned back against his pack, patted his stomach, and sighed contentedly. "That was a terrific dinner." They all lay around the campfire, which Otis stoked back up into flames, now that he had roasted the fish perfectly over the glowing hot embers. Even Paige had tried the fish and ended up eating her full portion. "I want my fish cooked like that all the time."

Otis grinned. "How do you usually eat your fish? Raw?"

"No, from a ca …" Jake broke off abruptly as Marcus kicked his foot. No canned tuna in this day and age, Jake remembered. "Just not over a campfire," he finished at little lamely.

"All right now, it's time we're down to business, ain't it?" Otis nodded at Becca. "Ask your questions, and I'll answer ye true."

Becca gazed up at the clear, dark sky, where it seemed millions of stars winked just for them. Stomach full, having spent the afternoon watching Otis Jennings and seeing little or no sign of the bloodthirsty pirate, her questions seemed like they might be too suspicious. And yet … this man had somehow been part of that murderous crew they had seen earlier today. She had to be suspicious.

"Who were those men this morning? Why were they so angry with you?"

"Those were my once-upon-a-time crew mates, buccaneers all from the brigand *Dark Falcon*. They fly the Jolly Roger, sure enough, and I once with them." Otis sighed. "Mistakes of my youth, miss, mistakes of my youth. I be a privateer now, sailing on the good ship *Bethany*."

"You've got a letter of marque then, Mr. Jennings?" Marcus asked.

"And what know you innocents of a letter of marque? 'Tis adult talk, that is. But yes, we've been approved by the King of England himself to take from our enemies, the bloody Spaniards."

Marcus told the others, "Privateers are approved by government, soldiers of a sort really. Any bounty they take from the enemy, they give a percentage to the Crown. Pirates are only out for themselves."

Otis cautioned, "Now, don't get this wrong. Privateers can be as vicious as a band of buccaneers when someone stands in their way. They'll take what they need and want, same as old Blackbeard."

"How did you get to be pira … privateer, Mr. Jennings?" Paige asked. "You don't sound like you approve of them."

Otis rubbed an old scar on his neck, remembering. "I first took to the sea as a young boatwright apprentice on the good ship *Atlantic Grace* out of London. Sailed her for many years, learning the art of shipcraft, repairs, and carpentry. Then one day, we were taken on the high seas by a Spanish galleon. They bore down on us with the speed of the wind. Such sailing I'd never seen." He shook his gray head, obviously seeing those sights of long ago. "And cruel … our meek merchants were no match for those ferocious killers. Killed most of the crew, but for me and the ship's doctor." His hand again went to the scar on his neck. "Pressed us both into service on their vessel, they did. Ships are always in need of repairing and crews in need of doctoring. We could join their crew or die a tortured death, worse than we'd seen." He shrugged. "We both decided to live. We worked that godforsaken ship for a couple of years, pressed into battle against our own countrymen." Otis hung his head. "I ain't proud of those months, my lads and lasses, I'll tell ye true. But I was young and wanted to live beyond my twenties, just as sure. Only good thing that came out of it is the doc taught me my letters, to read and write a bit. Then, one day, the galleon was taken by the good British ship, *Golden Sail*. Privateers, sanctioned by the king to battle with any Spanish vessel they found. Rescue, we thought, the doctor and me." Otis laughed mockingly. "Shiver me timbers! Rescue … pah. We were press-ganged once again, under penalty of marooning, rather than death, but pressed just the same." Otis leaned back, sighing. "At least I was working for my own true homeland once again. A few years of privateering, and you just don't go back to the merchant fleet. I ain't proud of it, but I'd grown to love the battle and the bounty. Not pretty, but there it is, true as anything I've ever said."

They all sat quietly for a moment, digesting this story of the high seas, of choices forced and choices made. Jake thought grown-ups always had a say in their lives, could always do as they pleased. He was beginning to see this might not be so, whether it was here in the tropics in the 1600s or at home in suburban Minneapolis.

"How did you end up with the crew on the *Dark Falcon*?" Becca finally asked. "Are they privateers?"

"Nah, not that scurvy lot." Otis spat in the sand. "As rotten a lot of picaroons as you'll ever see. We'll do well to steer a wide berth around them. I was with them only to right a terrible wrong, take back what rightfully belongs to my king and crew. And I done it all right," he said proudly.

"Done … uh … did what?" Paige asked.

"Took back the bounty that belonged right and proper to the *Bethany* and the cut that belongs to our sovereign king. Them bilge rats on the *Dark Falcon* raided our vessel, one night in port. Killed the two guards we'd left on board, took the Spanish gold we'd fought long and hard for. Took it like scurvy cowards, not even a face-to-face battle, like real men." Otis spat again. "So I took it back. Well, took back a like amount since they'd already spent their ill-gotten gains."

Marcus looked at Otis, eyes wide in surprise. "By yourself? Without a battle?"

"Certain sure, lad, certain sure," Otis laughed. "A boatwright has a berth anywhere he likes, pretty much. So I got myself signed on to the *Dark Falcon* and bided me time. Waited on a good chance, then run a rig on 'em."

"A rig?"

"Tricked 'em, right and proper."

Becca laughed. "Just like that. You just took it."

Otis looked across the fire at her. "Well, it wasn't as simple as that, you're right. I did have to do a bit of fancy sabotage to the ship's rudder linkage to make certain we all stayed in port overnight. And work a bit of encouragement and bribery to convince the guards they could take off for the nearest pub since I was on board anyway to make repairs."

"They were that dumb?" Jake asked.

"We'd been asea for some time. Them boys were missing the rum and the ladies." Otis grinned and Becca saw the wickedness in that smile. "It just took the proper convincing and old Otis knows how to convince."

"So you just walked off the ship with all the treasure?"

"Not all. I was making things even, not looking to rile up old Cocklyn any worse than I had to." He grinned again, that wicked look flashing once more. "Didn't work too well, as you saw today. Course, it's been a while he's been a-chasing me. That didn't make him feel any more kindly toward me."

Marcus asked, "How did you get the treasure away? It must have been a lot."

"I did have a friend to help and you can always hire some shoreman to move anything." Otis lay back, gazing at the stars, remembering his triumph against the pirates of the *Dark Falcon*.

"Give some men a bit o' gold, and they'll do a lot with no questions. My friend and I loaded the treasure on his ship and that very night, he gathered his crew back from their revelries, and we sailed."

"For England? To the king?" Paige asked.

Otis laughed. "No, my dearie, we've not yet gotten that far. Else I'd not be marooned here with you lot. No, it'd have been easy enough for Cocklyn to find out who had outfitted for that long a sail. No, we hid our booty away, waiting for Cocklyn to settle some. My friend went back to his sailing life, I went back to the *Bethany*, and we both stayed out of Cocklyn's way. But he's been so close—seems like his men have been everywhere I turned. What we thought would be a few weeks has turned into a couple of years. And I'm still at odds with the government."

Otis sat up and stirred the fire, reviving the flames and feeding a few more pieces of wood into it. He sighed and the grin the children had seen so often in the short time they'd known him slipped away. "It's time to be done with this. Whatever comes, I've got to fetch the treasure and get it to the king."

Paige put her hand on Otis's arm. "We'll help you. That's what we're here for."

Otis looked at her kindly, but Becca could see the laughter he held back in his eyes. "My dearie, you've a good heart. But it's best I get you back to whatever folks you have and move on with my own troubles."

Jake said, "But we don't have any folks here. We're alone."

Marcus cleared his throat. "Um … yes … that is true. There is no one for us here."

Otis patted Paige's hand where it rested on his arm. "Orphans? Every one of you? Och, my darlings, that just ain't right." He continued to hold Paige's hand as he fell quiet, clearly thinking about their situation. After a time, he said, "You did a good bit to help me with Cocklyn and his crew." He looked at them all. "If you sign on with me, as my crew, I'll not abandon you. We'll take

what comes together, until you're ready to find a home berth."
He released Paige's hand, stood, and gestured for all the kids to
stand also. "What be it then? Crew or just passengers until we
get to port?"

Marcus looked at each of his friends but knew what they had
to answer. This was the quest: to help Otis find his bounty so
they could go home. He turned to Otis and held out his hand.
"We'll crew with you, Captain Otis. Your mates until our quest
is over."

Paige reached out her hand and put it on top of Marcus's. "To
help you get your treasure back."

Jake put his hand on top of theirs. "The buccaneer's bounty—
we'll find it."

Becca looked at her friends and gave one last sharp look to
Otis. It rubbed her the wrong way to put their fates in the hands
of this stranger, but she had nothing else to suggest. Slowly, she
reached out and laid her hand on top of the others. "You have our
pledge, Captain Otis."

Otis grinned his toothy smile and put his hands beneath and
above the others. He gave them all one good shake and held fast.
"My very own crew. We'll do well together, we five. Certain sure
we will!"

CHAPTER 16

Otis roused the children early the next morning, prodding them awake with the toe of his boot and a cheery, "Show a leg, my dearies. Time for our rescue!"

Becca sat up and stretched her arms above her head, yawning. She blinked sleepily against the rising Caribbean sun. Around her, the other kids were stretching and yawning as well. Marcus got to his feet and headed quickly toward the woods, Jake following him. Paige pushed her hair out of her eyes and said, "I can't believe we slept on the beach! That's something new for all of us."

Becca grinned and looked around to see what Otis was doing. He was kicking the remains of the fire apart, scattering the ashes and remaining charcoaled sticks until it looked as though it were just a part of the sandy verge between beach and forest. The boys came trotting back out of the woods, and Becca stood. Morning preparations out in the wilderness would be something new too. "Come on, Paige, I gotta find a private spot."

When the girls came back to the beach, Otis handed them each a handful of fruit and pointed a short distance away to a small creek running out to the shore. "Just a quick breakfast this morning, my lasses. 'Tis fresh water there, if you drink back up by the tree line. We need to be up and away. A hard day of canoeing before us."

Becca heard rustling behind her and turned to see the boys already at work, pulling the brush and camouflaging grasses off of the canoe. She quickly ate her fruit, gulped some water, then rubbed her finger over her teeth. She waited impatiently while Paige took a last drink at the stream and then they headed to the canoe.

"I'll need one of you to reconnoiter a bit, before we shove off." Otis clapped Jake on the shoulder. "How are you at climbing trees, my lad?"

"Excellent," Jake said excitedly. He looked at a nearby palm. "Want me to climb this one?"

"Nay, not here. I'll need you to run up that hillock yonder— highest point on the island. Pick one of those big trees there, shinny on up, and check for the *Dark Falcon*."

"Okay!" Jake turned to run off when Becca stopped him with a loud "Wait!"

"You can't send him all by himself off somewhere. He's just a kid." Becca pulled at Otis's arm.

"Am not! I can do this. It's a cinch!"

Otis looked at them both then focused on Becca. "Young mother, are ye? He's a strong 'un. He'll be fine. And we are all needed here to get this canoe to the water's edge." He turned back to Jake. "You do this seriously and carefully, lad. Climb only as far as is safe. Don't be foolish."

"Yes, sir. I'll do it just right," Jake answered gravely. "I'm just looking for the *Dark Falcon*?"

"Aye, or any ship. We need to make sure Captain Cocklyn ain't just setting off the coast, biding his time. If you see any ship, take note of the flags and the bowsprit."

Marcus whispered to Jake, "The carving on the front of the ship. The *Falcon*'s looked like a big hawk kind of bird."

"Off with ye now, and we'll be to work here."

Jake gave Becca a quick smile and said, "No sweat, sis. See ya!" He ran off into the underbrush, pushing toward the hill and its tallest tree.

"Right then. Let's finish clearing this brush and get our rescue ship ready to sail."

The kids and Otis pulled the rest of the camouflaging foliage off the vessel and Otis began a detailed inspection of the hull of the overturned canoe. He ran his hands over the wood, picking at small chips, looking for any sign that the hull would leak. "Here, girls, pick this moss off wherever you see it. Grab a flat stone to help you scrape."

Now that the vessel was cleared of its disguising plant life, the children could see it was not a canoe in the sense they thought of canoes. It was larger than the two- to three-person vessel they were used to seeing on Minnesota lakes in the summer, longer and wider. The bottom came to a central keel board, more angled than the usual flat bottom of the classic Voyageur or birchbark-style canoe. The hull was made up of long, individual boards rather than a single smooth surface. Becca thought it looked far more like her uncle Jim's fishing boat than a canoe.

Marcus picked up a perfectly flat stone and tossed it to Paige. Becca found another, and they each took a side of the canoe to scrape. "Anything else needed, Otis?" Marcus asked.

"Aye, lad, we'll need a pathway cleared through that brush there. I don't want to rough up my pretty vessel dragging it through all that to the beach."

"On it!" Marcus attacked the nearby bushes and grasses with gusto. Otis fell flat to the ground and shinnied himself under the canoe. They heard him mumbling to himself. "Oh, those spiders. Out with ya! Where'd that oar go? Ay, are these mice? Get on, you scurvy vermin." Paige shrieked as several mice burst from under the canoe and ran across her shoe.

Otis poked his head out, grinning. "Don't like my pets, eh?" he laughed. "Well, that's the last of the freeloaders under here.

How's that moss?" He began to back out from under the canoe, pulling a large piece of canvas cloth with him.

"All gone, Otis," Paige said. "What's that?"

"It's our sail. Help me pull it out—careful now, we don't want to tear anything." Paige reached down to help him. Becca dropped her rock and brushed bits of moss from her hands. "Marcus, need a hand?"

"I'm almost through, but sure, there's a few more feet." Together, they pulled the last of the small brambles and twigs out of the way. A clear view of pristine beach and bright blue water rewarded them for their efforts. "Clear waters, sir!"

"Good work, young 'uns. Let's take a look at this sail now. Check for any tear, any spot that looks rotten through." They all pulled a corner of the large canvas, spreading it out over the ground so they could see all of it clearly. They ran their hands carefully over the rough surface as they saw Otis doing, feeling for any imperfections that might mean a problem. After they'd checked one side, they worked together to flip the canvas over and checked that surface as well.

"Shipshape!" Otis announced. "Good canvas, good voyage they say. Any sign of that youngster, Jake?"

Paige shaded her eyes and looked up toward the tall trees on the nearby hill. The tallest one shook, trembling as though under a stiff wind. Suddenly, she saw a pair of feet poke out from the leafy top of the tree, and Jake slid down into view. "Yes, sir! He's just coming down the tree now." She watched him safely climb down the trunk. "On his way back."

"Good lad. All right, mates, time for us to get this vessel upright. Everyone on the topside here." They lined up along the side of the canoe. "Bit of a lift now. Careful, wait for all of us to get a grip. Right ho, mates, and one, two, three!"

They groaned, grunted, heaved, and the side of the canoe began to rise from the ground. "Keep on, don't stop, heave to!" Otis shouted encouragement, and they kept the pressure on the canoe. Finally, with one last push, the canoe began to roll. It thudded over, its keel now resting on the ground, the inside seeing the fresh air for the first time in months. Becca and Paige leaned forward, hands on their knees, puffing with exertion.

Jake burst through the undergrowth. "Hey, you shoulda waited for me. I coulda helped."

Becca looked up at her baby brother, nearly jumping out of his skin in excitement. "Settle down, Jakie. You had your job."

"Ay, lad," Otis patted him on the shoulder. "And what's your report on that front?"

"I didn't see a thing," Jake told them. "Not a ship, not a cloud, nothing. I looked all the way around. Nothing."

"Good, lad! Won't do us any good to get the canoe into the water if the *Falcon* is hiding 'round the tip of the island to catch us." Otis reached into the canoe and pulled out a few last wisps of grass and cobwebs. "Right. This will take all of us now. She's a heavy vessel, but I've done it on me own, in a pinch. Easy with the five of us." Otis directed them each to positions around the sides of the canoe. They found their grips along the edge of the canoe and prepared to push. Otis went to the bow and righted the canoe straight up on to the keel. "Now push!"

They pushed, they leaned the other way, and pulled; they groaned, they shouted. The canoe seemed to resist their efforts on purpose, at first, but then finally moved grudgingly from its long resting spot in the woods. It was hard going through the bushes, even with Marcus's clearing work, but they kept at it. Once they hit the clean sand, it acted as small ball bearings against the hull and helped the canoe slide more easily. They pushed and pulled across the small stretch of beach and right into the gentle surf of the island's smaller bay. As the canoe hit the water, it lifted and floated, coming to life under their hands as if it were a living creature, finally coming home to its native habitat. The children cheered, raising their fists in triumph.

Otis laughed at their enthusiasm. "Long way to go yet, maties. Haul yourselves in while I hold her steady." Marcus and Jake boosted the girls over the side, where they turned and helped pull the boys up. Once in, Otis directed them to various bench seats, getting the balance of the canoe stable by the distribution of their weight. "Lean port," he told them, as he prepared to hoist himself over the starboard (or right side) hull. He sprang in, spraying and dripping water on his new crew. "Sun will dry you quickly enough."

Otis maneuvered two oars out from under the bench seats whose brackets had held them in place. Each oar had a metal fixture about two-thirds up the handle from the paddle end, a ring holding tightly to the wood with a metal peg hanging from it. "Help me fit these in the oarlocks," Otis directed Marcus and Becca, who sat nearest the center of the canoe. Near them, on each side of the boat, were two small metallic collars, just wide enough for the peg on the oar to slide in and rotate easily. Otis raised the handles, and the paddle ends slipped into the water with only a small gurgle. He flexed his hands, set his back to the front of the canoe, and pulled mightily on the oars. The paddles pushed against the water and propelled the large wooden vessel several feet further from shore.

As Otis raised his arms again to take another swipe at the waves, Paige could feel the boat surge backward, pushed by the waves back toward shore. "We're going back!" she said, frown lines creasing her forehead.

"Don't fret, lass. I'll get us through this surf—take a minute ..." Otis grunted with the effort he threw into drawing the oars back against the waves.

Marcus put a hand on Paige's arm. "Don't worry, Paige. Otis just needs to push us out past these small waves. Then we can put up the sail." He gestured to the canvas that pooled around their feet.

"See those short ropes attached to that pole?" Otis said. "Feed those through the holes along the top side of the sail and see if you can't tie them back around the pole."

"I'll tie," offered Marcus. He had been studying knots for a couple of months now and thought he could make the sail fast and secure. The other children crouched on the floor of the canoe, pulling the canvas taut and stringing the ropes through the sail in the correct order.

Otis watched Marcus make his first knot and nodded approval. "That's a pretty buntline hitch that'll hold that sail right." He continued rowing, having gotten into the rhythm needed to pull them out past the turbulent surf into the comparatively calm waters further out in the bay.

The children got the top side of the canvas tied off and began to look for the pole to tie off the bottom end. "Wait, maties. We'll get the mast up and tie the sail off after it's hoisted into place." Otis pulled on the oars several more times then flipped the paddle ends up and over the sides into the boat. He reached down alongside the keel line of the boat and pulled out a long, straight pole, carefully maneuvering it over the heads of the huddled children and swinging it around to fit in a fixture on the floor toward the front of the canoe. It stood tall, pointing up into the sky. "Here's the mast. Now lift that rigged canvas up to me." Standing on one of the bench seats, Otis took the pole from their hands and hoisted it to a fitting at the top of the mast. "Hang on to the bottom," he directed.

Paige watched in amazement as Otis stood, balanced, and not rocked by the constant motion of the waves against the hull of the boat. He shifted his feet just slightly from time to time but seemed to take most of the motion for granted. She noted that his legs were not straight but bent slightly, allowing him to shift his weight with a minimum of movement.

Otis jumped down from the bench and directed Marcus to one side of the sail while he went to the other. Together, they pulled out a third, slightly shorter pole from under the seats and began stringing it to the canvas. Soon they finished, leaving the canoe with a sail that was slightly wider at the top and with fixtures that allowed Otis to turn the sail back and forth. He turned the canvas slightly, and it caught the breeze, filling and billowing with a cheerful snap and rustle. The canoe leaped forward, and they began to move swiftly away from the island. The children clapped and cheered loudly, delighted with the speed and feeling of freedom.

As the children celebrated their escape from being marooned, miles and centuries away from their home in Minnesota, the Kincaid backyard was quiet. The sun shown brilliantly, the breeze wafted gently. On the bird feeder set in the middle of the lupine garden, a bright red cardinal fed his soft reddish-brown mate a sunflower seed and she trilled happily back to him. The lazy drone of a bumble bee grew loud, then faded as the bee followed its eyes and nose to its next flowery lunch counter. The leaves on the trees swayed lightly, but there was no movement to be seen in the deep green grass of the backyard.

There was no sign of the wild winds and snowy blizzard that had swept through the yard. No mounds of snow heaped at the fence, no branches snapped from trees. And no sign of any children. Not a broken shoelace nor a random giggle. No abandoned soccer balls, no dropped bicycles. The yard was so quiet, so empty, it seemed almost as if there had never been a child in the yard—ever.

CHAPTER 17

The canoe moved like a living thing, leaping above the waves, rocking as it landed in the troughs between the crests, vibrating as the wind filled its sail. Otis laughed in delight at the children's expressions as they turned their faces into the bright sun, relishing the heat and light, tasting the salt spray on their lips. Marcus called above the sound of the surf and wind, "I love sailing!"

Jake leaned as far forward as he could, feeling the wind blow through his hair. "Me too! I need to do more of this!"

Otis clapped Jake on the back. "You sound like you've never been at sea, lad. Surely you had your fill before you were marooned."

Jake looked stricken, caught in the awkward lie they'd told about how they had arrived on the island. Becca quickly spoke up. "He's always like this. Like everything is the first time. My little brother …"

Jake frowned at her superior tone but held his tongue, hoping her comment would divert Otis. He breathed a sigh of relief when Otis said, "Ah, the innocence of the young. I barely remember such a time myself anymore."

"How far do we sail, Cap'n?" Marcus asked, changing the subject.

"It should only take us a couple of hours to reach our destination."

"There's a port that close?" Paige asked.

"Nay, lass, but my crew—my other crew—" he corrected, with a nod to the children, "—was careening the *Bethany* over yonder." He pointed out across the horizon, to a seemingly endless expanse of ocean.

"Careening?"

Marcus explained, "They haul the ship over on its side then clean the barnacles and such sea creatures off the hull." Otis nodded at Marcus's explanation. "I hope the *Bethany* is still on its side. I'd love to see that."

Jake grimaced, suspicious that he was being made fun of. "Just how small is this boat?"

Otis said gently, "Ship, lad. She's a ship, and you'll find her plenty large. It's true that the crew pulls the ship on to the beach and over on to her side. It's a sight, for certain, but we'd best hope the crew is done with that hard work. I want to be out of the area before Cocklyn figures I've been left long enough and heads back."

Paige gasped. "Oh yes! Let's pray they're done and ready to sail!" She looked anxiously back toward the island they'd left, as though she was afraid the *Dark Falcon* would spring up from the surf behind them.

Otis patted her shoulder. "Don't fret, girl, Cocklyn is impatient, but he knows it'll take more than one night of marooning to break me down." He pointed suddenly across the stern to the waves ahead of their canoe. "Look quick! See the flying fish?" The children saw several silvery fish hanging above the water, looking for all the world as though they did, indeed, fly. Then they splashed back into the waves, sparkling drops flashing in the light. Suddenly several appeared again, leaping up out of the waves and falling back, time and again. The children laughed in delight.

Their small canoe continued to skim across the waves, and Becca almost felt like a flying fish herself as they bobbed up and down with the motion of the water. Salt spray blew off the hull of the boat, refreshing on her skin, tangy on her tongue. The sun slid higher and higher in the sky, its heat becoming like a weight on her shoulders. The wind kept the heat at bay, however, so the day felt pleasant and summery, rather than sticky and stifling.

At the rudder, Otis began to sing the same song they'd heard on the island. Even though he sang in another language—French, they'd thought earlier—it was clearly a happy tune. Soon they found themselves joining in the chorus, learning the words simply by listening. He laughed at a few of their pronunciations and corrected them. As they sailed on, they began to sound like they were singing actual words, not just making sounds.

The time flew by, and soon a small speck on the horizon appeared and then began to look like an island. The children knelt on the bench seats, trying to get a better look at their destination. "Sit yourselves down now, young 'uns, or you'll have us in the sea," Otis commanded. They settled, but even patient Paige found herself fidgeting, anxious to see more of this new place. How would Otis's crew greet them? Would they accept them or would the children find themselves marooned again on a new island?

The canoe drew close to the island, and Otis began to work the rudder. He turned the little boat out of the wind slightly, slowing its progress and turning them to sail along the coast.

"I don't see the *Bethany*," Jake said. "Have they gone without us?"

"Don't fret, boy. They're here. There's more than one side to an island, you know." They continued to sail along the shoreline, curving gently to the right as they began to round the island. As their direction changed, Otis maneuvered the sail to keep it billowing in the breeze. Marcus watched his technique carefully, storing away the information against future need. Becca watched the island, trying to think ahead to what they would do when they met with the rest of the crew of the *Bethany*. She felt Paige tremble as she huddled closer to Becca's side. Jake leaned as far as possible over the prow of the canoe, his eyes peeled for any sign of the crew or the ship. Suddenly, he jumped and pointed. "I see them, Captain Otis!"

"Dead ahead, lad! I see 'em. Now sit ye down and you'll all let me disembark first. Good men, they are, but suspicious of strangers—even young 'uns like you." Otis stood, balancing the canoe as it rocked under his movement and quickly pulled down the sail. He then placed the oars in the locks and began to row straight toward his crew. The children sat back out of his way, trying not to worry about his last statement.

Otis made quick work of the remaining distance between their canoe and the crewmen on the beach, working with the surf this time instead of against. "Ahoy, lads!" he shouted as the canoe drew close enough. "I see you've managed to keep your word and be where I need you for once." Several men ran into the surf and pulled the canoe up onto the sand, shouting greetings and exchanging good-natured insults with Otis. When the canoe was solidly beached, Otis leaped over the side, into the midst of his crew mates. Once they saw the men gather around Otis, ignoring them for the moment, the children climbed out of the canoe and stood together, awaiting their fate.

CHAPTER 18

The children huddled close to one another as Otis met his shipmates on the beach. The yelling and back-thumping was loud and raucous, and if Becca hadn't known better, she would have thought the crew was attacking their friend. Finally, the excitement subsided and the men began to move back toward their longboat, beached a short distance from the canoe.

"Hold, mates," Otis said. "Got room for four little 'uns?"

One man, with a gold ring piercing his ear and a scarlet bandana covering his long brown hair, turned and looked the children over sharply. "Since when have you grown a family, old man?" he asked.

"Foundlings on the island, Perkins," Otis replied. "And lifesavers too. Rescued me proper from Cocklyn and his scurvy lot."

Perkins surveyed them skeptically. "Rescuers? More in need of rescue, it seems."

Jake thrust his chin out. "We did rescue Mr. Otis and you can't say different!" Becca grabbed his arm, but he faced down the wry grin on Perkins's face.

"Well, pardon me, young master! I'll not judge what I have not seen." He turned back to the men preparing the longboat for launch. "Hold fast, boys! We've got passengers." He waved the children forward, bidding them step into the foamy surf. The men helped them into the boat, where Perkins directed them to the middle seat. "Ye'll stay driest there, if the waves heave up. But if the captain decides against ye, you'll be getting more than a light splashing—a good soaking might be all you're bound for!"

All the men laughed loudly, and Paige did her best to keep a smile on her face rather than let her worries show through. Otis turned back from the canoe at the sound of laughter. He eyed his young charges then told the other men near the canoe, "Take the canoe to the ship for me, lads. My wee ones need their pappy nearby." The men laughed again, but Otis made his way to the longboat and pulled himself in by the children. He put an arm around Paige's shoulders as he settled onto the bench next to her. "Don't worry, lass," he whispered. "I'll stick by my crew." Paige leaned against him briefly, grateful for his touch.

Perkins pulled himself into the longboat and told the other men, "Come on, lubbers. Let's shove off this pile o' sand!" He manned the rudder on the longboat, and Otis pitched in on the oars. The boat bobbed up and down with the waves that rolled their way toward the island. The oarsmen kept a steady pace, for if they faltered, the boat would have been pushed back to shore. The children faced the back of the boat, toward the island, like the rowers. They watched the island retreat from them, as surely as if it had sprouted arms and was swimming in the opposite direction.

Otis leaned closer and told the children, "Look forward. There's the *Bethany*." They all turned on the bench seat and saw the ship closely for the first time. She rode gently on the waves of the sheltered harbor, rocking up and down with the water.

On the front end of the ship—the bow, Marcus had told them—hung the wooden carving of a young woman's head and torso. Her hair flowed back against the sides of the ship as though waving in the wind. She was smiling gently, her face alight with expectation. The carver had angled her so she was leaning forward, urging her ship onward toward the horizon. Suddenly, the *Bethany* no longer sounded like a strange name for a ship but like the name of a beautiful young woman, excited about her future and what it held for her. The crew served her dream of sailing into adventure, driving her forward through skillful handling of the canvas, riggings, and rudder. The love of the sea stirred in the children's hearts, like an old dream awakening.

In very short order, the men brought the longboat close to the side of the *Bethany*. As they drew right alongside, crewmen on the ship dropped ropes and tackle attached to pulleys. The boatmen quickly attached the tackle to the bow and stern of the boat. With a shout, the men on deck high above them pulled on the ropes and the longboat began to rise up from the waves. Marcus watched with interest as the boatmen used oars and arms to keep the boat from swinging into the side of the great ship. Paige gasped as she looked over the side, seeing the sea retreat from them so quickly. Suddenly, the *Bethany* seemed to be a very tall ship indeed.

With a last strong pull, the longboat rose to the level of the short fence that surrounded the ship's deck and the men made short work of tying the boat off, secure until the next time it was needed to go ashore. The men in the longboat jumped onto the *Bethany*'s deck and several of them turned to lift the children out. Otis jumped out last and raised a hand in greeting to a man striding across the deck toward them. It was clear as the crew made way for him that he had high status among them. His brown hair was neatly trimmed, especially when compared to the rest of the crew. He wore a white shirt with loose sleeves under a dark leather vest, with black close-fitting pants. He wore a pair of knee-high boots, rather than the bare feet or soft moccasins the other men wore. This must be the captain. His tanned face was stern as he eyed the children gathered around Otis.

"Otis, you old seadog. What have you brought home with you?"

"Cap'n Penner, sir, it's good to be back on the *Bethany* where I belong." He put out his hand, and Penner grasped it firmly. "I owe my life to these wee tots, I must admit. Kept Cocklyn from woolding me eyes out with the prettiest bit of tomfoolery you've ever seen. I've pledged to see 'em safe to whatever destination seems best."

Penner looked Otis steadily in the eye, and the silence stretched long and uncomfortably. When he finally spoke, his voice was low and intense. "Would you turn the *Bethany* into a nursery then, ignoring our mission?"

"Oh no, sir, not for a moment. These brave ones have pledged their loyalty to our mission. We'll fulfill our duty to the king and crew, then find a final home for these poor orphans." Otis looked at his young friends. "I'll warrant we'll find them more help than hindrance, sir."

Again, Penner held his tongue. He turned his gaze on the children, and they stood quietly before him. Jake raised his small chin, meeting the challenge of the captain's stare. When it became clear they would be not intimidated by his glare and silence, Penner nodded once and turned back to Otis. "Well, we'll have to bring them before the entire crew tonight for a final vote. But you might as well get them some food and drink. It'll not do to have them starve before we make our decision." Penner turned on his heel and strode back across the deck, calling orders to weigh anchor and prepare to sail to his crew as he went.

CHAPTER 19

The children kept out of the way as the *Bethany* set sail, left uncertain of their status by Captain Penner's pronouncement that the crew had to decide if they could stay. "Why doesn't Captain Penner just say yes or no?" Jake complained. "Then at least we'd know."

"Buccaneers and pirates don't work that way," Marcus explained. "They are actually quite democratic. The captain may have the say in running the ship, but major decisions are made by a vote of the crew. Like where their next destination should be or who should they attack next."

"At least we're a major decision," Becca grumped. "But how do we get everyone on our side? Shouldn't we be talking to them, making friends, getting in good with the men?"

Paige frowned. "They look awfully busy. I don't think we should get in their way."

"I agree." Marcus nodded. "We'll have to trust Otis to plead our case."

Becca shook her head firmly. She couldn't stand not having any say in what was going to happen to them. "We can't just leave this to him."

"Hey, Otis is our captain! He made a deal with us," Jake said angrily.

"He's a pirate. Can we really trust him?"

Jake got to his feet, his hands fisted, arms stiff at his sides. "A privateer, not a pirate, and I believe him."

"You're a child. You trust anyone who smiles at you." Becca's tone was so condescending that Paige flinched. Jake had heard her speak like this before and hated it. He wasn't about to let it slip by quietly now. His face grew red and his eyes narrowed. Marcus quickly stood and stepped between Jake and Becca.

"This is not a time to fight among ourselves." He put a hand on Jake's shoulder. "Becca, if we want to get home, we have to help Otis. We've already been through this."

"Yes, but we've got to do something. We can't just sit here." Becca was on her feet now, her anger flaring. Paige knew this Becca—didn't really like her much, but she knew her. She'd seen Becca pick fights with girls from middle school when she was in this kind of mood. Caught in the middle of something she couldn't change. Becca never was one just to go with the flow.

Paige pulled the snow globe out of Jake's backpack. "The poem, Becca. Remember? 'A treasure's been lost. A buccaneer's bounty.' Otis fits that picture perfectly." She held the snow globe up, and it shone brightly in the sun.

Marcus shielded his eyes as the globe blazed in Paige's hand. "Is that globe shining?"

The children sat again, even Becca, mesmerized by the glowing snow globe. Paige placed it on the deck, where it was blocked from the crew's view by the tight circle formed by the children's crossed legs. Its smooth glass glinted brightly in the sun, sparking light as though it had fireworks in its interior. But even in the dazzling sunlight, beneath these sharp flashes, the globe continued to glow softly. It wasn't simply the inner glow of a well-hidden light fixture. Everything shone—the glass, the wood base, the beautifully crafted miniature ship, the carved yet lively ocean waves. They all radiated a definite light that had no obvious source.

"Did it do this back home?" Paige asked. "I don't remember …"

Becca shook her head somewhat impatiently as she kept her eyes on this small puzzle in the midst of their greater mystery. "No, it didn't. I know it didn't. What does it mean?"

Marcus leaned closer and waved his hand near the globe without touching it. No shadow marred its surface or interrupted the glow. "I can still feel the tingle we felt back home," he said. "But I concur that there was no glow."

"Did it glow on the beach?" Paige asked, thinking of the beach miles away, where they first landed.

Becca shrugged. "Uh, we were kind of busy to notice."

Jake nodded definitely. "But it was glowing."

"Sure it was, Jake."

Jake shoved Becca. "I saw it. I did."

"Why didn't you say something then, shrimp?"

Jake grimaced at the hated nickname. "Because I knew you'd—" He shoved his sister again. "You'd just say it was the sun or something. You'd have laughed."

Marcus spoke quickly, heading off the scornful comment that would certainly spring to Becca's lips.

"Jake, I get why you didn't say anything." He gently slapped his buddy's shoulder. "But you have to speak up when you notice something." He looked intently at the girls as well. "We must all speak up. We're in a situation filled with unknowns. We have no way of knowing what may turn out to be important, so we must observe and note it all. And we must share those observations with the group. No secrets." Marcus continued to gaze closely at the others, letting his words sink in. They remained silent, each of them realizing how right Marcus was. They knew so little of what was happening and even less of what was to come. The tiniest misstep, the smallest unnoticed clue could mean the difference between going home and staying in this place and time forever.

Jake said, his voice tight, "I'm sorry." His brow wrinkled with worry and his eyes pleaded forgiveness.

Marcus pushed Jake's shoulder, rocking the younger boy where he sat. "Aw, nuts to that," he grinned.

Jake's face immediately brightened, and he pushed Marcus back. "Yeah, nuts to you too."

Paige rolled her eyes. "Boys." She reached across their little circle, careful not to knock into the snow globe. She patted Jake's knee. "Don't sweat it, Jake. Could have been any of us."

"Ah, nuts to you!" Jake laughed but gripped Paige's hand briefly in thanks. He could always count on Paige to take the sting out of Becca's harsh comments or his own mistakes.

"Well, this is certainly interesting," Becca said. "But we still don't know if Otis is our ticket home. I say we need to keep our options open. Maybe it's someone else. Maybe the treasure is somewhere else."

"I don't believe it's just coincidence that the globe dropped us practically at Otis's feet," Paige said. "We need to stick with him—and keep our word to him."

"It's a poem, Paige. They write those things on purpose so that no one can understand them. Otis may just be a distraction."

"Uh, guys," Jake said.

Marcus said, "Though it is hard to apply logic to what is obviously a magical process, it doesn't seem likely that whatever power it was that sent us here wouldn't have placed us where we could begin our quest immediately. Otis seems to be our most logical quest."

"Guys ..." Jake said, a bit more forcefully.

"You're right, there is no logic here. Otis has all his crew mates to help him. Why would he need us?"

"Guys!" Jake shouted.

"What?!" all three said.

"Look at the globe." They did and saw a dull, nonglowing snow globe sitting before them.

"What happened?" Paige asked, worry evident in her voice. What would they do if they'd lost their magic?

"What did you do?" Becca said harshly.

Jake kept his eyes glued on the globe. "Marcus, say what you think about sticking with Otis."

"What are you talking about now, Jake? Just tell us." Becca sighed.

"No, you have to see. Look at the globe. Marcus, say it."

Marcus cleared his throat. "I said I believe Otis is our quest. We need to stay with him."

The snow globe flared, sparking brightly once again.

"Now you, Becca."

"I … I think it's a mistake to stay with Otis. We don't …" She gasped as they all saw the globe fade as quickly as it flared, dull and dead-looking once again.

Paige said quickly, "No, we have to stay with Otis. Help him find his buccaneer's bounty." The globe flashed and shone steadily, nearly blinding in its brightness.

Jake grinned. "I think it's trying to tell us something."

Becca nodded slowly. "I think you're right. Good catch, Jake."

His grin grew even wider. "Okay, I guess Otis is our quest."

The globe flashed and sparked, fireworks shining approval for the children's decision.

After several hours of sailing, during which the children kept a watchful eye on the crew as they went about their work, Otis found his way up to them on the foredeck. "Been pretty quiet on the whole, ain't ya?" he said, grinning at them.

"We didn't want to get in the way," Marcus said. "We don't know enough about sailing to be helpful."

"Ah, we'll change that soon enough. You're quick learners, I've seen."

"If we get to stay," Paige said.

Otis patted her hand. "Have you been fretting about that all day? There's no need."

"I don't know," Becca said. "No one seemed all that interested in having us here." As she finished speaking, a young crewman bounded up the stairs to stand before them. He wore a vivid red shirt, covered by a short brown vest and tucked into canvas pants that were cut short at the middle of his calves. He wore no stockings or shoes, and seemed not to notice how hot the boat decking was beneather his feet. His freckled face smiled shyly, and he tugged at his blond hair as he gave them a small bow in greeting.

"Good day, young ladies, gentlemen."

Otis introduced the young man. "This is Jeremiah, the ship's cabin boy. Captain's aide, cook's assistant, all-round crewman. A good lad, learning the ropes."

Jeremiah ducked his head, trying to hide his pleased grin. "Aw, Otis, just doing my job."

"Doing it well, boy. No shame in taking that compliment."

Jeremiah's face reddened even more, and he looked away quickly. "Well, uh ... Pierre sent me up. Told me to have our guests come down to dinner. He'll feed them in the first seating."

"Right nice of Pierre. Might irritate the crew some ..."

Jeremiah laughed. "Like that will bother the quartermaster! More likely the reason he'd do it." The teen leaned close, speaking in a loud whisper. "I think Monsieur Pierre wants to test the meddle of these young 'uns for himself."

Paige looked alarmed. "Test our metal? I don't have anything metal. What will he want from me?"

Marcus suppressed a laugh. "Not metal, Paige. Meddle, with a D. It means he wants to get to know us, see how we react."

Jeremiah looked shyly at the pretty redhead. "Aye, miss, don't vex yourself. Pierre can be your best friend, next to the captain hisself."

Otis stood and the children followed suit. "Breakfast was a long time ago. I suggest we go and tuck into one of Pierre's fine meals—and if we can do so early, so much the better." Otis and his small crew trooped down from the foredeck, and he led them to the doors of the main cabin. The doors stood wide, and the children could see that the large room was used for many purposes. To one side, there was a four-poster bed, with curtains drawn around it. Next to it was a tall cabinet that appeared to be a free-standing closet. On the other side, an elaborately carved desk stood, covered with rolled documents and an instrument case of some sort. Straight across from the doors was a wall of windows, looking out under the bowsprit, the spray of the waves splashing and sparkling in the sunshine. The center of the room held a few long tables and many chairs, seating for the meal.

On the other side of the room, Jeremiah crossed over to take his place behind a large table, filled with bowls and plates of food. Another man already stood there, slicing a crusty loaf of bread. He wore a bright yellow kerchief on top of his head, tied at the back and holding his long, brown curls off his face. A silver ring pierced one ear, and he sported a thin mustache above his pleasant smile. He wore a white shirt, much as they'd seen on many others, but he also had on a leather apron, looped around his neck and covering his chest. The front of the apron had several large pockets just below the waist, and the children could see the handles of various utensils—some recognizable as kitchenware, others not so easily named.

He looked up as Jeremiah made a quiet comment to him. The tall man set down his knife and came across the room toward the children. Jake tried not to stare as the older man stumped across the floor, his artificial wooden leg clunking hollowly as it hit the decking. The man noticed his gaze, however, and stopped short.

"Eh, *mon ami*," he said, his accent announcing loudly that he was from France, not England, as so many of the other men were. "It is a leg most belle, is it not?" He held the wood leg aloft, balancing on his good foot. It was indeed beautiful, intricate carvings up and down and around its surface. Jake gulped and nodded, unable to speak a word in his embarrassment.

The Frenchman laughed and set his peg leg back down. "Otis, you must tell your boy to blink or his eyes will pop right from his head!"

"Jake, this is Pierre. A fine sailor and musketeer until a cannonball took his leg." Otis gestured to the carved peg leg. "But the sea is in his blood, so he got himself this artwork and came back aboard as our fine chef and quartermaster." He turned and surveyed the dishes that Pierre and Jeremiah had placed on the table. "And he's showing off his best today, I see."

Pierre smiled proudly. "It will never be said that guests on the *Bethany* were not well-fed. And these petites have been marooned, I am told. They need a good meal. Come, *mes enfants*, satisfy yourselves."

Pierre had given them a meal fit for special guests. Whole roasted chickens were the centerpiece, golden brown and juicy looking. Several flagons of gravy steamed next to them. There were bowls heaped with boiled potatoes and others with carrots. Large, rustic loaves of freshly baked bread gave off their fragrant aroma. Despite their worries, the children's mouths began to water and their thoughts turned to dinner rather than what their future held.

Jeremiah filled tankards of water for them as Pierre filled their plates, taking the opportunity to smile again at Paige. "Come sit here," he said, showing them to spots at the table. No sooner had they gotten seated than other members of the crew began filing in. Jeremiah hurried back to help Pierre serve the men, the line moving quickly as they filled plates and tankards. The noise level grew, and the children tried hard to listen to as much of the conversation as they could. But they couldn't help but notice that no one came to speak with them or Otis directly.

Captain Penner swept through the doors, calling for water. He noted the children sitting at the table and crossed to them with his tankard. "I see Pierre is taking good care of you," he said with a brief smile.

"Yes, sir," Paige piped up quickly. "He's a very good cook, isn't he?"

"Aye, he is that. He's also a very good quartermaster."

Jake swallowed his mouthful of bread and said, "Otis called him that earlier. What does that mean, sir?"

"A quartermaster is charged with many tasks. He supplies the ship, makes sure we are stocked for our voyages. He negotiates for work needed when we're in port, and he aids me in signing on new crew. But most importantly, he divides up any bounty we obtain, making certain all shares are divided out per the ship's articles—the agreement we've all signed on to."

"An important man," Paige said, sorry she'd called him a cook. "He's been kind to us."

Penner nodded. "He is that as well. Enjoy your meal, children." He turned and went back to the table to fill his own plate. The children and Otis were left in solitude to finish their meals. Becca didn't think this was a good sign.

As they were cleaning their plates, Pierre came over with a pitcher of water. "*Très bon, mon petites.* You have eaten well. A chef likes to see his creations enjoyed so fully." He poured each of them more water. "You have enjoyed your dinner?"

"It was wonderful, Pierre," Paige assured him. "Where did you get chicken here at sea?" Paige knew that, in this time, there were no such things as refrigerators to keep meat fresh.

"Have you not heard them, in the hold? We will keep some for eggs, to be sure, but we have several cages of the birds. We kill them as we need them."

Paige gulped, trying hard not to think of the delicious food she had just eaten as a living creature just hours before. Marcus saw her discomfort and changed the subject quickly. "Do you know, Pierre, when the crew will meet? To discuss our status?"

Pierre nodded, his cheerful countenance becoming solemn. "It will be tonight. You will know before we sleep."

Becca asked, "Why didn't anyone sit with us? That's not a good sign, is it?"

Pierre and Otis exchanged a glance, then Pierre laid a reassuring hand on Becca's. "Do not read omens in all things, *ma cherie*. Go on now. Enjoy the sunshine and the sea spray. You'll know how the men feel soon enough."

CHAPTER 20

After a few more hours of sailing, as the sun was nearing the horizon, the *Bethany* drew close to another beautiful island. Captain Penner's first mate began to shout orders to the men, making it clear they would be anchoring in the calm harbor the children saw over the bow. Paige turned to Otis, who had come up once again to check on his young charges and asked, "Won't the *Dark Falcon* find us if we stop sailing?"

"Oh, darlin', don't fret yourself. Cap'n knows what he's doing and the *Falcon* isn't looking for us just yet." He paused and made sure all the children were looking at him. "Now, once we've dropped anchor, you all will have to hold yourself ready. The crew will be meeting to decide if you'll join us as crew or be dropped at our next port."

"Can't we come?" Becca asked.

"No, lass, ye're not crew so there's no place for you in our meeting." Otis patted her shoulder. "Trust me, dearie, the vote will go our way."

"How can you be so sure?"

Otis smiled his mischievous smile. "Oh, my girl, I know more than a bit about getting people around to my way of thinking. You're my crew now, as well as these men, and I'll make certain we stick together."

"Otis!" the first mate called to him from the main deck. "Leave your orphans now. There's work to do to make harbor." Otis gave Becca's shoulder one more pat and went to his chores. The children sat back down to await their fate.

The crew efficiently brought the ship to anchor in the small bay. Marcus moved back and forth, trying to keep an eye on everything that was going on. He took note of how the men climbed up (or swarmed as he knew it was called) the rigging and furled the sails. As the sails folded in on themselves, the ship slowed, no longer running before the wind. He watched as they unwound the chain to release the heavy metal anchor, which would dig into the soft sand bottom of the bay and hold them steadily in place on top of the gentle waves. They all watched as every single member of the crew finished their work and headed into the captain's cabin below the aft quarterdeck.

"Can't we do anything?" Becca said angrily as the last two men made their way into the cabin and closed the doors with finality.

After a brief silence, Paige said simply, "Pray."

For the next half-hour, they alternated between prayer and despair, and they waited. It was the longest thirty minutes any of them had ever lived through. Finally, the doors opened again, and one of the crew men waved to them. "The captain will see you now. Look lively!" The children jumped up and ran across the deck to the cabin. Becca searched the buccaneer's face, hoping for a clue as to the final decision. But his eyes were hard and his face expressionless, and she could not guess what had passed behind these doors. She was also surprised to see, beneath the skin made dark by the hot sun and scrubbed harsh by the wind, a very young man looking back at her. She wondered what had carried him away from his mom and dad to this hard life on the sea.

The children were ushered into the captain's great cabin where the entire crew was crowded, looking them up and down. Paige looked to Otis immediately but could not read his facial expression. Were they in or out? He gave them no clue but looked

SECRETS OF THE SNOW GLOBES

solemnly at them along with the rest of the crew. Captain Penner sat just before them, sprawling easily in his chair.

"So Otis has told us his tale. Now you'll each have a chance to tell us why you should stay." He jabbed a finger at Becca. "Name and your reason, lass."

Becca lifted her chin and took a step forward. "I'm Becca, sir. I think we should stay because … um … well, we made a promise to Otis. And we'll keep that promise here with all of you. It's important to keep our promise."

Penner nodded once and waved Jake forward. "You, boy, give us your line."

"I'm Jake, and we can help you and your crew. We'll do what you tell us."

Marcus got the next nod. "I'm Marcus. I'm a fast learner and know a bit about sailing, tracking, and most things. I'll be useful."

Penner looked at Paige. "And you, gingertop?"

"I'm Paige. I guess I think we should stay because we need you. I mean, yeah, we've promised to be Otis's crew and that means we'll be your crew, since you're Otis's captain. But if you abandon us, we'll never have a home again." Paige ducked her head quickly, hoping this room full of rough men did not see the glint of wetness in her eye.

If Penner had seen her tear, he seemed to remain hardened to it. He looked each of them in the eye once more then nodded and turned to his men. "You've heard it all now, me boys. What say you? Is it yea or is it no? Speak up now!"

A crash of sound from the throats of the men made Jake flinch, so much so that for a moment, he could not tell if it was a yes or no. But he realized that the sound he was hearing was a long "a," not a trailing "o." He looked quickly for Otis, who was now beaming ear to ear.

"Seems the crew has been moved by your plight," Penner said, a smile now curving his lips. "If you'll pledge faith to the *Bethany*, you'll be crew, right and proper." He stood and held out his left hand, palm up. "Pledge now!" Marcus laid his hand on top of the captain's, Jake next, then Paige, and lastly Becca. Penner laid his right hand on top, palm down. With a firm grip and single shake up and down, the children became crew. As he released them, the crowd of men broke into a loud cheer.

Suddenly, Otis was by their sides and gathered all the children into his arms. "That's me, hearties," he crowed. "New and old crew united, as it should be." He laughed out loud at the rather stunned expression on Paige's face. "Confused, my lass?"

"I thought … it kinda looked like they all hated us. They all seemed so serious." Marcus and Jake joined in Otis's laughter. "What? What's so funny?"

"It's just guys, Paige," Jake said, giving her a gentle push. "It's how we are."

Paige looked at Becca, who just shrugged. All around them, the noise level wound higher and higher, as the serious business that had been before them was now completed. Bottles and tankards of rum were being passed among the men. Otis stopped a couple of bottles and quickly poured a bit from each of them into cups, which he handed to the children. "Here ye go. A wee nipperkin will do ye good." When they hesitated, he pressed. "Come on now. Ye're crew now. The captain's taken you on. Show 'im he's nothing to regret."

Becca raised her cup to her nose, smelling cinnamon and a dark sugary fragrance. She also smelled the rum. "Otis, can't we just have water?"

Otis grinned. "Old Otis knows how to take care of young'uns. Ye've got grog—just a wee drop of rum with your sugar and spice." He gestured briefly behind. "Look around now. The crew is watching. Are ye with us or are ye outsiders?" The children looked around and saw that the crew was indeed watching them as they raised their own glasses.

Marcus hoisted his cup and shouted "To the *Bethany*!" He tipped his cup and swallowed quickly.

"It's okay, guys, tastes pretty good," he told the others as the crew erupted into cheers, toasting their ship. Paige and Jake gulped their grog, again to the crew's approval. "Becca, just drink it." Marcus leaned in and spoke in her ear. "It won't hurt you." Becca scowled, held her nose, and swallowed her drink. She coughed as the mixture hit the back of her throat, and the crew shouted with laughter.

Captain Penner roared above the chaos. "All right, me hearties, we've had our fun." The crowd cheered. "These lads and lasses have done as we asked which is no more than you can ask of any crewman. So they've got a vote same as any of us." The privateers shouted their approval. "And they'll have their share in the bounty, just as is fair." Again, the men cheered.

"We don't want any of the treasure," Becca tried to say above the noise. "Otis, they don't have to give us anything."

Otis laid his finger on his lips. "Hush now. If you're crew, you take part of the responsibility and part of the reward. These men will not find it in your favor if you refuse it. You'll only make them suspicious. We're as fair a ruled ship as you'll find on the high seas. Captain Penner manages this motley bunch, but he'll do as the majority says or find another ship."

"So, you four," Captain Penner was addressing them directly. "Even though we already have a majority, your voices will be heard. You know we seek the lost treasure, to return what's due to the king in London and split the rest fairly amongst us. What say you on this plan? Will you sail with us on this?"

"Aye, aye, Captain! Yes, sir!" All four agreed quickly, their voices clear and loud.

"Then rest well tonight, all of you," Penner said to the full room. "Tomorrow we sail for treasure!" Another loud cheer went up and more rum flowed. Penner looked at Otis and said, "Perhaps our new crew could use more sleep than the rest of this scurvy bunch. The forward hold should do nicely." He looked at each of the children, his eyes more gentle than Paige had yet seen them. "Sleep deeply and well, my little friends. Tomorrow you'll learn what it truly means to crew on the *Bethany*. Hard work, but you'll find the rewards worth it in the end. You've made many good friends tonight, so sleep securely." He turned back to his crew's celebration, and Otis herded the children back out of the cabin into the clear, dark night.

CHAPTER 21

Paige leaned back against the gunwale in the bow of the *Bethany*, taking a short break from washing the dishes used for breakfast that day. She gazed over the deck stretching below and away from her. There was activity everywhere—men climbing the rigging to check the canvas, others scrubbing the deck with bucket and brush, still others working to mend some small sails from one of the longboats that hung along the side of the ship. The captain stood at the helm, leaning alertly on the wheel, which she knew worked the rudder. His eyes were fixed on the horizon, head lifted into the brisk wind, guiding the ship through the shining waters, ever closer to the treasure—and to completing their quest.

They had been sailing for several days now, and Paige felt as though they'd truly become part of the crew. She saw Marcus sitting near Otis, examining the ropes coiled around the main mast. As she watched, he laughed at something Marcus said, his dry old man's cackle rising to her ears even against the wind. He pulled the rope higher then began to show Marcus how to tie a complicated knot. Jake was working with Jeremiah, swabbing the deck with salt water they'd hauled up by bucket, from over the side of the ship. Becca was peeling potatoes, working alongside one of Pierre's assistants. They were all working crew members, and it felt good to be a part of this new family.

The wind blew her hair back off her face, drying the sweat that had begun to form on her forehead in the bright Caribbean sun. Before them, the ocean swelled and rolled, whitecaps shining in the light. She looked down into the spray that flew off the bow where the ship sliced through the water. What a day to be alive! What a place and time! Paige almost felt like she wouldn't mind if they never completed their quest and had to stay here forever. She knew it was wrong, but the crew felt more like family than her own mother often did. Paige knew her mom's life was hard, since Dad had left them. But Paige also often thought she had become just another task on her mom's "to-do" list rather than a beloved daughter or even a helper, like she was here. She closed her eyes and lifted her face to the sun, putting aside these darker thoughts and let happiness warm her very bones.

Suddenly behind her, a cheerful shout raised from the crew. She turned and saw that one of the crewmen had brought out a small box with two wooden ends joined by leather flexible tube. He pulled the wooden ends apart and pressed them back together, and a squeal of music issued from his small instrument. An accordion? The man sat on a convenient crate and began to play. His hands moved back and forth, pushing air through the instrument and his fingers flew over small ivory buttons on the wooden ends. A joyous tune filled the air and the men began to clap in time with the melody.

Otis jumped to his feet and danced a few steps in place. "Miss Becca!" he cried, holding his hand out to her where she sat on a coil of rope, potato and paring knife in her hand. She blushed but rose, setting those things aside, and went to take his hand. Otis bowed deeply, then took both her hands in his and led her on a merry jig across the deck. The men laughed and clapped all the louder. Jeremiah, blushing furiously, dropped his brush and ran to the foot of the stairs that led to Paige's perch at the bow.

"Miss Paige, you'll not sit out a good concertina tune, will you?" He held out his hand, and Paige moved forward to take it. The young sailor swung her off her feet, down the steps, and led her out on to the deck. She had no idea how to dance to this kind of music, but her feet seemed to have developed a mind of their own. They twitched and stomped, following her partner's lead. More men began to dance, spurred on by the merry music. Soon, even Marcus and Jake were on their feet, stomping and jumping with all the others. It seemed the whole crew had gone mad with joy. Paige laughed in sheer delight.

The bright, free day was suddenly shattered by a cry from the crow's nest—"Ship ahoy! Off the port bow!" The music stopped, and the crew all turned to the left side of the ship and saw a large vessel sailing toward them. The children rushed over to the gunwale, peering through the spindles of that fence to see.

Captain Penner had pulled out the glass—the long brass-encased arrangement of lenses that brought things afar into closer focus. It was the forerunner of the binoculars Jake carried in his backpack. Marcus had warned him seriously, however, not to pull them out. These had not yet been invented in this time, and they would be very hard to explain. But Jake sure wished he could use them now, to see more about this ship bearing down on them.

"I see a Dutch flag," the captain announced, gazing through the glass. "They're tacking prettily, heading toward us, but not at an unseemly speed." Pirate vessels often ran fast along the waves, unburdened by much cargo. They carried cannon, ammunition, food, and crew—the minimum they could carry, the better to chase down their prey. "I see no obvious gun ports ..." He lowered the glass and handed it to Otis. "Is it the *Falcon*?"

Otis peered across the waves, trying to focus on the bowsprit. He could not see one, though not all ships carried one on their bow. And he knew many pirate vessels—the *Dark Falcon* included—had bowsprits that could be removed to fool potential victim ships. He tried to bring some of the men on deck into focus, but the glass was not that good. "Can't be sure, Cap'n. We'd best keep an eye on her."

Penner nodded, and the first mate relayed the message to the lookout high above them. If the ship began to speed up or move toward them more directly, he'd shout the change for all to hear.

The Dutch ship continued its course toward them, seemingly unhurried, but it worried Otis. With all the great wide ocean to choose from, why did they seem so intent on coming alongside the *Bethany*? As he reached the children, he said, "Keep a sharp eye now. This vessel sets me on edge. If I say, you get below decks and hide yourself in the deepest dark." They nodded solemnly.

The watch in the crow's nest kept a sharp eye indeed because it wasn't but half an hour later that he again called urgently. "Ship ahoy, Cap'n. She's coming on strong!" The crew and the children ran to the port rail, straining for a look. Indeed, the Dutch ship seemed to be moving faster, coming more directly at them. Captain Penner stepped to the rail, raising the spyglass. The other ship was so close now, that it was hardly necessary. Everyone could see hurried activity aboard the Dutch vessel, more crew than was noticeable before. Suddenly the Dutch flag, flying from the main mast dropped, and they could all see a deep black flag rising in its place. A crossed cutlass emblem blazed white against the ebony flag.

"Pirates!" the watchman shouted. "Pirates upon us!"

"Battle stations, lads! Look lively now!" The calls went out from the captain and the mate, hurrying their men into position to do battle with the pirates. The menacing black flag was closer now, the ship moving faster than seemed possible.

Marcus was watching intently. "How can they be going so fast now? The wind hasn't changed."

"Do they have a motor?" Jake asked.

"Ssh, no, nothing like that exists," Becca said impatiently.

Otis responded to Marcus's question. "They were towing cargo. Flip towlines filled with mattresses, pots, and sea anchors over the back of the ship, dragging against the sea. That slows them down even under full sail. Made them look like a fat merchant vessel, not an attack ship." Otis started to pull the children away from the gunwale. "Now they're close enough so's we can't outrun them. So they cut the towlines and the ship comes up to full speed." Otis spat over the rail into the sea. "A devil's trick, used to great advantage by these demons." He tugged on Marcus's shirt. "Come, now's the time for you to hide yourselves. Don't argue—this lot will eat you alive."

Otis chivvied them down the hatch and then ran for his pistol and his saber. He saw portals opening in the sides of the pirate ship. Well disguised gun ports swung wide as cannon barrels began to bristle from the ship's sides.

Marcus led the others into the dark shadows below deck, seeking a hidden spot he'd prepared for just this kind of emergency. He had pushed and pulled water barrels, crates, and bales of hay into place, carving out a snug cave of protection, out of sight and out of the way of the sailors rushing to open the gun ports in the *Bethany*'s side. "Come on, this is as safe as we'll get," he told the others. Paige shoved into the dark, close space first then turned to face Jake as he poked his head through the opening. He scrambled through, falling half into Paige's lap. She wrapped her arms around him, and he stayed quietly in her embrace. Becca slithered through, sliding aside as Marcus backed in, pulling a hay bale across the opening. They huddled in the dark, listening to the shouts of the crew and prayed for safety.

Topside, Otis put the children from his thoughts. He needed to focus fully on the battle before him now, keeping his step sure and his eye sharp. The pirate ship was close enough now for him to see faces of the crew. There he was—that ugly blighter, Hargest. Another searching look and Otis found Captain

Cocklyn, standing smug on his quarterdeck, shouting orders to his men.

Otis swayed slightly as the *Bethany* turned broadside to the enemy vessel, pushing her own cannons into position. A quick count, however, showed the *Bethany* to be badly outgunned. Nevertheless, Captain Penner ordered the guns fired, hoping to mortally wound the brig before they could get off a shot. As the *Bethany*'s cannons roared, so did the pirate cannons'. The heavy iron balls flew through the air, an eerie silence in the moments before they hit. Most splashed heavily into the ocean, raising huge sprays of water, drenching the decks. One of the *Bethany*'s cannonballs smashed through the very end of the bow of the pirate brig—a blow, but not a killing one.

The *Bethany* did not fare so well. Only one ball hit her as well, but the shot was better placed. It dropped through the quarterdeck, smashing a gigantic hole through the deck and out through the ship's side, just above the waterline. Screams of men hit by the ball or the shrapnel it blew through the ship filled the air. The ship's doctor ran to the area to do whatever he could for the wounded. Otis ran in that direction as well to see if any repairs could be affected on the ship, even in the midst of battle.

As they worked feverishly, nearly side by side, their efforts seemed almost the same. The doctor bound holes in men's arms and legs, quickly staving off the immediate danger of bleeding to death. Otis and several able men quickly began to nail planking back over the hole in the ship's side, trying to raise the level of protection against waves trying to flow into the ship's hold. Above them, through the gaping break in the deck, they could hear the battle rage on. More cannon fire, though none was accurate enough to cause further damage to the *Bethany*. Men ran back and forth, shouting orders and encouragement to one another. Otis kept his eye on his work, but his mind was with the children that he prayed had done as he told them.

In their dark cave that provided so little protection, Paige held tight to Jake, whispering every Bible verse she knew. Jake leaned against her and when she began the Twenty-Third Psalm—"the Lord is my shepherd"—he joined her with vigor. Their prayer brought tears to Becca's eyes as she wondered if this would be the last time she'd hear these words.

Marcus peered through a space between the water barrel and crate, trying to see what was happening. "That shot hit the aft quarterdeck."

"Are we sinking?"

"No, the damage is mostly from above. Some of the men are putting planks back up over the gap." Marcus gasped. "I see Otis!"

"Is he hurt?" Becca crowded next to him, trying to get a look.

"No, he's leading the repair team." They both cringed back as they heard another set of cannonballs fly. Paige came to the end of the psalm and began again. Jake paused then joined her, though his voice quavered.

"How can the *Bethany* survive this?" Becca asked.

"Can't you feel the movement? The captain is maneuvering out of range, I'd say."

Suddenly came a terrible tearing sound, as though giant claws were ripping at the wood of the hull. "Gaff hooks!" they heard Otis shout. "To the gunwales, lads!"

"Gaff hooks?" Becca wondered what new terror this could mean.

"The pirates have gotten close enough to the *Bethany* to throw ropes across the sea, tying the two ships together," Marcus told her. "They'll try to swarm across those lines and bring the battle over here, hand-to-hand. This will get rough."

Otis and his helpers abandoned their carpentry work, for now it was time to fight. If they could not hold off the pirates, the hole in their ship would be of no import. They would all be dead. The men swarmed up from the hold, pistols and swords held high.

The pirates were preparing to make their crossing. The crew of the *Bethany* had begun to cut the ropes, but there were so many enemies, so many pistols. The pirates strung multiple pistols from ribbons that they wore hanging around their necks. They didn't have to pause to reload as they shot at the crew, keeping them away from the gaff hooks. Some of the pirates began to crawl over the ropes, swaying above the ocean waves. With a roar, the crew of the *Bethany* charged the ropes, braving the flying buckshot, knowing they had to stop this invasion.

The children stared at the deck above them, trying to determine what was happening just from the noises they were hearing. Suddenly, Marcus grabbed Jake's backpack and began searching through it. "Jake, have you still got that can of charcoal lighter fluid? And the butane lighter?"

"Of course." Jake pulled the pack away from Marcus and zeroed in on an inside zippered pocket. He pulled out a slender wand, small opening on one end, a trigger on the other. He pulled that trigger and a small bluish flame shot out. "Working." He unzipped one of the outer pockets of his pack and brought out the can of flammable liquid. "What are you thinking?"

Becca hissed, "Why do you have this stuff? It's dangerous."

"Let him be," Marcus said as he began to pull handfuls of straw out of the bale that covered the opening of their hiding place. He tossed them at Becca and Paige. "See if you can kind of braid these into some sort of stiff brush. I need something to tie them on to."

Jake scrabbled in his pack and pulled out several pairs of chopsticks. Marcus took them with slightly raised eyebrows. Jake bobbed his head as he handed them off. "Never know when you'll need a good stick," he said. "Mr. Chen always sends me extras when we get takeout."

The children worked quickly, making small makeshift torches, wrapping dry straw plaits around the chopsticks. Marcus grabbed them up as they finished, stuffed them in his pockets with the lighter and fluid, hissed "stay here," and began to snake out of their hiding spot. Paige grabbed his ankle.

"What are you doing?"

"I've got to try and help them get rid of those ropes. I'll be all right."

"Marcus!"

"Just pray!" He scrambled out between the bales and ran across the hold to the stairs. The other three held hands and began to pray fervently for his safety and the success of whatever plan he had in mind.

Marcus crawled up the stairs, carefully poking his head above the decking. He saw the *Bethany*'s crew at the gunwales, shooting at the pirates trying to swarm across the ocean gap along the ropes. He quickly pulled out the torches and fuel, dousing each straw-headed stick with the extremely flammable liquid. Staying low, he crawled across the deck to the gunwale, where the grappling hooks held the ropes taut that held the ships together. He quickly lit a torch, which exploded into flame. He jammed it between the hook and the rope, splashing a bit more fuel on the rope. It burst afire, burning quickly through the dry, tarred hemp. As he crawled past the feet of the fighting sailors to the next hook, the first rope began to slump as the fibers parted under the flames.

Scrambling to the next rope, Marcus glanced up and saw Otis, cutlass hanging from his belt. "Otis, cut the ropes at the fire!" Otis looked down then dropped behind the slight protection of the gunwale.

"Lad, what're you doing?" He looked behind Marcus and saw the flaming rope. "It'll never burn through in time."

"I've added a bit of something so it burns hotter. But if you hack at the burning spot with your cutlass, it'll part even faster." Otis nodded and pulled out his cutlass, crawling back toward the first rope as Marcus moved on to the next. When he'd started that on fire, he began his scramble to the next rope. Suddenly, he heard a whine past his ear, and he fell to the ground. That shot was close! He began moving forward again, this time crawling on his stomach.

He and Otis made their way carefully across the deck, under the feet of the battling sailors, dispatching the eight ropes from the pirate ship. Marcus could hear the shouted curses of the pirates as they watched their ropes fall. The occasional scream, ending in a great splash, indicated that some of the ropes carried a pirate or two down to the sea with them. The crash of pistol fire dwindled as the ships began to drift apart, too far from one another to warrant the waste of ammunition.

Finally, the last rope parted, and the sailors raised a cheer. "Good work, lad! I don't know what magic you worked, but I've never seen hemp part so fast!" Marcus grinned, tucking the lighter fluid and lighter back into his pocket. The captain shouted "To the sails, men!" and the sailors swarmed up the rigging, pulling sails full against the wind. The captain spun the wheel of the ship, moving her before the wind to put some distance between her and the pirates' cannon. The canvas flapped noisily, the rigging ropes creaked as they pulled tight, and the beautiful *Bethany* began to move swiftly away.

"The *Bethany* can outrun that barge, even with damage, now that we've got some distance between us," Otis said proudly. "And now that we know it's a race." He shook Marcus by the shoulder. "Thought I told you to stay safe below."

"I hoped to help," Marcus said, with a small smile.

"And you did, lad, you did. But you worry me. The others?"

"Safe below. I made sure of that." He raised his head over the gunwale, looking for the ship. Over the rail, lagging farther behind them, the pirates' vessel sailed away, tacking against the wind. Pirates often used surprise and overwhelming numbers to frighten their victims into submission. Clearly, neither was going to work with the *Bethany*, so the pirates cut their losses and turned tail. Marcus breathed a sigh of relief as he turned to go below and tell his friends that they were safe—for now.

CHAPTER 22

The relief of their escape from the *Dark Falcon* gave the children and the crew the boost they needed to recover quickly and do everything they could to get the *Bethany* to the port of Nassau at all the speed she could muster. It was clear that they would not be able to continue their quest for the treasure until major repairs had been made. Marcus and Jake worked alongside Otis and other sailors, making temporary repairs that would help them get to safe harbor. Marcus broke off splintered wood and nailed spare planks in its place. Jake helped the gunnery crew clean and prepare the cannon for the next time they were needed. The men worked swiftly, putting the ship to rights, making sure she was ready for whatever came their way.

Becca and Paige worked with the doctor, doing what they could to help him with the wounded sailors. Thankfully, none of their new crew had been killed. At first, Paige was sure she couldn't look at the bloody gashes in the men's arms, legs, and bodies. But she concentrated hard on their faces—the drawn, pained faces of these men who had become friends. She was doing well, really keeping it together, until she turned to the next man who needed bandaging—and it was Jeremiah, the cabin boy. His face was covered in blood from an open cut in his forehead. "Jeremiah!" she cried, her eyes immediately stinging.

"Don't fret, Miss Paige," he said weakly. "It's nothing."

Paige quickly grabbed a clean rag and rinsed it in the basin of water at her side. She gently wiped at his face, trying to clean it without irritating the wound further. "Oh, Jeremiah, it's not nothing. It's a great big something across your whole forehead."

The doctor appeared by her side. "Naw, don't fright the lad, young miss. Just enough of a mark to give your face some character, Jeremiah. Give you a story for the ladies." Paige looked up at the doctor, shocked to hear him talk so lightheartedly to a badly wounded man. The doctor looked back, directly into her eyes, and shook his head just slightly. "We'll get you bandaged and on your feet in no time."

Paige kept her head down, continuing to clean Jeremiah's face while the doctor dressed his wound with a large bandage, wrapped bandana style, around his head. She had to admit, while she had first thought the doctor's words harsh and even untruthful, they seemed to be having great affect on Jeremiah. The boy's eyes seemed more alive, and even his voice sounded stronger as the doctor worked on him. Soon, he was sitting up, leaning against a coil of rope. As the doctor drew Paige away with him to the next patient, Jeremiah raised a hand and said cheerfully, "As I said, Miss Paige, don't fret!"

Paige smiled and waved back at Jeremiah then turned to the doctor. "How could he be feeling so well? That wound is horrible."

"Aye, lass, it's pretty terrible, and he'll be spending some time ashore until he recovers from it." The doctor looked kindly down on his red-haired helper. "But sad words and worried faces don't do him any good. He needs to believe his lot ain't so bad—it's as good a medicine as I've ever seen." He patted her hand. "So smile your pretty smile and help these men believe in their recovery. That's the best way to be helping them." Paige nodded, put a smile on her face—though it felt quite false—and moved to help with the next man.

Sooner than Paige could have believed, the doctor was washing his hands after bandaging the last man, and Jake and Marcus came and flopped down wearily next to her and Becca. "Are you guys okay?" she asked, still thinking like a nurse.

Jake flipped his hand. "Of course. No sweat." But he settled back further against the hay bale they had gathered around.

Marcus just shook his head. "I can't believe some of the repairs we made. These men are geniuses when it comes to creative patching."

"But will it get us to port ahead of the *Dark Falcon*?" Becca asked, worry evident on her face. She looked across the deck to where Pierre, the quartermaster, and Otis were debating if the sail that had been shredded by the *Falcon's* cannon shot could be salvaged or if they would have to fully replace the tattered canvas. They could hear that the argument was coming down to money versus time. That seemed to be the case in so many grown-up discussions, Jake thought.

"Otis told me that the *Falcon* is not going to sail for Nassau. The authorities are just waiting for them to try something as foolish as that," Marcus said.

"Still, there's so much to fix." Becca continued to worry. "We can't just sit in port for days while the men repair all this."

"It'll be okay," Paige soothed. "Our crew will take care of us."

Becca just shook her head, rose, and walked up to the bow to watch for land.

As they sailed, Pierre recruited the children to help him serve a meal to the wounded men. He had made a thick stew, easy for them to eat and nourishing. It helped pass the time, but Becca couldn't keep her mind off the long delay she saw stretching before them.

Finally, the seaman in the crow's nest cried "Land ho!" and the children all crowded to the bow. Soon they could all see the island, as though it was rising up out of the ocean. They'd made it! Their poor limping *Bethany* was going to make it to shelter.

At the lookout's call of land, the crew had jumped into activity. They began preparing the unshredded sails to be furled, checking the temporary patch on the ship's port side, gathering (at Pierre's shouted directions) goods that could be sold or bartered for a new sail and other repairs. Suddenly, Otis came up behind them saying, "Survived another one, maties. Old Otis has more lives than a cat."

"How will the men get all this repaired in time for us to continue our quest?" Becca asked. "Things are so wrecked …"

"Oh, my dearie," Otis sighed. "Try to stop fretting yourself." He ruffled her hair gently. "Darlin', we're going to find our treasure. Now all of you keep your eyes over the prow and enjoy the sight of coming into harbor. 'Tis a lovely vision." Otis left them to help the other sailors bring the *Bethany* into port. Becca, Paige, Marcus, and Jake turned their attention to the sight of Nassau port before them.

At first, all they could see were a collection of masts and sails. But as they drew closer, the details of the ships and people came into focus. Small pinnaces—small boats that helped the larger sailing ships when in port—darted between ship and shore. Rowboats were coming out into the harbor, loaded with gear and victuals, to restock ships getting ready to set sail once more.

Behind them, the children heard the sailors rushing about, readying the *Bethany's* longboats for landing. The captain called to the helmsman, "Bring a spring upon her cable," and the helmsman spun the ship's wheel to turn the ship about. Marcus said, "I've read about this. Captain Penner is making certain the *Bethany* is berthed in such a way that we have a clear pathway to sail back out of harbor. He's preparing an escape, even when he doesn't know if there's danger. That's so smart."

"Why would we need to escape from here?" Jake asked.

"A privateer's life is extremely uncertain in many ways," Marcus answered. "The governor here in Nassau or even the king himself in England could cancel their letter of marque."

"Why would they do that?"

"Nations are always changing from enemies to uneasy partners and back again, even in our day," Marcus explained. "Politics. So if Spain is now suddenly an ally, their ships are no longer fair game for any privateer. Sometimes to show good faith, a governor will put privateers on trial, even though they were once considered soldiers in the war."

"You mean the governor could make them dance the hempen jig?" Jake said, eyes wide.

"What is that?" Becca asked sharply.

"It means they could be hanged," Marcus said seriously.

"Jake, why do you know words like that?" Becca was shocked.

"Dunno. Just heard it from the crew, I guess."

"Well, I don't like you saying things like that."

"Oh, Becca," Paige sighed. "Let him be. Marcus, is it true? Could they be hanged?"

"It is possible, I imagine. We have to remember that many privateers are a pretty lawless bunch. Our crew is different, but we've all heard the stories now. Most of them see nothing much wrong with taking what they want, when they think they can get away with it."

Becca nodded solemnly. "Yes, from what Otis has told us, most privateers have gone easily from soldier to pirate and back again.

"I'd imagine that doesn't make them many friends among the local law," Paige said.

Marcus nodded. "So I'd say each trip to port is, even in good times, an uneasy return. And a captain serves his ship and crew best if he's prepared to set sail at a moment's notice. This is at least part of why there's always a watch kept on the ship itself, the crew taking it in turn to guard the vessel and keep it ready to sail."

Suddenly, at their feet, a thick cable began to run out the hawsehole as the anchor dropped into the sea. A huge splash and the children felt the ship jerk slightly as the anchor bit into the soft sea bed. The *Bethany* had reached harbor.

The children felt their own uncertainty as they approached their first encounters with regular society. Would the authorities take them away from Otis? Did they have child protective services in this day and age? And if they were separated from Otis, how would they complete their quest and make it back to their own time? These questions and more weighed heavily on their minds.

CHAPTER 23

Otis joined them, once again, as they waited in the bow. "Didn't I tell you Nassau port was a pretty sight?" Looking at their serious faces, he sighed and shook his head. "You just can't stop a-worryin' at this, can you? You just let me and our mates take care of it. A few days and we'll be right as rain." Becca's jaw tightened and she bit back the sharp response that sprang to her tongue. Otis talked big, but clearly he didn't have a real plan, if he wouldn't tell them about it. But Becca knew from past experience that, if you called an adult out on that kind of thing, they just got more stubborn and even less likely to tell you anything or listen to your suggestions. She swallowed hard, trying to keep her anger in check. That wouldn't help anything at this point.

Marcus looked at the sun sinking lower on the horizon. "We'll have to wait until morning to start anything, won't we?"

Otis saw his glance and grinned. "You're becoming quite wise in the ways of the sea. No, we'll not have time to more than put into harbor and secure the *Bethany* for the night. As a matter of fact, we five will sleep off-ship tonight. Most of the crew will. Less activity on her now, the better, until we get her into dry dock."

"Dry dock?" Jake asked. "That sounds like you're taking the *Bethany* out of the water. How?"

"Ah, in morning you'll meet Master Merrick, and he'll explain all. The damaged wood will need to be pulled out entirely and that means below the waterline. So it's dry dock for us."

Becca shook her head. "This is going to take a really long time, isn't it? How will we get to the treasure?"

"Again the worries. The treasure has been waiting for us for a long time and will wait a while longer. So if it takes another week or two, rather than a day or two, it's really no matter."

"Doesn't matter? How can you say that?" Becca felt her voice rising and Paige's hand on her arm.

Otis looked quizzically at her. "Have you something else to be doing, lass? I thought we'd thrown our lot in together as a crew. Are you looking to be elsewhere so soon?"

Becca gulped, reminding herself that Otis couldn't know about their need to get home, to be swirled away by the snow globe once more. He'd think they were crazy and probably abandon them as quickly as he could. "No," she labored to say. "No, Otis. I … I'm just anxious to have your name cleared."

"Ah, my dear," Otis laughed as he stroked her cheek softly. "A few days more or less on that won't matter either. Soon enough, the treasure will be back in the hands of the king's men, and I won't have to shy away from the soldiers in port." He stepped up to the gunwale to watch the sailors busy at the longboats. "Children, gather some bedding and Paige, run off and ask Pierre for some victuals for our dinner. We'll camp on a likely stretch of beach tonight."

Several hours later, the children and Otis stretched out on the sand next to their campfire, fed and content to watch the flickering firelight. Their sail into port had been pretty uneventful, considering the condition of the *Bethany*. Captain Penner had assigned a number of men to stay with the vessel, but the rest were off in various places in port. Jake had asked where they might be, wondering what kind of hotel there was in Nassau. "I don't know this word *hotel*, lad. Many of the taverns offer rooms.

But a good portion of our crew will be at their homes, with wife and family."

"Family?" Paige said. "I didn't think … how can they be away from their families when they're at sea for so long?"

Otis shrugged. "They're sailors. It's what they do. The womenfolk know the way of the sea, most of them having grown up in this port city. Makes their time at home all the more sweet, I'd say."

"Did you ever marry, Otis?" Paige asked.

"Naw, never landed anywhere long enough. Always tried to visit my brothers and their young 'uns so I'd have some family … But you lot, you're my first real taste of family." Paige slid closer to Otis so she could take his hand. He smiled and squeezed her hand lightly. "Glad to have had the chance here before the end of my days."

Jake and Marcus also slid closer to their friend, happy to be a part of this small, thrown-together clan. Soon they were joking and laughing with their friend as he told them tales of his days as a boy in Ramsgate, the English port city where he grew up.

Becca sat on the opposite side of the fire from the others, barely visible at the edge of the firelight's glow. Her legs drawn up, she rested her chin on her knees. Her eyes were half-closed as she squinted into the fire, listening to the others. It almost seemed as if they were happy to be here, on this beach many years past, instead of in their own homes and own beds. Had they really forgotten that their quest was to get home again? Clearly, no one—adult or child—was concerned about the delay in getting the treasure. So it was up to Becca, as usual, to fix the problem. She rose and brushed the sand off her shorts. "I'm going for a walk," she announced.

"Want company?" Paige asked, though Becca was sure she had no real desire to leave her cozy little family group.

"No, just want to stretch my legs." *And think*, she said to herself. *I've got to think of a new plan.* She turned away from the fire and her friends and headed down the beach. Soon she had walked around the point of the island and could no longer see or hear her friends. She felt completely alone. Alone with her cares about the delay. Alone with her worries about losing the treasure. And alone in her desire to get back to their right time and place apparently. So she alone would have to find the solution. But how?

As she kept walking, she began to hear other voices and see a light flickering in the distance. She rounded another point in the beach and saw the source—a group of soldiers! Becca looked inland and realized she had walked around to the point where the island's fort sat. Past the soldiers, in a small bay pulled up into the shadow of the fort, she saw a military sailing ship, riding gently on the waves.

Her eyes widened, and she actually slapped her hand to her forehead. Of course! Here's what they needed. The sailors had a ship and the treasure was going to them eventually anyway. Why not just enlist their aid now? The soldiers could give them the ride they needed to the treasure island, Otis could show them the hiding place, and then the soldiers could bring Otis back to the *Bethany*. The children, of course, would be long gone, having been flown back home by the magic of the snow globe. All Becca had to do was convince the soldiers that she knew what she was talking about.

Briefly, she wished she had the snow globe with her, so she could see its shining approval of her plan. Glowing to show that they were finally back on the right track. But she was sure this was the right solution. Hadn't she been led to walk down the beach? Hadn't she … ? But she had no doubt that this answered all their needs. And Becca was sure she could make this all come out right. She was really very good at making a plan and making it work. Determined to solve all their problems right away, she took a deep breath and headed toward the soldiers and their campfire.

The moonlight sparkled off the tips of the waves rolling onto the beach, dancing like fireflies in the spray. Becca watched the men in uniform from the shadows, trying to determine who might be in charge. Their white breeches reflected red-orange from the fire, and the gold buttons on their red jackets glinted in the flickering light. She heard a murmur of comment from the men, followed by a good-natured burst of laughter. She decided the leader must be the tall, dark-haired one at the center of the group. She headed toward them, thinking of the words she would need to convince them of her story.

"Boys, look." One of the men pointed in her direction. "We've got a visitor."

"Well, lass, where did you come from?" Her choice for leader, the dark-haired man, came toward her. She'd been right. He held out his hand. "Do you need help?"

Becca felt her eyes sting suddenly, moved by his kind tone. "Please, sir, yes. I … I don't know where to begin exactly, but if you'll hear me out …"

"Of course, child, of course. Come close to the fire, rest yourself. Then tell us your tale." The soldier drew her close to the fire and had her sit on a log placed as a seat. "Give me a draught of water, won't you?" A solider handed him a canteen, which he in turn pushed into Becca's hand. "Settle yourself, dear. How can we help you, young lass?"

"Well, sir, I've got some news that I think the king's men would be glad to hear." All the soldiers moved closer, intrigued by her opening remark. She took a long drink of water, which flowed cool and sweet down her throat.

"We *are* the king's men, every one. So your message comes to the right ears here." The soldier sat down next to her. Becca was somewhat surprised and disappointed to realize how young he was, now that she saw him more clearly in the firelight. He barely looked older than Marcus!

"Um … maybe someone in charge?" she said, uncertainty evident in her voice and her wrinkled brow.

The tall, dark soldier drew himself straighter, glaring at one of the men who snickered at her remark. "I'm in charge of this unit, miss. Lieutenant Baker, in charge and in command tonight."

Becca flinched. She'd insulted him and that was a bad way to start her story. "Oh, of course, Lieutenant. I'm sorry, you just have such a young face. But surely, if you've made lieutenant at such an age, you must be very, very capable. Just the man to tell my story, I'm sure."

Baker's rigid back loosened slightly at her words. "Well, yes, I am the man to help you. Will you tell us your name?"

"Yes, sir. Becca, sir. I'm seeking help for my friends and me." The soldiers looked around at her mention of friends. "No, no, they're not with me. I came out by myself, but when I saw you and the fort, I knew this was just the help we needed."

The soldier looked down on her. "Perhaps you'd best tell me your whole story."

She looked shyly at the others, suddenly aware of their keen interest focused all on her. She felt them weighing everything she said, ready to jump at the slightest misspoken word. "Maybe … could we talk on our own?"

Lieutenant Baker glanced back at his men, gesturing for them to step away. "Of course, my dear girl. It's hard to speak in front of so many curious eyes, isn't it?" The men moved away from them reluctantly. But they stood outside the fire's light and Becca could focus fully on the young lieutenant. Now she only had to convince him of her story, and he would do the work with the others. "So can you tell me now, lass?"

She settled herself to begin her story. She couldn't, of course, tell him everything. If she tried to explain the magic of the snow globe, he would think she was crazy and ignore the rest of her tale. It was important that he believe her, in order to help all of them.

"I have some friends—four of us altogether—who were marooned with me on a nearby island. Our boat … our ship wrecked with all hands lost."

"What vessel was this?" the lieutenant asked, concern furrowing his brow. "I've not heard of any one missing."

"Um … a small private sloop, sir. The … uh … Kendrick. My aunt and uncle were sailing here from the Spanish Main. Anyway, we were wrecked, and my friends and I alone saved. We met an old sailor who had also been marooned there, by pirates. He saved us with a canoe he knew of."

"Pirates! They bedevil us throughout the Caribbean. But they usually maroon their own, not good honest sailors."

"Well, our rescuer may have once been forced to serve on a pirate vessel." Becca gulped, knowing this part was tricky. She needed the lieutenant to believe in Otis's honesty. "He himself had escaped them when he rescued us. He's not a pirate."

"Hmm … your friend may not have been fully honest with you. But go on."

"Well, he saved us and has told us the tale of a stolen treasure. He wishes to save it from the pirates and bring the rightful tithe to the king. We've been trying to help him …"

"A tithe to the king? Doesn't sound like pirates."

"Oh, not pirates, sir. Otis sailed with a privateer crew—we saw the letter of marque, sir. Stamped and sealed by the governor in the name of the king."

"Letters of marque have a way of being used for pirates' convenience sometimes, lass. But you say this man's name is Otis—are you talking of Otis Jennings?"

"Aye, sir, that's him." Becca hoped that his recognition of the name was a good sign. But she must step carefully now. "We've gotten separated from the crew we were sailing with. I don't know how we'll find the treasure now, without a crew to help us. I thought perhaps you could help us."

He took her hand tightly. "Where is this treasure?"

Becca tried to pull her hand loose casually. "Um … I don't know. Otis knows, but I think he's afraid to ask for help from anyone else."

"I'm sure he is," the lieutenant said. The man stood suddenly, releasing her hand. "So old Jennings is trying to return his stolen treasure to the king, is he? A pretty story for children, but I think we know better."

"No, Lieutenant Baker, he is sincere. We just need to help him regain the treasure, and he'll return what's right to the king. We just need a vessel." Becca stood also. "I thought perhaps we could meet on the pier tomorrow afternoon. We'll be there in the afternoon. If we're out in the open, Otis won't be nervous. It won't feel like a trap. Then we could talk it all out there."

Now it was Baker's turn to seem uncomfortable. "Yes, that could perhaps be arranged. I'd have to check ..."

"Check? I thought you were in charge here, sir," Becca said carefully. "Can't you just order it?"

Lieutenant Baker faced her, his spine straightening once again. "I am in charge here." He gestured to the sand. "This unit, tonight. But Major Hale is in charge of the fort and the garrison. He must issue the orders." He looked down his nose at her, daring her to mock his authority.

"Oh, oh, of course. I see." Becca mentally kicked herself. She should have realized the person in charge of the fort wouldn't be standing a nighttime watch on the beach. But she really didn't want to go into the fort. She had to be getting back or Otis and the others would come looking for her. If the soldiers got a hold of Otis before she'd had a chance to explain the plan to him, it could mess up everything. So she must get Baker to be her messenger to the major. "Well, sir, I'm sure you can explain this all to Major Hale. Obviously, he trusts you, or you wouldn't be in charge here. So just explain it to him, and I'm sure he'll issue the right orders."

"It'd be better if you'd come up to the fort yourself. Major Hale is sure to have his own questions." Baker took a step toward her, his hand outstretched.

Becca took a step back. "Oh, sir, I don't think so. My friends will be missing me."

"So they'll come to the fort too. None of this nonsense of waiting until tomorrow at the quay."

Becca bit her lip and thought quickly. "Um, no, they won't ... um, can't come. Otis wants us to stay close ... Yeah, we have to stay with him. I just slipped away, but he'll keep a much closer eye on the others now. He worries ..."

"Are you in danger, girl?"

"No. No! Not danger. But ... um ... Otis wants to be sure the pirates can't use us to force him to give the treasure to them. He's been keeping us very close, but he'll still be afraid to come to the fort. Please, *please* do it my way."

"Well ..."

"Honest, Lieutenant Baker, I know I can convince Otis to come to you tomorrow. I'll talk to him, and I know he'll feel safe out in the open. I know it."

Baker suddenly looked every bit as young as Marcus. He looked over his shoulder at the others, obviously uncertain about what to do. Becca made her final push. She stepped back from the fire and began moving inland. "Just tell him, Lieutenant, I know you can convince him. I'll see you tomorrow afternoon, on the docks. Wait for me, I'll come to you." She turned quickly and began to run. "Tomorrow, Lieutenant Baker."

As she'd hoped, the young man's uncertainty gave her the few seconds she needed to get away from the firelight. She was quickly swallowed up by shadows. Lieutenant Baker took a step or two, almost called to his men, but realized he'd let her get away. He could not admit that to the unit. He'd have to convince Major Hale to meet the young girl on the docks tomorrow.

CHAPTER 24

Becca lay quietly in the sand, her eyes squeezed tight against the urge to peek out through her eyelashes. She'd made it back to the campsite on the beach without raising too many questions. "I just got turned around in the dark a little bit" was all she said when Paige asked why she was gone so long. Everyone seemed to accept that, but Otis had raised an eyebrow, even though he'd made no comment. So now she kept her eyes closed, in case sharp-eyed Otis still lay awake, wondering about her walk. She'd have to talk with Otis in the morning, convince him of the wisdom of her plan, but tonight she didn't want to raise his suspicions. But she had one more thing she had to do tonight, after the others were asleep.

A crackle and a sudden whiff of smoke signaled that Otis was stirring the fire one more time. She'd been right about him still being awake. A thump that must be the stick he was using, as he tossed it into the sand. A brief cough—Jake, who always did that right before he fell asleep, Becca didn't know why. Otis grunted as he lowered himself to the sand and breathed a loud, weary sigh. Paige exhaled softly, humming a couple of notes that sounded like part of the jig they'd danced to back on the deck of the *Bethany.* A happy sound that scraped raw against Becca's jangled nerves. Characteristically, she heard not a peep from Marcus.

Becca suspected he was already asleep, with the logic of a boy who knew he needed rest, so he rested. He would have laid down his head, intertwined his fingers over his stomach, closed his eyes, and simply gone to sleep. Becca envied him that ability—to shut it all off so he could reenergize to meet the challenges of the next day.

Becca waited, waited, willing herself to stay still and not move too soon. Her ears strained to filter out the sounds of the waves lapping on the shore, the occasional snap of a dying ember in the fire, the bugs buzzing and chirring in the forest. The breeze whooshed gently, cooling the sleepers, but adding another background sound to sift out. She lay quietly, controlling her breath and her thoughts, not thinking beyond this one moment. Wait for it. Wait until they've settled. Make sure it's safe. Be patient. Be calm.

Becca started, twitching awake. She'd dropped off—for how long she didn't know. Nothing seemed different, the sounds, the breeze. She listened, impatient now that she didn't know how much time she had lost. She heard nothing from her friends or from Otis. Unable to bear any longer delay, Becca rolled as naturally as she could to face the smoldering fire and the others sleeping around it. She paused again, holding her breath, listening for other movements. Finally, with a false silent yawn, she stretched and opened her eyes, trying to look as natural as possible, in case one of the others was awake. She blinked and squinted past the barely burning fire to see Otis sprawled facedown on the other side. Just past her feet, Paige lay curled in a ball, looking more like a sleeping kitten than a young girl. Becca looked up just beyond her head to see Marcus, lying straight and tidy, just as she'd thought. His chest rose and lowered rhythmically, in the slow, steady breathing of a deep sleeper. Past Marcus lay Jake, his backpack nearby but, for once, not attached to his back.

A sudden snort nearly jolted Becca upright. Otis snorted again, then gasped, then began to emit a steady, sawing snore that promised he was deeply asleep. Becca calmed her breathing, willing her heart to settle down and stop jumping so hard in her chest. She sat up slowly, trying to keep her eyes on all four of the others at once. Gently, carefully, she pushed herself up into a crouching position and began to move carefully around the fire toward Jake's backpack—and the snow globe. She had to be sure she wasn't ruining their chance of getting home. The globe would tell her if her plan was right or wrong.

She crept around Marcus, watching carefully not to put a foot or hand on a twig or knock any pebbles to skitter across the sand. The pack was within her reach, if she'd just stretch her hand to it. But again, she held her impatience in check. *Don't pull it to you,* she mentally warned herself. *Go to it and lift it carefully.* Becca took a deep breath, three more steps, and stood upright. Then she leaned over and carefully lifted the pack straight up, pulling it into her chest, corralling the dangling straps and buckles to prevent any stray jingle or entanglement. She cautiously stepped back from Jake, moving away from the fire and toward the dark of the woods behind her.

When it was clear no one had heard her movements, when none of the others would wake to see her go, she turned her back on the fire and her friends and headed into the shadows of the trees. Becca continued to step very carefully, keeping her eyes peeled for branches that reached across the barely cleared trail she followed into the dark. When she looked back over her shoulder and could no longer see the small, dying flames of their campfire, she stopped and lowered herself and her precious cargo to a fallen log. She held the backpack carefully in her lap and searched by touch for the zipper to the main compartment of the bag. When she found the tab, she pulled it only briefly, stopping abruptly at the loud *zzzttt* of the metal zipper teeth coming apart.

Becca held her breath, sure the sound had echoed back to the small camp, and waited to hear confused voices. What would she say? She could explain the trip into the woods with a bathroom break, but why did she have the backpack? What could her reason possibly be? Once again, her ears strained for the slightest sound for thirty seconds, one minute—surely they would have reacted by now, if the zipper had woken them. Ninety seconds … Becca blew a lungful of air out in relief. She'd worried for nothing. The sound of opening the pack had not carried much beyond her own ears. She shook her head, trying to clear her thoughts and calm her nerves. She pulled on the zipper again, ignoring the noise this time, opening the pack wide enough to see the globe inside.

But there was something wrong. The inside of the pack was dark, with no gentle, otherworldly glow to show the globe's presence. Where was it? The radiance shining in the dark night. Their guide and their way home. Becca blinked back sudden hot tears. She couldn't deny it. The snow globe was not glowing any longer.

She pulled the globe out of the pack and shook it lightly. A faint glimmer was the only result. The snowflakes settled lightly on to the deck of the miniature *Bethany* and then even that faint light extinguished. Becca shook the globe again, harder this time, agitating the snow, bringing about a slightly stronger light. The characteristic tingle from the globe barely tickled her hands. "No. This can't be." She shook it harder. "Please, please shine. You have to shine." She got a few weak flickers for her efforts, then the globe settled into a barely noticeable glimmer.

"That's enough, isn't it?" she whispered, as she held the globe tight to her chest. "You're still lit up, so it's enough. It has to be." She rested her forehead against the glass orb, feeling its coolness, even in the evening's heat. "Please … please let it be all right." She sat for a long time, trying to think, to decide what to do next. She had to have made the right decision, the right choice. The globe had to glow, now that they had a ship, a vessel to finish their journey to the treasure. Now that they had the soldiers' help.

But maybe they didn't. Maybe the globe was telling her that the major hadn't made his decision yet. That must be it. Baker hadn't convinced Major Hale to help them yet. Once they met tomorrow, once Becca had talked the major into helping them— then the globe would glow again. Wouldn't it? It had to.

She finally placed the globe back into the backpack and zipped it closed. She'd just have to make sure that Major Hale and his men helped them. That's all there was to do. She wiped the tears from her eyes and made her way carefully and quietly back to the campsite.

CHAPTER 25

The next morning, the children and Otis had a quick breakfast on the beach, and no more mention was made of her solo walk the night before. After eating, Otis led them back to the *Bethany*. Becca kept her eyes open for soldiers, hoping not to run into them before she'd had a chance to talk with Otis. She hadn't been able to find a way to bring up her nighttime visit with everyone else around. She hoped to be able to have a few moments alone with Otis as they worked on repairing the ship.

But once they reached the *Bethany*, it became clear very quickly that they were not there to begin repairs. The crew had been busy already and the children found themselves laden with fabric, pots and pans, and other household goods, rather than a hammer or lumber. Becca became just one of a large group, Otis leading them and others from the *Bethany*'s crew, out onto the pier and heading inland. "Stay close behind me now," Otis said.

They marched past swaggering sailors, who were delighting their fancy dress lady companions with wild talk of ocean-going heroics. Bright golden earrings glinted in the earlobes of men and women alike, though many women also sported flashing jewels on their necks and rings on their fingers. Other sailors hauled on ropes, loading and unloading cargo. Large-roped packs swung wildly off decks or dock, dangling dangerously over the water until their short trip to the pier was completed. Several of the fancy ladies made invitations to Otis and his crew mates. One or two even cooed over Jake's baby face or Paige's bouncy red curls. "Mind them not, my young 'uns," Otis warned them. "'Tis not a pretty life they'd offer ye. You're better off at sea."

The children obediently followed close behind Otis along the pier, drinking in the sights and sounds of the bustling seaport. Wind-whipped canvas snapped and rustled. Ropes creaked and anchor chains rattled loudly. Men called harshly.

"Avast, ye lubber!"

"Step lively now!"

"Furl that jib proper, you!"

As they walked, Otis pointed out various examples of his, the boatwright's, trade. He brought them by a ship whose bilge was being searched for any sign of leakage. They saw a lad no older than themselves, stringing the cordage for the sails, his hands quick and sure. On another ship—a sloop, Otis informed them—they saw men mending and recutting the huge pieces of canvas that made up the sails of any ship.

And all around them, the business of loading and unloading cargo and crew went on, a constant hum of sound and sights and smells. On their left, Becca saw crates of chickens being hauled up the tall side of a ship, squawking and flapping their wings at the odd sensation. To their right, Jake watched in awe as a sailor crawled over the ropes that held the sails on the ship. High above their heads, held up in the sky by a fantastic manmade web of cords, moving surely and confidently as if he were on solid ground. The ropes swayed and bounced as the man moved swiftly along them, apparently checking for damage as he went.

As they moved further along the dock, closer to the wharf and its conventional shop buildings, the dress and manner of the people seemed to change as well. Certainly there were still sailors and fancy women, but their numbers grew smaller. Men wore breeches and long coats over white shirts rather than the colorful shirts and waistcoats the sailors wore. Their feet were shod with hobnail shoes rather than the boots, soft shoes, or even bare feet that sailors sported. The women were clothed in soft, subdued colors, dresses with modest necklines, white aprons, and bonnets. Few walked alone, and they walked with purpose, not the lazy stroll of the women out on the piers.

They passed the open door of a bakery, and Paige felt she might faint from the wonderful smells wafting out into the open air. "Mmmm—fresh bread …" and her steps slowed. The other children slowed as well, relishing this homey fragrance. A young woman popped out the door, a tray of small rolls in hand. "A bit of a taste for your children, sir?" she asked Otis. He nodded and dug in his pocket for coins. "And for my bigger boys too." He laughed, as the seamen had all been gazing with longing at the fresh rolls. Each of them took a roll and politely thanked the young lady—and Otis.

"Onward now," he commanded, and they all continued their march through the wharf area. They passed countless and varied shops. A watchmaker who also sold sextants (a strange mix of lenses and metal arms used for navigation) and spyglasses for seafaring. A tailor's shop with breech coats and sailors' canvas pants in the window. A cooper, working on his barrels in front of his shop, hammering the slats of a barrel into place. A gunsmith selling pistols and long guns for hunting and fighting.

At the very end of the wharf, where the water deepened again, they came to a long warehouse, where Otis stopped. The long building stretched from the water's edge back into the wharf area, several times larger than any of the shops they'd passed already. The building had a small door in its side, with a sign that announced "P. Merrick, Boatwright" in bold black letters. The front of the building faced the water and had two large doors that reached through both stories of the building. Peering around the corner, the children could see these large front doors opened straight out on to the water and now, at higher tide, the water of the harbor blocked entry there. Waves actually licked up into the building itself. Marcus could see small wooden rails under the water, and wondered at what he saw. Otis leaned around the corner and shouted.

"Peter Merrick!" Otis cried out, his voice echoing through the dark recesses of the warehouse.

"Who's asking?" came the sharp response.

"The crew of the good ship *Bethany*, come to purchase your wormy wood and rusting supplies."

Laughter cackled out at them and suddenly the small landward door in front of them swung open. A small brown man pulled the door wide and gestured broadly with his arm. "Welcome, welcome, ye scurvy rat, and all your fellow crew. As long as you've got barter, you can call my goods what ye like." Merrick's eyes lit upon the children. "What's this?" he chirruped. "Otis Jennings, don't tell me you've been a father all these years."

"Go on with ye. You're more likely to have begat this 'un than me" Otis replied, gesturing to Marcus's dark skin. "And there's never been a redhead in my family. Just offering a bit of aid and comfort to some young orphans. Crew's kind of taken with them, so now I'm stuck." Otis winked at his young friends.

"Well, good on ye, old man. The Lord may have some mercy on you for your kindness. Now what can I do for you? Lumber? Sails? Pitch and pegging?"

"Aye, all of that." Otis led the way into the shadowed warehouse. "And likely your dry dock as well."

"Mind your step at the edge," Peter Merrick said to Marcus as he peered into the water outside the large main doors, hoping for a better glimpse of the rails beneath the surface. "The water's deeper there than you might think."

"I am fascinated by these rails," Marcus said. "Is it a ramp?"

"Oh, aye," Peter nodded. "A barque will slide along here, neat as you please." He skipped from the solid floor to dip the toe of his boot in the water, landing on the rail and jumping lightly to the far side. "Designed her meself, if you'll pardon a small boast."

"'Tis this kind of thing that keeps Master Merrick in high demand," Otis told the children. "Smart he is and has new ideas that always work."

Merrick cocked his head to one side, eyes sparkling, mouth pulled into a guarded smile. "Now I wonder what it is Master Otis is after, smoothing the way with so many flattering words." He looked past Otis to the other men, laden with goods. "A rather large barter stock, I see. Are ye looking to buy my goods or me?"

"Are you for sale?" Jake asked, shocked. He knew of slavery from school, but he never expected to see it firsthand.

Merrick laughed heartily and skipped quickly back across the watery boat cradle. He put an arm around Jake's shoulders, hugging him. "Oh, my lad, your offended tone does you credit. Ye'll not be a slaver in your life, will you?"

"You can't own people! God didn't make people to be property." Jake was a bit afraid that he was being made fun of, but the very thought of one man owning another made him feel a little sick. "It's wrong." He turned to Otis. "You can't buy Mr. Merrick, Otis. I won't let you."

Otis grinned and ruffled Jake's hair before he had time to duck away. "Hold now, young firebrand. I'm not planning to purchase Merrick."

Merrick crouched so he looked Jake directly in the eyes. "Bless you, my boy, for your fierce heart. God will use you for His own good, I'm certain. But Otis is no slaver either. I merely meant to ask if he was planning to barter for my services." He straightened and held out his hand. Jake shifted the fabric he was carrying and gripped Merrick's hand firmly, hoping he seemed more grown up than he was feeling. "Thank you, young master."

"Jake, sir. My name's Jake."

"Thank you, Master Jake. I'm pleased to call you friend." Merrick released his hand and turned to Otis. "So let's relieve these fine people of their burdens and talk business, Otis." He gestured to tables along the side of the warehouse. "Set things down here. There are some fine alehouses back along the dock, if your men are so inclined, while we talk business. But I can offer your children a bit of tea and sweets here with us."

"That will be much appreciated, friend Merrick."

After they'd set down all their bundles, the children were drawn back to the water's edge. Marcus explained. "See, they sail the ship right up here in high tide. Then, they anchor and wait until the tide ebbs. The water drops away and the ship is left, held by the rails, safe. Then they can work on all areas of the ship, nothing underwater. Terrific, isn't it?"

"So you're saying they can get the boat out of the water?" Becca asked. "That must make it easier to work on."

"Yes, much easier. And faster." Marcus and the others didn't notice Becca step away from the water. She turned and went back toward the back of the warehouse, where Otis and Peter Merrick were discussing the repairs needed and the best way to make them. She listened quietly as Otis explained the damage, sketching images out for Mr. Merrick to see.

"Oh, aye, we can have the *Bethany* in and back on her way," Merrick said. "If your men stay nearby and all hands ready to work when the tide's out, we'll make short work of it."

"Short work?" Becca said quietly. "Like, how short?"

Otis and Merrick turned to look at her. "Didn't see you there, lass. From what Otis has been telling me, I'd say two days should set us right."

"Two days?" Becca's eyes widened. "That's all? Just two days?"

Otis laughed. "I told you, girl, this was nothing more than a minor setback. And you had to keep fretting, didn't you?" He turned to Peter. "Smart as a whip, this one, but she will worry. Always looking for something to fix."

Becca heard his voice, but all she could think was "Only two days. Just two days and we'll be on our way. The *Bethany* will be fine." She nodded at the men and turned away, not really seeing anything. What had she done?

CHAPTER 26

Becca stumbled away, deeper into the warehouse, away from everyone. If the *Bethany* would be sailing in two days, there had been no need to pull the soldiers into this. No wonder the globe barely glimmered. She had ruined everything. They weren't going home; they would be stuck here in the 1600s forever because she tried to fix things. Things that didn't need to be fixed. She tripped over a coil of rope and fell. She put her face in her hands and began to cry.

Becca didn't know how long she sat there, crying. But eventually, even the tears stopped, as though she had no more liquid in her. And she just sat in the semidarkness, staring at nothing, completely out of ideas and not knowing what she should do.

"Young lady, come now, what's all this?" Peter Merrick's cheery tones were quiet as he came up to Becca a few minutes later. He seated himself on the coiled rope and laid a gentle hand on her shoulder. "Setting back here in the dark, away from your friends?"

"I can't call them my friends, Mr. Merrick. Not anymore."

"Well, that's some fine how-de-do. You all seemed a pretty tight little family when you came in. Whatever could have gone wrong in the short time ye've been in Old Merrick's shop?"

Becca felt a tear slide down her cheek, followed quickly by another and another. Apparently, she wasn't completely dried up after all. "I've made a mess of it, all of it," she cried.

"Surely not all of it," Mr. Merrick said. "Not every bit of it." He patted her arm. "Tell me, perhaps I can help."

"Nothing can help."

"Oh, now, I'm quite good at fixing things, darlin'. Give me a try, won't you?"

His gentle voice and kind words were too much for Becca to resist. She turned to him and buried her face in his coat. With sniffles and sobs, she haltingly confessed what she had done, how she had betrayed Otis, how she thought she'd known best. "But now I don't know what to do. The soldiers are going to find us, and I'll get Otis arrested and it's all for nothing. For nothing!"

Merrick had put his arms around the young girl, letting her blurt out the story in her own way. He let her cry for a few more moments then said firmly, "Enough now. That's enough crying, child." He pushed her upright, settling her back against the corner where she'd fallen. "There's always a way, young lady, if you'll just quiet yourself. We'll find a way."

Becca wiped her eyes with the back of her hand. "How can I make this right? I can't tell Otis what happened."

Merrick reached into his pocket and pulled out a large, red kerchief. "Wipe your eyes properly, lass. Seems to me that's exactly what you must do. Tell Otis."

Becca stared at him. "No, I can't. I can't tell him I planned to get him arrested. I have to tell him something else. Something that will keep him safe."

Mr. Merrick looked at her, his bright brown eyes unblinking. "You think it's wise to tell him some made-up farradiddle?"

Becca tried to look back at him as directly, but found she couldn't hold his steady gaze. "Well, no, but ... What am I gonna do?"

"Try the truth, lass. Otis deserves that, and you know that's the right thing to do." He patted her hand. "You know it's what your heavenly Father expects of you. You don't have to face this alone." Merrick stood and held out his hand, eyes sparkling once more. "Come now. Face the devil and tell him, 'Run'! That's the way to live."

Becca gulped, wiped her eyes once more, then took Mr. Merrick's hand. What was it Jesus had said? The truth will set you free. Well, she was about to find out if this was a promise she could trust.

"Ah, you've found her!" Otis greeted them as Merrick and Becca returned from the depths of the warehouse. "Running off becoming a habit, Miss Becca? I'll have to keep my eyes on you, eh?" He smiled until he saw the somber lines of Becca's face. "What's this, friend Merrick?"

The little brown man gently pushed her forward. "Time for straight talk between you two, I venture. I'll go give the others that tea and sweeties I promised so you'll not be disturbed." Becca turned to look at him, yearning on her face. "Face up, darlin'. Make your Father God proud." With that, he winked at Otis and disappeared toward the front of the warehouse.

Otis gestured to the chair next to him. "Have a seat, my girl. Something serious is afoot, it seems."

Becca tried to speak but found her voice was choked back in her throat. Instead she nodded sadly. Otis waited, saying nothing. She hung her head, unable to meet his steady, clear gaze. She wished she could look at him. This would be the last time she would see the friendship and care in that gaze. What she had to tell him now would destroy all that forever. She tried again to speak, and this time found her voice.

"I … I've made a mistake, Otis." Good start, but she didn't know how to go on. Otis waited. "I … I meant to help. I wanted us to find the treasure quickly, to clear your name, to …" her voice trailed off. She knew that wasn't the real reason she'd pushed ahead. She knew she'd really only been worried about getting herself home. Not even the others. She'd really just been thinking about herself. But she couldn't say that to Otis. Again, trying to introduce the magical elements of their quest would do more harm than good. "I wanted to clear your name, but I was really just thinking about myself."

"Well," Otis interrupted. "Your cut of the treasure will make a nice nest egg for you. And nobody ever died from a healthy desire for what's their own, I guess. But I don't believe that's the mistake you mean to tell me about."

"No, sir," Becca pushed on quickly. "I just wanted to get us a ship. The *Bethany* seemed so damaged, so hard to repair." The words wouldn't stop now. Now that she'd determined to tell him all, she couldn't get the words out fast enough. "I was worried that the pirates would find us again before she could be repaired. And I knew you meant to turn over the proper tithe to the king. So I thought the king's men would be willing to help. So last night, while we were on the beach, I went to the fort. I found some soldiers on the beach, and I told them that you wanted to turn over the treasure, and we just needed a ship and could they help me, help us …" She stopped, out of breath and out of words. Now that she said it out loud, she realized how lame it sounded. Why had she thought she knew best? Why hadn't she discussed this with the others? If she'd said it out loud last night, she would never have gone. Her head hung even lower than before. She couldn't possibly look at Otis now.

They sat there silently for a long time. The shipyard was so large that no sounds from the others trickled back into their private corner. Becca thought maybe she should say something more, break this silence. But she had no more words. What else could she say?

Then, as if a quiet voice whispered in her ear, she knew what she must say. Head still down, she said, "Otis. Sir, I'm sorry. I've probably wrecked everything, and I know 'I'm sorry' won't fix anything. But it's all I can say. I'm very sorry, and I don't deserve to be forgiven. Ever." And she fell silent again, words truly gone now.

Again, the silence echoed between them. Becca felt as if she wanted to crawl away, back into the darkness deep in the shipyard. But then, she felt a touch on her shoulder. Otis laid his hand on her shoulder, squeezing gently. "Darlin' girl," he said, his voice rough. "Look at me." Becca could only shake her head. "Girl, do as I ask. Look me in the eye now."

Slowly, reluctantly, she lifted her head. At first, she kept her eyes closed, but then knew she must meet his gaze. She opened her eyes, prepared to see the anger and hurt she knew she deserved.

Instead, Otis's eyes sparkled, not only with his characteristic love of life, but it appeared from a few unshed tears. They crinkled then as he smiled at her. "That's better, dearie. We've come too far together for you to hang your head in front of me now. So tell me, what is the plan you hatched with this soldier?"

"We … uh, I told him to meet us on the wharf this afternoon. That we'd meet out in the open so you wouldn't …" her voice stumbled, "fear a trap. And you'd explain to them, and they'd agree to take you on their ship and all could be well. The soldier even knew your name, so he believed me about the treasure."

Otis stroked her cheek lightly then simply took her hand and held it as he talked. "Oh, I'm sure he knew my name. The soldiers at this garrison have been looking for me for a very long time, it seems." He looked thoughtfully into the lamplight, "How to use this … how to turn it …" he spoke to himself.

Becca sat quietly, relishing the feel of his hand over hers. He hadn't said he forgave her, but surely his hand on hers meant something. She'd take whatever she could get, since she knew she deserved nothing but his hatred. She waited for him to speak again.

"Well, my lass, you've presented me with a pretty pickle. But I think I can see my way clear. It'll take some cooperation, and you'll need to do as you're told, no questions." He looked piercingly at her. "Can you do that now, lassie?"

"Aye, sir, yes, I can. I'll do just as you say."

Otis gave her his crooked grin. "It'll be the first time since I've met you, but we'll take you at your word." He rose and pulled Becca to her feet with him. "It's not so bad as you think, child. But I hope you've learned it's not always wise to make your plans all on your own. We all need help from time to time."

"Yes, sir. I know that now. I'd give anything to take it back."

Otis shook his head. "No sense wishing for what can't happen. What matters is what you do from here on." He held her hand between both of his and, again, looked directly into her eyes. "We'll say no more. The others have no need to know what's passed between us here. So put on your prettiest smile and help me put a new plan into action."

CHAPTER 27

Becca's promise to obey Otis without question was immediately put to the test. Otis gathered his little family around him quickly and hurried them back to the *Bethany*. He told none of them anything, other than arrangements had been made with Mr. Merrick to bring the *Bethany* into dry dock and make repairs. When they reached the ship, Otis spent a short time alone with Captain Penner, then came back out and told them they'd disembark shortly.

"Aren't we sailing back around to Master Merrick's?" Marcus asked. "I was looking forward to watching him work."

"Aye, lad, some other time. I'm sure he'll be happy to have you back for another repair. But for now, we need to be elsewhere." With that, Otis ushered the children off the ship once more and led them across the docks again. They hurried after him, trying to keep up with his long, determined strides. The sun in the sky showed that it was still well before noon, but Becca knew that Otis had to put his plans in place before the soldiers came to the docks to meet them. In short order, however, they reached another ship, apparently their destination.

Paige's eyes widened as they came to a halt before a tall, gorgeous ship, with a carving of a dolphin on its very front. "It's beautiful." The bowsprit, the carved dolphin caught in the act of leaping high into the air, gleamed bright in the morning sun.

Becca tried to see the smiling face of the dolphin as welcoming, but the expression seemed scornful and mocking. What were they doing here? What did Otis have planned? And how would this help with the soldiers? But she bit back all her questions, resolved to keep her promise to Otis.

Otis looked up at the dolphin. "Aye, she is. That bowsprit is the captain's pride and joy." He cupped his hands around his mouth and called, "Ahoy the ship!" at the man standing far above them on the deck.

The man looked over the side, shading his eyes from sunlight glinting off the turquoise blue water. "Ahoy yourself, you old scalawag! Can that be Otis Jennings I see, surrounded by a sea of young 'uns? Did you get yourself married off, old man?"

"You'll not see a band of gold 'round any of my fingers," Otis said. "These 'uns are in my care, no doubt of that, but with no mother to coddle 'em."

"Well, whatever your happenstance, you're not welcome here on the *Dolphin*, children or not."

"Perhaps your captain would prefer to talk to us himself," Otis said. "Seems to me Captain Trevor is fully in charge of his own decisions."

A dark-haired, sharp-eyed man appeared at the sailor's side. "I am in charge," he said. "Never doubt that." He pushed his crewman aside and gestured for him to leave. The pirate gave one final, nasty look to the children and then stalked off down the ship's deck. "What have you to do with the *Blue Dolphin*, Otis? It's been many long months since we've had dealings with one another."

"Might we speak face-to-face and not shout our business to the whole docks?" Trevor disappeared briefly as they waited for his response.

"The *Blue Dolphin*," Paige whispered. "It's a beautiful name."

Marcus gazed at the ship with a measuring eye. "A beautiful ship. A brigantine by the confirmation. See the three masts? Would have a crew of twenty to thirty if it's a merchant ship. But if it's pirates … Could be as many as eighty."

Otis hissed a warning at Marcus. "Be quiet now, boy. You mustn't let on how much ye know about such things. You'll only make Cap'n Trevor suspicious." He looked to all the children. "This is a rough crew, make no mistake. We need their help, but this is not the crew of the *Bethany*, I warn ye."

Suddenly, a sailor aboard the ship tossed a rope and board ladder over the side of the *Dolphin*. "Come aboard then, ye lubber, and bring your packet of babies as well. Cap'n says he'll see you, who knows why." Otis swarmed up the ladder, moving swiftly despite its swaying and turning.

Becca looked at the ladder skeptically. "A Jacob's ladder," Marcus said. "A typical method of getting on and off a ship in port. Different than the *Bethany*." He took hold of the bottom of the ladder, stopping its movement. "Go on up, Becca. It's fine."

Jake pushed ahead of her. "I'm not afraid." He climbed up about half the rungs. He swung around, hanging by one hand gripped around the rope. "Come on, Becca. It's easy!"

"Jake, hold on. Don't fool around." She grabbed hold of the ladder and followed Jake more slowly. "You'll fall off!"

He laughed happily and scrambled up the remaining distance as though he'd been boarding ships all his life. The sailor at the top grabbed him by the arm and swung him over the gunwale onto the deck. The man then leaned back over and offered his hand to Becca. "Come up, lassie. I got ye." His tobacco-stained teeth grinned at her. She stifled a shudder and reached out to take his hand. He reached past her hand, gripped her upper arm, and swung her off the ladder, out over the strip of water that glimmered between the ship and the pier, then over the rail on to the solid wooden deck of the *Blue Dolphin*. Paige and Marcus followed quickly and soon they all stood together on the deck.

Captain Trevor stood, arms folded across his chest. His broad, immovable stance made it clear he did not intend to invite them any further onto his ship than necessary. He frowned, clearly waiting for Otis to speak.

"Trevor, I come to you to beg a boon. I—me and my little crew—we need a ship and a crew to aid us in our final quest."

"A boon. You ask a boon of me? And why would I give one to you, the man who robbed me and nearly took my life?"

The children crowded close, hoping they would hear the full story of what had passed between these two men in past years.

"Perhaps to repay me for the robbery you've done and the near-fatal wounds you've inflicted on me over the years."

The two men stared at one another, never flinching, barely blinking. The air seemed to grow quiet and thick around them. The children held their breaths, sensing the battle of wills that was taking place in front of them. Instinctively, they knew that the first man to break the silence would somehow be conceding the win to the other. Paige silently prayed that Otis would stand strong and true. Captain Trevor's hard face, with its intense blue eyes, dark black brows, and trailing scar across his chin, seemed carved from stone. Otis's open gaze, sun-lightened hair, and small smirk was more pleasant to look at, but seemed just as unbending now as the other. Paige felt the tension stretching between the two men, stretching and expanding until she thought she would scream to break the spell. Then, suddenly, when she thought she could stand no more, Trevor stepped back and gestured for them to come further onto the deck.

"I'll hear you out, old man," he said. "For old times' sake."

CHAPTER 28

"What is it you've come for, old man? And why trail your wet nursing charges here to my ship? We've no need for babies here."

Jake bristled. "We're not babies. We take care of ourselves—and Otis!"

Trevor reached out and hoisted Jake a few inches off the deck by the straps of his backpack. He shook him slightly, and Jake balled his hands into fists. "Slow down, youngster. I've no quarrel with you." He dropped the boy. "I've already heard the tales of how you and Otis care for one another. But Otis Jennings never does anything without reason." He looked at Otis speculatively. "What have you in mind, you scoundrel?"

Becca noticed that several other of the *Dolphin* crew stood nearby, their hands resting casually on the hilts of their knives or the butt of a pistol. She shuddered but kept all expression off her face and her eyes on Captain Trevor.

"Afraid of one little boatwright, still?" Otis teased Trevor gently.

The captain smirked. "No fear, Jennings, just informed caution. You'll not forget that I've seen you in action. I want no trouble here in port—the authorities are just beginning to leave the *Dolphin* be when she comes in. It is ... convenient ... for me to stay on their good side for the time." Trevor clapped a heavy hand on Otis's shoulder. "And you have been known to stir up a bit of fuss then slip away with no dirt clinging to your fingers."

Otis laughed out loud. "You've a long memory, my friend, a long memory. No trouble today, I'll warrant. My crew here—surely they're proof enough I want no trouble either."

Marcus and Paige were following this lively exchange carefully. They could tell there was a long relationship between these two men—and that it was not always a friendly one. Both itched to know more but knew this was not the time to question anyone.

"You know I come about the treasure," Otis stated flatly. "Have you touched it?"

Trevor looked away from Otis and the children, out over the ocean that stretched wide and clear beyond the mouth of the port. "Otis, do you trust me so little?"

"It's a lot of booty," Otis said. "A temptation to any man."

Trevor looked back at his old acquaintance. "I know what it means to you, old man. Clearing your name. Getting right with the Crown." He turned away again. "Your interests have changed over the many years, Otis. Some would call these wishes the dreams of an old man. Are we old men, Otis?"

Otis took a step and laid a hand on Trevor's shoulder. "Old for this game, Trevor. Old for this." He stepped back and straightened his spine. "But not so old that I don't know what's right. And it's right for the Crown to have this loot. With all we've done, we know that."

Trevor turned again and surveyed the four children, waiting wide-eyed, for his response. His lips curved again in their mocking sneer. "Aye, we know. But it's only to you it matters. Yours is the only name known to be associated with this fiasco. I hold your future, Otis."

Otis faced him calmly. "You do." The two campaigners held each others' gaze, an adult version of the child's game to make each other blink. Neither did. The silence stretched again, pulling the day tight around Becca until she thought it would choke off her ability to breathe. She realized she was holding her breath, waiting to see if Trevor would give Otis what he needed.

Trevor's white teeth flashed—not quite a smile, almost a grimace. "You win, matey. I'll not prevail over you in this coward's way. The treasure remains where we placed it. You'll have your vindication with the Crown."

Otis nodded. "I thought I knew my man. Our early agreement to leave the treasure be has held us both. But now, it's time to fetch it home. And I'll need your help."

Trevor raised a suspicious eyebrow. "You'd not come to me lightly. Let's go below decks and discuss your business behind doors." He turned and led them all to the captain's cabin. When they entered, there were several crew members there, eating breakfast, playing cards. "Mates, I need the room. Give us some space, will you?"

There were grumbles, but the men gathered their plates and cards and grudgingly shuffled out of the room.

"What were they doing in the captain's cabin, anyway?" Jake whispered.

Marcus answered, "A captain gets the cabin for his sleeping quarters, but mostly to conduct the business of the ship. But a buccaneer crew is very democratic, so the captain is expected to share and share alike."

Paige nodded. "Pierre told me that the cabin was mess hall, meeting room, social spot, and actually belongs to everyone on the ship."

"The captain is given preference simply because of he's proved he can run the ship and bring in the treasure the crew is always after," Marcus continued. "If a captain fails in a campaign against an enemy, he'll be demoted without a second thought—or even killed.

Becca put a warning hand on Jake's shoulder. "These men can be ruthless. We can't ever forget that."

Captain Trevor glared at them. "Children, always nattering about something." He waved them to seats and sat himself at the head of the table, slouching casually in the carved fancy chair that was his right. "So tell me, Otis. I want the whole story, not your fancy lies."

Otis grinned at his mate. "Why, Trevor, would I lie to you when I come beseeching your aid?"

"Yes."

Otis's grin became a laugh. "Well, that's fair enough. But, Trevor, I've nothing to hide here. I simply need your help to get to our treasure."

"Our treasure, you say now. Why not the *Bethany*?"

"The *Dark Falcon* scuppered her for the moment. Me and the kids, we need to keep moving. We can't wait for the repairs."

Trevor grinned, an evil look, not at all a happy expression. "Cocklyn still on your tail, eh, mate? Not a good enemy."

"Makes a worse friend, I'll wager. No trusting that scoundrel. But if I can make them believe the treasure is gone, he'll give me some space to breath."

"And how to you plan to do that?"

"By actually making sure the treasure is gone. I want to put it somewhere where the soldiers can stumble on it—without attaching any particular sailor to it."

Becca started when Otis said the word "soldiers" but kept herself still, not giving anything away.

Trevor snorted. "Give up perfectly good bounty. You've gone soft, Jennings."

"No, now hear me out. The soldiers are looking for the gold from the El Coronado. They don't know how much more we gathered in our travels. If they find the gold, they'll be satisfied. We can split what's left—and you know that's no trifle."

Trevor stroked his chin thoughtfully. "Only the gold, eh? As I recall, there was plenty of silver, yard goods, some jewels …"

Otis leaned in. "Plenty to satisfy the crew and keep a nice parcel for yourself. A bit for me and the kids, our crew … this can work."

"We'll have to put it to the *Dolphin* crew. No guarantee they'll think it a good idea."

"That's why you and I will work out all the details, make sure they can see the benefit." Otis clapped a hand on Trevor's shoulder again. "You're in command of this crew, Trevor. You can make this happen."

Trevor glanced down at Otis's hand on his shoulder then looked coldly back up into Otis's eyes. "You'll not forget who is in command."

Otis took his hand back and raised them both, palms forward, a gesture of surrender. "Nay, Captain. You'll have no trouble from me and mine." He looked away to the children. "Though I might suggest a change in command on land."

Paige gasped at Otis's nerve. Surely Trevor would be offended by such a bold suggestion. Instead, he nodded sagely.

"Aye, you know the terrain better. You'll be major of the expedition on land." In fact, what Paige didn't know was that captains of pirate ships often gave over leadership when their battles moved to land. A ship's captain developed one set of skills; a commander on land had to know a fully different set of battle plans and tactics. "Let's work out the full plan, and we'll talk with the crew tonight. Draw up ship's articles then." Trevor looked sternly at the children. "And this lot? Part of your cargo, I imagine."

"Aye, they come with me. But they needn't sit here and fret through our plans. Your crew will leave them be for a bit, if they keep to themselves on the aft deck?"

Trevor nodded. "Aye, they'll be left alone." He rose and crossed to the door. "Here, Bowers," he called to one of his crew standing nearby. "Put these children up on the aft deck. Keep the others away from 'em. I want no trouble."

"Aye, Captain." Bowers looked at the children with a sneer on his lips. "Come on then, you picaroons."

"Otis?" Becca asked once before she left.

"Go on now. This here's adult business." His voice was harsh, but he winked at her behind Captain Trevor's back. She turned and left with the others.

CHAPTER 29

The kids gathered closely in the very rear of the quarterdeck, away from most of the prying eyes of the crew. The pirates were all engaged in the maintenance needed on a ship in port, preparing to set sail soon. Loading hogsheads—large barrels—of rum. Hauling crates of hard tack—a biscuit that kept well on long voyages—into the hold. Belaying or tying barrels of water to the masts to have handy as they sailed and worked in the hot Caribbean sun. The children heard cackling chickens and grunting pigs that had already been stowed below to provide fresh eggs and meat for the sailors when they were days, even weeks, from port. Some of the crew swarmed the rigging, inspecting sails and yardarms. But they kept a wary, if distant, eye on the children huddled together.

They were unsure why their captain allowed them on board or why he was dealing with that scoundrel, Otis Jennings. But Captain Trevor had made them rich men in the past, and they would trust his judgment as long as that held true. Still, they kept watch, not trusting even these youngsters, since they were strangers to the crew.

Paige shuddered and turned away from the glaring men across the deck. "They look at us so … I don't know. It makes my skin crawl."

Jake nodded. "They're not like the crew of the *Bethany*."

Marcus agreed. "They're not. These are full-blown pirates. Our friends on the *Bethany* work for crown and country—most of the time. At least Captain Penner, Otis, Pierre, Jeremiah, a few others do. They work as soldiers for the king. But not this bunch."

"I don't like being away from Otis like this." Paige continued to worry. "Why wouldn't he let us stay?"

"I wish we knew what was happening. I don't like not knowing what he's planning," Becca agreed. "But I guess we have to trust him."

Marcus nodded slowly. "Yes, but ... Listen, I don't like to bring this up, but ..." He stopped, giving his friends a solemn look.

"What? Cough it up," Jake said impatiently.

"It's possible ..." He glanced over his shoulder at the crew on the other end of the ship. "They might not let us go with Otis."

"They can't!" Paige said. "We have to stay with him!"

"And I believe Otis will want that as well. But it's possible, and I thought we'd better be prepared for it."

"But how do we know the globe will still work?" Paige said. "If we're separated, how do we know it'll work?"

"That's a good thought, Paige. We don't know, really, do we?" Marcus poked Jake's arm. "Let's see the globe now, Jake."

Becca drew in a sharp breath. Now they'd see. They'd know something terrible had happened. The globe would barely glow, and they'd know something was terribly wrong. What would she say? How could she explain it?

Jake pulled the pack off his back and tugged the zipper open. Becca squeezed her eyes shut as he carefully lifted the globe out into the sunshine. She waited, expecting to hear their disappointed shouts. But all she heard was ... nothing. She opened her eyes.

The globe was once again glowing beautifully, visible even in the bright sunshine. All of them smiled happily to see its beauty, but Becca felt sharp tears sting her eyes as well. She hadn't ruined everything. By going to Otis with the truth, she'd changed the course of their history, but for the good this time. The globe would still get them home despite her mistake. She nearly cried out loud in her relief.

"We're separated right now from Otis," Jake said. "Doesn't that mean it'll work anyway?"

"Mmm, not so sure this is really separated, kid," Becca said. "He's still on the ship with us."

"Wait, let's think this through," Marcus said. "Have we been away from Otis at some point or away from each other and know that the globe still glowed? Think back ..." They sat quietly for a moment, casting their minds back over their adventure so far.

"Yes. Yes!" Paige suddenly said. "Remember just after the *Bethany* picked us up? We landed on that island to get fresh water?"

"Oh yes," Marcus said. "Yes, we were on the island and the *Bethany* sailed off with some of the crew, Otis included, to go hunting on the next island over. Yes! Did anyone look at the globe?"

"Yeah, I did," Jake said. "I reached into my pack to grab my own canteen to fill it with water. The globe was really bright, there inside. It was nearly like a spotlight!"

"That's great!" Becca said. "Good memory, guys. So maybe it means even if they separate us from Otis, we can still all go home."

Paige's brow wrinkled, her expression deeply unhappy. "I don't want to split up. I don't like it."

Becca took her friend's hand, squeezing it gently. "None of us want to, Paige. But we might not have a choice."

The four friends all sat silently, each thinking about the unthinkable. What would they do? What could they do? Paige reached out and took Marcus's hand on one side and Becca's on the other. "Let's pray, guys. I ... we can't do anything, but God can." Becca nodded and grabbed Jake's left hand while Marcus took his right. They bowed their heads together, seeking comfort from their heavenly Father when so much that lay ahead of them was unknown.

CHAPTER 30

After what seemed like hours, Otis and Captain Trevor finished their business and they all left the *Dolphin*. They'd be back soon enough—the *Blue Dolphin* would sail with the tide later that day. The children quietly followed Otis from the *Dolphin*, each lost in their own thoughts. What had Otis planned with Trevor? Would they be able to stay together, or would they have to split up to save their quest? Would they ever see home again? Doubts that had been pushed to the back of their minds throughout their adventure came flooding back, as they wondered and worried about what Otis had in mind.

Becca slowly noticed that Otis was not leading them back to the *Bethany* directly. He seemed to be on a wandering course through the wharf, strolling up and down docks as though seeking something. "What is it, Otis? What are we looking for?"

Otis stopped in his tracks, eyes focused across the pier. "There they are," he whispered. "I knew they had to be here somewhere." Becca and the others followed his gaze and were shocked to see the bright red coats of the soldiers only two docks away. Their backs were to Otis and the kids, but they were obviously searching for something or someone too.

"Otis, we've got to hide!" Becca grabbed his sleeve and tugged urgently. "Before they see you."

"Now mind what I told you earlier, girl. You do as I say and do it right smart. You and Paige run on ahead and move over there closer to them redcoats. Be sly about it, but make sure they see you."

"What!?" Both girls reacted in shock.

"Do as I tell you. Make sure they see you and then run back to where me and the boys will be waiting for you. I need those redcoats to see you with me. They need to follow us back to the *Bethany*."

Marcus shook his head. "I'm afraid even I don't follow your reasoning here, Otis."

"Matters not right now. Hurry on, ladies, do as you're told. Right quick. Don't let them catch you but lead them back to me."

The girls reluctantly began to move away from Otis and the boys, looking back over their shoulders, concern etched on their faces. Otis made a final impatient shooing gesture then moved himself and the boys over to the top of the pier that led back out to the *Bethany*. Becca, uncertain but determined not to foul Otis's plans again, pulled Paige by the arm and moved more quickly to the dock where the soldiers still remained. Sneaking up behind a sailor with an armload of canvas, the girls moved closer to the soldiers, positioning themselves to come under the men's gaze as they swept the docks in their search.

About four yards away from the redcoats, Becca grabbed Paige's arm and directed her attention to a cage full of chickens. "Look at the chicks, Paige," she said loudly, hoping to catch the ear of the searching men. Paige exclaimed her delight loudly, with a mild squeal that brought the soldiers' eyes around to see the two young girls standing so close to them. Becca almost hoped they would keep on searching, their eyes moving past the innocent sight of girls and chickens, but it was not to be. They were, in fact, the object of the soldiers' search. Becca quickly averted her eyes so the men would not know she had noticed them and turned back to Paige. "Come on, Paige, we'd better find Otis and the boys."

Paige made one last cooing sound at the birds and fell into step beside Becca. Her lighthearted skipping step belied the concern they both felt, but she acted the part of a carefree child, one who was not the object of the soldiers' manhunt. Becca was amazed at Paige's ability to play the part. She did her best lighten her own heart and step, to match Paige's cheery pose.

One of the soldiers called out, "Young miss!" But Becca and Paige kept moving away from the soldiers as though they had not heard. But Becca had heard and recognized the voice of young Lieutenant Baker. So they had come—her story had been believed. It took all her concentration to keep her eyes front and not glance back to see how close the soldiers were and if it was just the two of them. Had Major Hale come? Would he seize Otis on sight? What did Otis have in mind, drawing the soldiers to him?

Paige grabbed Becca's hand and said quietly, "Smile, Becca. Jeez, you look like you're walking your last mile." She swung Becca's arm and broke into a full skip. They began to move more quickly through the crowd, and Becca worried they'd lose the soldiers. But no—she could hear their boots clomping loudly on the wooden pier. Always there, not too close but never far away. She concentrated on keeping a natural-looking smile on her face.

As they came to the end of the dock, ready to turn toward Otis and the boys, Becca saw several more soldiers out of the corner of her eye. She heard Lieutenant Baker say, "It's her!" and saw the new men move swiftly toward her and Paige. "They'll get us!" she hissed at Paige.

"No chance!" Paige changed from a skip into a trot. "We're almost there." She pointed halfway down the pier that led to the *Bethany* to where the boys stood. She pulled Becca forward, ducking under the arms of a sailor pulling a load up onto a ship's deck. They quickly twisted around a stack of crates and wove in between several men who were laughing wildly about something. Becca snuck a peek backward and saw that these quick maneuvers had put some distance between them and the soldiers. She laughed out loud as well and put on more speed, racing toward the boys.

Otis turned and smiled broadly as he saw the girls speeding down the dock. His smile didn't falter as he noticed the soldiers disentangling themselves from the rowdy group of men further up the dock. "There's my darlin's, just as I thought." He wrapped his arms around the girls' shoulders and hurried them all down the dock that led to the *Bethany*. "Nicely done, my brave lasses," he said quietly. "Now they'll see us right and tight onto the *Bethany* and no more expect to see us wandering about the wharf."

"Aren't they just going to grab you?" Becca whispered back. "Now that they've found you. Now that we've led them right to you."

In a louder voice, Otis said, "Just a day or two for repairs and we'll be underway. No need to fret on that account. We'll be off after our treasure sooner than you can blink an eye." Otis looked at Becca and winked. He whispered, "Now they'll just wait to follow us is all. No need to fight a crew that might not be wanting to let us go."

CHAPTER 31

B ut Becca did not relax until they were actually standing on the deck of the *Bethany*, with no challenge from the soldiers. Though *relax* wasn't exactly the right word. Pierre put them to work immediately, helping to prepare the evening meal for the crew, who had been working hard to prepare the *Bethany* to sail for dry dock the next day. It wasn't until after dinner that Becca had a chance to look overboard and see if the soldiers were still about.

They were. She didn't see them out in the open, but by watching carefully, she could see them peering out from various hiding places. There was one behind the bales of fabric, sitting at the far end of their dock. There was another, loitering along the second pier over, keeping a wary eye on the *Bethany*. She thought she could even see one on the deck of a merchant vessel that was moored in the vicinity. Otis was right—they were just going to keep an eye on the *Bethany* and follow them to the treasure. But she still didn't understand how that helped Otis's overall plan.

As the sun began to set, Otis gathered the children into the captain's cabin, where Captain Penner and Pierre waited. "Well done today, crew," the captain said as they entered. "But there's more to do—and you'll need to be very brave now."

Pierre nodded encouragingly. "*Mes amis*, you will be able to do this thing."

"What thing?" Jake asked suspiciously. "What's going on?"

Otis looked at them, his expression grave. "When we pledged to each other as crew, and then ourselves to the *Bethany*, you promised to obey orders." The children nodded. "Even if you didn't agree with them, right?"

"Now just a minute. What is this all about?" Becca protested.

Otis fixed her with a steady gaze. "You made me an added promise, didn't you, girl?"

Becca rolled her eyes, but had to nod. "But why are you reminding us of this now? What is it?"

Captain Penner said, "You must trust us, children. Trust that we know our warfare and how to make battle plans." He stood, drawing himself to his full height. "Paige and Jake, you'll be staying here on the *Bethany*. Marcus and Becca, you'll go with Otis on the *Dolphin*."

There was a moment, but only a brief moment, of silence. Then all four children began to talk at once.

"No way!"

"Unacceptable, sirs, really."

"Not going to happen."

"What? Why?"

The captain stood silently, letting the children shout themselves out. When at last they quieted, it was simply because they weren't getting any answers and finally realized it. Marcus asked quietly, "Sir, may we have an explanation?"

Penner nodded and Otis spoke. "I need to leave and the *Blue Dolphin* will take me. But Trevor seems to feel he needs you young 'uns to guarantee my good behavior."

"Then we'll all go with you, Otis," Jake asserted.

Penner held up a quieting hand. "No, we need the soldiers to believe that you're all still here, at least for a time. If they see a couple of children, they'll assume all of you are together."

"And, with a few appearances of one of our men in Monsieur Otis's chapeau"—Pierre twitched Otis's straw hat from his head—"we can convince the soldiers not to go seeking you elsewhere."

The children exchanged distressed glances.

"The logic is flawless," Marcus said.

Jake looked at him, stricken. "You're okay with this?"

"I think it is well-thought-out arrangement," Marcus answered, putting his arm around his younger buddy's shoulders. "I wouldn't say I'm okay."

Paige looked from Otis to Captain Penner to Pierre, her eyes shining with unshed tears. "Can't we please just all wait for the repairs and stay together? Please?"

Pierre laid a gentle hand on her head. "*Mon amour*, no tears now, *s'il vous plaît*. We must give Otis some room to move about without the soldiers."

"Aye, I can make all things right with the king, soldiers, and get Cocklyn off my back. But I can't do it with Hale and his men breathing down my neck." Otis nodded confidently at the children. "This will work, certain sure, but you must do your parts."

Becca looked again at her friends, then back to the men. Her voice shook as she said "All right. So how do we get to the *Blue Dolphin* without being seen?"

CHAPTER 32

The night was now full dark outside the windows of the *Bethany*'s cabin. Pinpoints of light—distant stars—had just begun to pierce the darkness. The cheery twinkle depressed Paige, and she turned from the window and back toward her friends. Maybe for the last time. Her mind quickly snatched at that thought, trying to stop it. But it was no good—she'd thought it. This could be the last time they were all together. She caught her breath, choking back a cry.

Becca sat close to her brother, not touching him but drawing comfort from his nearness. Yeah, they fought a lot, but she loved him. She could see that he was working hard to keep a brave face. He looked up and caught her gaze on him. A quick grin, then he looked away and pulled out his backpack.

"We'd better check the globe," he said. "Just to be sure …"

"What'll we do if it's not glowing?" Paige worried, as Jake unzipped the bag.

"Hush," Becca said, her eyes glued to the bag. "Let's see before we worry."

Jake carefully reached into the bag and pulled out the globe. It was ablaze with light, as though it was filled with fire. The little ship was barely visible, so bright was the glow. All the children sighed with relief.

"Looks like this must be the right thing," Becca said.

Marcus laughed. "I'd say so!"

Jake set the globe down carefully then shook his hand energetically. "Whew! That tingle almost hurts!"

Marcus held his hand close to the globe then snatched it back. "A lot of power there. It's really radiating. I believe we have our confirmation." He stood and held his hand out to Jake. Jake took it, and they shook solemnly. "Take care of yourself, bud."

"You make sure my sister is safe," Jake responded. "Or I'll track you down and make you pay."

Becca grinned and gave Jake a quick hug. "Goofball. You behave. Do as Paige and Pierre tell you."

Jake pulled out of her hug and gave her a shove. "Okay, *Mom*." Then he grabbed her back into a quick hug. "Come back in one piece."

Marcus had turned to Paige and hugged her. "We'll all be fine," he whispered into her ear. "Don't worry."

Paige blinked furiously, trying to keep the moisture that welled up in her eyes from spilling over into tears. "I know," she replied. "But you guys are all I have. Please don't get hurt."

Becca tapped Marcus on the shoulder. "Um, can anyone get in on this hug, or are you and Paige going together now?"

Paige grinned sheepishly and gave Becca a hug. "Jealous much?" She held onto Becca's shoulders and looked into her eyes. "Do what Otis tells you, okay? Don't mess around with this. You won't have the globe to tell you what's right or wrong."

"I'll be good, I promise." She grasped Paige's hands and gave them a quick squeeze. "Jake, better put that globe away. Otis will be back for us any minute."

Jake slipped the snow globe back into the bag and pulled the zipper closed, just as Otis and Pierre came back through the cabin door. "All right now, children, you've said your fare-thee-wells? Paige darlin'. Jake boy." Otis crouched and wrapped his arms

SECRETS OF THE SNOW GLOBES

around them. "We'll be back before you know it." As Otis stood, Pierre put his arms around Paige and Jake, drawing them close.

Otis turned his attention to Becca and Marcus. "Now, my crew, I need your best tonight. We'll be dropping over the bow into a waiting longboat that will take us to the *Dolphin*. It's the one side of the ship the soldiers can't see from the pier. But we'll need to move quietly, keep a low profile. And in darkness, no lights."

"Over the bow?" Becca said uncertainly.

"Be fearless now, girl. I know you've got it in you." Otis took her hand and gestured to Marcus with the other. "Here we go." Otis opened the cabin door, and Becca took one last look at her brother and her best friend before the door closed on them and safety.

Becca and Marcus followed Otis at a fast glide across the deck, ducking low to blend with the shadows cast by the gunwales, the water casks, and the masts. All around, she heard the sounds of the port—ropes creaking on the *Bethany* and nearby ships, the occasional burst of rowdy laughter or rough shouts from a group of sailors elsewhere on the docks, the waves lapping against the flanks of the ships and the pier footings. She knew all this would be good cover for their escape, but she wished it would all stop for just a moment so she could listen for the careful footfalls of soldiers' boots against the wooden planking. All too quickly, they were at the bow where one of the other crewman from the *Bethany* waited to help them over the edge and away.

"Marcus, over you go," Otis hissed. He lifted the knotted rope that trailed over the gunwale alongside the bowsprit's head. "Let yourself down easy. Perkins waits below in the boat." Marcus quickly climbed up and over the railing, pausing to give Becca a grin before he disappeared from her sight. She listened to the rope chafing and creaking against the wooden rail as it moved under Marcus's weight. It shifted and rubbed then stopped and went slack.

"All right, Miss Becca, step up. Let yourself down, hand over fist. Hold fast to the knots, use them as little steps, and ye'll be in the boat afore ye know it." Otis and the other crewman helped her over the side of the rail. For a moment, her feet swung free and she couldn't feel the rope at all.

"I … I can't …" But then, her searching toes found the rope, and she stood almost firm against the side of the *Bethany*. Becca thought that it was a good thing that it was so dark. If she could have seen the long drop to the ocean, her courage would have surely failed her.

"Oh, and sure you can. Go on now. I'll follow right after you." Becca began to let herself down the rope, finding the knots more easily than she thought. Three knots down, six, then ten—she wondered how many it took until she reached bottom.

Suddenly, she felt a hand on her ankle and a firm grip around her waist. "Got you, miss," a voice whispered. It must be Perkins, helping her into the longboat and seating her next to Marcus. She gratefully took his hand in the dark and listened as the rope whispered and slid under Otis's weight. The boat shifted and rocked as he let go of the rope and found a seat in the boat. "And we're away," Perkins said softly, as he and Otis began to work the oars to push them away from the *Bethany* and toward their fate on the *Blue Dolphin*.

CHAPTER 33

As they slid across the water, Becca's eyes adjusted to the dark, and soon she could see the large ships that surrounded them in the port. Most were quiet, with only a man or two visible on deck. When in port, most of the sailors would be given shore leave, taking it in turns to walk guard duty. Here and there, however, she glimpsed vessels that were centers of activity—men returning from the town and swarming up the Jacob's ladders, orders being shouted to rig the mainsail or stow the cargo. The *Blue Dolphin* would not be the only ship sailing with the tide that night, it seemed. All the better for their escape.

Soon, Perkins brought them alongside the *Blue Dolphin*, gliding in under the leaping bowsprit that it was named for. Several men waited on the dock to hold the boat as Otis, Marcus, and Becca scrambled out. With a cheery but whispered "Good sailing," Perkins pushed off again and headed back toward the *Bethany*. The *Dolphin*'s crewmen led them to the rope ladder and, in short order, they stood on the deck of the *Blue Dolphin*, under the watchful eye of Captain Trevor.

"All going as planned," he said to Otis, half a statement, half a question.

"Aye, and from your end?"

"Aye. My crew has been out and doing their jobs today. You children," Captain Trevor gestured toward the main cabin. "Keep yourselves out of the way in my cabin. I don't want you underfoot while we make sail. If you must fall asleep, it had better be on those blankets on the floor and not in my bed."

"Yes, sir," they said in unison and hurried off, his rough laughter following them across the deck.

"Marcus, close that door," Becca said. "Captain Trevor's going to see."

"I'm not in the way," Marcus said, looking back at her over his shoulder. "I just want to see what they do differently for sailing at night." As he turned back to the open doorway, a gruff "Kill that light!" was growled at him, and he quickly pulled the door shut and Becca doused the lantern. "Oops …"

"Come to the window. There's enough moonlight to see." Because the captain's cabin was at the bow—at the very front—of the ship, the windows actually curved around to the sides. While they couldn't see what was happening on the deck of the *Dolphin*, they could see activity on the decks of a couple of other ships also preparing to leave. It was clear there was a lot of noise, light, and action on those vessels.

"Captain Trevor must be taking the extra precaution of masking our flight with the other sailings," Marcus said, gesturing in the direction of the other ships. "Obviously, night sailing doesn't normally require keeping lights out."

They soon felt the *Blue Dolphin* shift and saw that they were, indeed, moving out of port between a frigate and a brig. With no lights and little sound, Becca imagined it would be very easy to miss the fact that three ships were leaving port, rather than just two. She had to give the captain credit. He was taking no chances. But that only meant he thought this was as dangerous as she did. She shivered.

"Don't worry, Becca." Marcus moved closer to her and put an arm around her shoulder. "The globe says we're doing the right thing."

"But we don't know what's happening from here. Things could change and the snow globe could go dark at any point from here on out." Becca sighed as she turned back to gaze out over the wide sea. "I feel so … so out of control."

Marcus chuckled. "And you hate that, I know. But we have to trust Otis and Captain Trevor. They know their enemy and the warfare of these times. We don't."

Becca made a growling sound. "I hate that." Then she laughed. "But you know that."

"We should try and get some sleep." Marcus slid off the window seat and bunched up some of the blankets the captain had pointed out earlier. Becca grabbed a few and curled up beside him. "Becca … will you pray with me?"

"Of course." The two children lay side by side, holding hands, and poured their hearts out to their heavenly Father, who was closer to them than their time-lost home, than their sea-separated friends and even than each other. They prayed and were able to sleep.

Becca roused slightly when the cabin door opened what felt like moments later. She heard Otis's rough voice whispering but couldn't understand what he was saying. Trevor responded to him, his voice soft but clearer. "The *Falcon* is there." Becca tried to wake herself, but the arms of sleep held her too tightly. She tried to speak, to ask what had gone wrong. How could the *Dark Falcon* have found them? How close were they? But all she managed was a slight moan, and Captain Trevor immediately closed the cabin door. Becca fought against the fog in her mind, but sleep claimed her once again, and she drifted into dreamlessness.

CHAPTER 34

Becca and Marcus stood on the stern quarterdeck, searching the horizon. "I'm sure he said the *Falcon* was here," Becca said. They had been sailing for several hours since Marcus and Becca had awoken. But they hadn't seen a glimpse of another sail.

"Maybe he meant they had been in port."

Becca shook her head. "No, it seemed more like ... I don't know. It was weird."

"You were asleep. Did you dream it?"

"I don't think so. He sounded like it was a good thing. He said it like Otis should be glad the *Falcon* was here." Becca turned from the sea, rubbing her eyes. "It just doesn't make any sense, does it?"

They were interrupted by the cry "Land ho!" from the crow's nest.

"We're here?" Becca and Marcus looked forward, trying to see what land the lookout saw. "It's this close to Nassau Town?"

Marcus shook his head. "That doesn't seem right. Nothing is making sense this morning." They left the quarterdeck and went looking for Otis. They found him, with Captain Trevor at the bow. Trevor was using his spyglass to look ahead.

"There she be!" he exclaimed excitedly. "Otis, you dog, we're going to pull this off."

Otis grinned and clapped Trevor on the back. "We still make a good team, don't we?" He saw the children coming up behind them. "There ye are, young 'uns. Our work is soon done. There's our island, on the horizon." From the front of the ship like this, the children could now see the island.

"It's awfully close to Nassau, isn't it?" Marcus asked.

"Just where no one would think of looking," Trevor said. He turned and called, "Prepare the longboat!" to his men. "We'll be in the lagoon quick as wink." He smiled, but Becca wasn't sure she liked the look of it. He was a hard man, and his smile seemed false somehow. Something felt off, but neither she or Marcus could figure out what it was.

They did reach the island quickly. The men of the *Blue Dolphin* swarmed over the rigging, furling the sails quickly as the anchor was dropped from the bow in the lagoon of the small island. They hung there, swaying in the breeze while others prepared one of the longboats. "Only one?" Becca asked. "Isn't a group of us going to fetch the treasure?" She stood next to Otis and Marcus at the gunwale near the boat.

Otis didn't answer but quickly jumped over the rail into the boat. Another couple of men boarded the small boat as well. "Otis?" Marcus climbed up on the rail. "What's happening?"

"Be good, lad. Stay and take care of Miss Becca." The boat lurched as the crew began lowering it away from the *Dolphin*.

"Otis, no!" Marcus vaulted the gunwale, leaping toward the boat as it sank from sight.

"Marcus!" Becca screamed as she felt the heavy hand of Captain Trevor on her shoulder. She pulled against him but only succeeded in dragging her way to the rail. There she saw that Marcus had made it into the boat, and Otis was scolding him. The longboat continued to drop and landed with the splash in the waves of the lagoon.

Becca turned furiously to Trevor. "What are you doing?! Why did you lower that boat without us?"

Trevor held her back from him, eyeing her balled fists carefully. "Your argument's not with me, young miss. This was the plan of your precious Otis."

"I don't believe you."

"Well, believe me or not, as you like. But I can tell you that Otis wanted you two to stay safely on board ship while he checked into the circumstances of the treasure. As your mate noted, we're awfully close to Nassau, and there's no saying the treasure is still there."

"Okay, fine, whatever. But you need to launch a longboat for me right away, then."

Trevor barked out a hard laugh. "You're not going anywhere, lass. Otis'll have his hands full with that Marcus. He don't need you for added trouble." Trevor turned and shouted to his men, still hanging in the rigging. "Sails up, boys!" He turned to the navigator and crew man standing on the foredeck. "Weigh anchor, gentlemen!"

Becca did hit at Trevor this time. "Stop this! We can't sail. Otis and Marcus—and some of your own men—are on the island. We can't just leave them!"

Trevor grabbed her hands and held them tightly, hurting her. "You'll stop now, miss. I've been good to you for Otis's sake, but I'll only tolerate so much. I'm captain of this ship, and I'll decide when and where we sail. You'd do well to find yourself a corner and stay out of my way."

Becca started to retort but bit her tongue as she sized up the look in Trevor's eye. This man was closer to pirate than sailor, and she had no one now to take her side. She pulled her hands roughly out of his grip and turned from him before he could see her fear or the tears that stung her eyelids.

She held her back straight as she marched away from him and found a spot on the rear quarterdeck once again. She watched, pale and silent, as the longboat landed on the beach and was hidden in some tall grasses at the shoreline. She couldn't believe

Otis hadn't turned around and rowed back to the *Dolphin* when he'd seen the sails unfurled. He had to have heard the anchor chain creaking loudly as the sailors pulled it back up. He didn't even look to see the *Blue Dolphin* sail out of the lagoon and back into the open sea. And then, suddenly it seemed, they were gone. She couldn't see Otis or Marcus or soon even the island. She was alone.

CHAPTER 35

Marcus heard Otis's voice, rebuking him for jumping into the longboat. But his eyes were on the *Blue Dolphin*, where he could just see Becca's face, leaning out over the gunwale. She'd screamed his name as he'd jumped, and it had sounded to him like the last word ever to be spoken. Otis finally reached out and shook him.

"You'd better pay attention to me, lad. Trevor'll watch after Miss Becca. But if you want to stay safe, you'd better do exactly as I say."

"What's going on, Otis? Why is Captain Trevor sailing without us?"

"Well, he wasn't going to sail without you, but you made some changes to our plan. I don't know if our treasure is still safe here. I wanted to check it out without having to worry about you lot." He looked away from Marcus as he spoke, and Marcus wondered what he wasn't being told. "Mind my words now, mate. We may be treading dangerous paths, and you need to obey me to stay safe."

"Otis, what's going on?"

Otis now looked him directly in the eye. "Just what I'm telling you, son. Don't endanger yourself and our quest here."

"Aye, sir." Marcus agreed, reluctantly, as he watched the *Blue Dolphin* sail away. But he couldn't help but wonder if he'd been part of endangering Becca by leaping into the longboat without her.

After the *Blue Dolphin* had been sailing for a few hours, the lookout in the crow's nest suddenly shouted, "Sail ahoy!" Quickly, another crewman swarmed up the mast, bringing the captain's telescope with him. It seemed the whole crew waited, holding their breath, to hear whose sail this was. Becca nearly cried out when the call came: "They fly the Jolly Roger!" Then, nearly immediately, the man reported, "I see the *Falcon* on the 'sprit! 'Tis the *Dark Falcon* a-comin'. Two leagues out, Captain!"

"Let 'er run, boys!" Captain Trevor shouted. The wind was filling the *Dolphin*'s sails fully, and the ship seemed to fly. But the *Falcon* was being helped by that same wind, and as the smaller ship, it moved faster, closing the distance to the *Dolphin* quickly. Trevor called up to the man in the crow's nest. "Wave the flag for parley. And Jacobs, bring my glass back down to me."

Becca didn't know that word "parley" and ran down to Trevor's side, as the man high on the main mast gathered in their vessel's flag and re-rigged a smaller, white flag with red border.

"What's happening?" she asked the captain.

Trevor glanced briefly at her, took his glass from the sailor, then walked back up to the aft quarterdeck. Becca followed, asking, "What does *parley* mean?" He continued to ignore her and raised his glass to his eye, looking back at the *Dark Falcon*.

"What do you see?" Becca persisted.

She might as well have not been there, for all the attention Trevor paid her. He continued to gaze at the *Falcon*, as though waiting for a particular sign. Becca squinted at the other vessel, trying to see what it was that Trevor was watching for.

Suddenly, he turned and shouted at his men. "Parley! Furl the mainsail. Drop the sea anchor. They'll parley!"

Becca pulled at the sleeve of Captain Trevor's shirt. "What does that word mean?" she asked insistently. "What is parley?"

Trevor pulled his sleeve out of Becca's grasp and headed back down to the main deck. She followed, growing more and more concerned about what was happening. As they stepped off the stairs onto the main deck, Trevor made a fast gesture to one of his men, who stepped up and took hold of Becca's arms. "Hey, what the …" Becca tried to twist away, but could not break away from the strong grip of the sailor. "What's going on here?"

Trevor finally looked directly at her. "You'll do yourself a favor if you keep yourself quiet for the next some time." His voice was low and mean, his gaze cold. "This is talk for men, not babies, and if you're good, you'll live through it all."

Becca kicked the shin of the man holding her, who roared in pain and lifted her off the deck. Trevor laughed harshly. "Put 'er down, Bixley. Can't you take a tap from a little girl?" Trevor stepped over to Becca and put a heavy hand on her neck. "Settle yourself, girl. There's nowhere to go. We're going to parley with Cocklyn and his vile crew before they run us down. Keep our lives in trade for something he wants."

"What do you have that they want?" Becca demanded.

"What has he wanted all along?" Trevor sneered at her.

"No!" Becca tried to charge Trevor, but her guard held her fast. "You can't tell him. Otis needs to find his treasure."

Trevor laughed again, and Becca was surprised to discover that laughter could hold no joy at all. "I suspect Cocklyn will let him find it all right. Save him some work." Trevor grabbed hold of her chin and forced her to look upward into his face. "Here are the hard facts, young miss. The *Falcon* is faster than us. We can parley with the information we have to sell and live. Or we can try to fight it out, still give up our information, and die. I'll take that first bargain any day. You behave yourself, and I'll let you live as well. Take you back to the *Bethany* and their baby nursery. Squawk and I'll let Cocklyn take his frustrations out on you." He released Becca and said to his men, "Lock 'er in the hold. I don't want to have to bother with her while I talk with Cocklyn."

The burly sailor dragged Becca across the deck to the open hatch, which led to the hold. What would happen if Cocklyn took the treasure? Would they ever be able to get home? As the sailor pushed her down the ladder into the hold and began to swing the big hatch closed, she felt as though the light was going out of the whole world.

Once again, Becca could only guess what was happening from the sounds she heard through the decking of the *Blue Dolphin*. She heard the clunking sound as grappling hooks hit the gunwale, as the *Dark Falcon* came alongside the *Dolphin*. Gruff voices and thuds as the pirates swarmed across the ropes and landed on the *Dolphin*'s deck. Scuffling, hard footsteps, and then suddenly she heard Trevor's voice, muffled, but right above her. He was obviously standing near the hatch that had just been battened above her. "No need for your ruffians, Cocklyn. We're under the flag of parley."

Becca shivered as she heard Cocklyn's harsh voice in response. "You're not giving the orders here now, Trevor. What is it you have to parley, ye scurvy bilge rat?"

"I know you only care about the treasure. My *Dolphin* is not what you're after."

"Your *Dolphin* is worth no more than a stinking fish. What know you about the treasure?"

"I brought Otis to it this morning," Trevor replied, as Becca bit back a cry, mindful of Trevor's threats.

"Don't tell," she whispered. "Don't tell him …"

"Tell me, then," Cocklyn growled.

"San Miguel."

Cocklyn roared his contempt. "You lousy knave. There's nevermore no treasure on that sand pile than in my hold."

Becca heard Trevor grunt and assumed that Cocklyn must have grabbed him or even hit him. "Tell me true, now, or I'll slit your scurvy throat."

"I can't tell you different, you scoundrel, because what I've told you is true. Otis thought he was clever, hiding the treasure in plain sight. You know where we were when you sighted us. Where else would I have been dropping old Jennings? And you know he was on the ship when we shoved off last night."

Cocklyn made a wordless sound of frustration. "You knew we were on to ye?"

Becca could hear the smirk in Trevor's voice. "Of course. I know what goes on around my vessel. I also knew I could deal Jennings to you, if your pathetic little scupper of a boat managed to make it to sea."

"Why so anxious to give him up?"

"Not anxious. But I've no love for the old man, and I'd rather you took out your vengeance on him than me and my crew. So head back to San Miguel and gather up your treasure. Me and my boys will not bother you."

Cocklyn paced back and forth a few steps. Becca could hear his boots clumping over her head. "Fine. But I'll take those children with me, to keep you and old man Otis in line."

Becca gasped. How did he know? They'd been careful to make sure there were children still on the deck of the *Bethany*—Paige and Jake.

Trevor sounded calm as he lied to Cocklyn. "No children on my ship. I'm not running a nursery."

"Hmmmph ..." Cocklyn grunted. "I'm not sure you ain't trying to run a rig."

"You've got your treasure. Get off my ship." Then suddenly, Becca heard Trevor grunt and a thud, like a man falling to the deck. This was quickly followed by shouts from the crew.

Cocklyn snarled above the noise. "Shut yer faces, ye scurvy animals. We'll search this ship before we leave. Let us do our work and you'll all live to see another sunrise. Men ..."

Becca backed quickly away from the hatch, trying to see into the dark around her for a hiding place. But she couldn't see more than a foot in front of her, as the hold was well sealed and the gun ports all shut tight. She stumbled over a bale of hay and crashed noisily into a pile of empty crates. Before the last crate landed, the hatch was thrown open and a pirate swarmed down the steps. "Got 'er, Cap'n!" he shouted as he reached out and grabbed Becca's arm. He pulled her up and into the sunshine. She blinked and squinted, trying to see what was happening. The pirate shoved her forward, and she found herself face to ugly face with the terrible Captain Cocklyn.

Becca looked past his scowl to see Trevor and his crew being held at pistol and sword point by Cocklyn's crew. "I thought parley meant you didn't take each other captive."

Cocklyn's faced was not improved by the wicked grin that crossed it when he saw Becca. "Here she is. Jennings's little charmer." Cocklyn grabbed her arm and pulled her close. She winced away from his anger and bad breath. "You're not here to tell me what parley does or doesn't mean, so watch your tongue." He shook her harshly. "Where's the other one now, girlie? I know Otis left two of you on the *Bethany*, but there's the dark one. Where's he at?"

Becca struggled to pull out of his grip. "Let me go. I'm not telling you anything."

Cocklyn roughly pulled her closer. "You'd be wise, little girl, to make nice with me. I can make things … very unpleasant for you if you ain't nice." He looked around at his crew. "Bring Trevor over here."

Two of the pirates manhandled Captain Trevor over to Cocklyn, who handed Becca off to the pirate who'd found her. He pulled a long, sharp dagger from his belt and held it up to the light. "Hmmm … here's my dilemma," Cocklyn said casually. "Which of you will talk first, with the right … encouragement? The seasoned sea captain?" He waved the blade under Trevor's nose. "Or the baby girl?" He watched Trevor's face as he pushed the knife close to Becca's cheek. "All I need to know is where the boy is. Simple question. No need for anyone to get hurt here."

Trevor shook his head. "Of course not. The boy is with Otis. You find Otis, you'll find the other kid."

Becca cried out, "Don't tell him anything!"

Cocklyn laughed. "And that tells me you're not lying. Don't worry, girlie, you'll see your friends soon enough. Bring 'er back across the ropes," he told the pirate holding her.

"For what possible reason would you saddle yourself with the child?" Trevor asked, his tone and facial expression showing only curiosity.

"Same reason you did, I imagine," Cocklyn replied. "Help keep Otis in line. He seems to fancy these children, from all I've heard."

"Aye, he does that," Trevor shrugged. "But both of them? I'd think one was enough to manage Otis."

"Well, I'd agree, but I think he might be a softer touch for the girl. So I'll have to deal with both of 'em." He snarled at the pirate, struggling to pull Becca over to the side of the ship. "Are ye a weakling, ye lubber? Get her across to the *Falcon*."

"She'll have us both in the water, the way she's wiggling," the other pirate said.

Cocklyn reached out to Becca, holding the knife close to her face once more. "Girl, if you want to live, you'll belay this nonsense. You're going over the ropes to the *Falcon*. But if you go in the drink, I'll leave you there to drown." He looked directly into her eyes. "Believe me, girl."

Becca gulped, seeing the truth in his hard gaze. "I ... I do."

"Right. Then let Smythe take ye over, nice and calm, and we'll let the crew of the *Dolphin* go on their way."

Becca looked at Captain Trevor one more time, hoping to see some fight, some hint that he wouldn't let this happen. But he wouldn't return her glance and seemed only interested in getting Cocklyn and his crew off the *Blue Dolphin* as quickly as possible.

Then she was at the gunwale and the pirate was pushing her up, past one of the grappling hooks and out onto a rope stretched across the rolling sea.

"Wait, wait—I can't do this!" she said urgently. The ropes swayed in rhythm with the sea that rolled and rocked the ships. Becca didn't see any way she could crawl across these loose lines to reach the deck of the *Dark Falcon*, thirty feet away.

"I'll see you across," the pirate said gruffly. "But you need to do as I say and no guff from you."

"All right," Becca said meekly. She could see no way to escape this situation and thought it better to live to see Otis and Marcus again.

"Crawl up on my back then. Hold on to my shoulders." Becca shifted back off the gunwale and climbed up, piggy-back, on her captor's shoulders. She clung to his shirt, trying to ignore the smells of old sweat, tobacco, and unwashed hair that wafted into her nostrils. As he crawled up on top the gunwale and started across the ropes, Becca bit back a cry of fear and squeezed her eyes tightly shut. But somehow, the swaying of the ropes seemed magnified with her eyes closed, so she soon opened them again. One glance below at the rolling, racketing waves almost made her lose her grip, and she bit back a squeal.

"Hang on and keep still," her pirate rumbled. "Keep your eyes on the *Falcon*."

Becca did as he said and looked up toward the *Dark Falcon*. The ship did seem to be a steady and stable destination, compared to the staggering waves and the swaying ropes. She fixed her eyes on the *Falcon*'s deck and prayed they would make it across quickly.

It ended up being the longest thirty seconds of her life, Becca thought. It was almost like the ship kept retreating, moving further away, though she knew that wasn't possible. The ropes held the *Falcon* and the *Dolphin* together and one could not move further from the other. But there were moments where she thought they'd never reach the deck of the *Falcon*. And even as she thought that, she realized that, only a few minutes ago, she would have hoped they'd never reach it. What would she do, once aboard the *Dark Falcon*? Would she ever see any of her friends or family again? Becca didn't know what to expect or what to do next.

CHAPTER 36

All too soon, Becca's pirate and all the others were back on the *Dark Falcon* and the crew of the *Blue Dolphin* couldn't get the grappling hooks off her gunwales fast enough. Becca strained against the clinging hands of her captor, trying to see some sign that Captain Trevor wouldn't just abandon her to Captain Cocklyn and his evil crew. But she never saw the captain, only heard his voice, calling out for his crew to unfurl the sails and take the *Blue Dolphin* out to sea—out of her sight and out of her life. Her eyes stung, and she blinked rapidly to keep the tears from overflowing. As the *Dolphin* sailed straight away from her, she turned to face her captors, her eyes clear, her face set.

Captain Cocklyn was busy as well, urging his crew to hoist the sails and begin tacking against the wind, back to the island where Otis and Marcus were seeking treasure. The pirate who had been holding her pushed her down on to a bale of hay and said, "Sit here and stay out of the way. None of us thinks that much of Otis that we need you to manage him." He grinned meanly and ran a thumb across his throat. "If you're trouble, we'll get rid of you, no second thoughts."

Becca did sit quietly, hoping only to stay under everyone's radar, thinking furiously about what she could do to improve this situation. She decided there was really nothing she could do until they were on the island. She had to connect back up with Otis and Marcus, make sure they were okay. Maybe together, they could make a plan. But here, alone, she couldn't think of one thing she could do to make a difference to the situation they were in.

After a long afternoon of sailing, Becca finally heard the lookout cry "Land ho!" and she ran to the bow to see they had, indeed, returned to the island where Otis and Marcus had been left. There was still no sign of the longboat on the beach or of any of the crew that had landed with them. Becca assumed they were all back in the forest, seeking Otis's treasure. How could she warn them? Could they avoid Cocklyn if she could let them know?

The pirate that had carried her across the ropes came up to the bow, grumbling. "Don't know why I got to play wet nurse. He wants you, he ought to drag you around." He jerked a thumb at Becca. "Get over here and come with me. Cap'n wants you in the longboat with him now."

Becca went with the pirate, glad to at least be going to the island. As long as she was there, she had some chance to make a difference. She meekly allowed herself to be handed over the gunwale into the hands of another pirate, already in the longboat. He dumped her unceremoniously onto a seat and said, "Stay still. Don't rock the boat." Becca did as she was told, as a number of other pirates loaded into her and another longboat. Soon, both boats were lowered to the ocean's surface and away from the *Falcon*. Becca tried to ignore the raucous calls of the pirates, as they made their threats and bragged about how they each would be the one to catch Otis.

When they hit the beach, all the crewmen jumped out and pulled the boats up on to shore, out of the reach of the waves. Cocklyn made a curt gesture, and one of them pulled Becca off her seat and out on to the sand. "How will we find 'em here, Cap'n?"

"This island ain't that big," Cocklyn said. "I think we can bring 'em to us." He grabbed Becca by the arm. "Give us a scream, girlie. Come on …"

"No way. I'm not helping you." Becca pulled away from him and crossed her arms.

"I think you will, girl," Cocklyn said as he stepped closer to her and gripped her wrist. "Now give us a scream." He pulled her arm away from her body then twisted it harshly, bending it sharply behind her back. Becca grunted but bit her tongue against anything louder. Cocklyn leaned into her and twisted harder, making Becca cry out. Still she kept the tone low, a sound that didn't carry more than a few feet. Cocklyn cursed, then pulled a knife from his belt. "Enough! Sing out, or I'll slice you until you do." He bent Becca's arm even further and stuck the tip of the dagger into her arm.

Becca screamed then, despite herself. Cocklyn laughed then twisted the knife to draw another scream from her. He pulled the knife tip out of her arm and a trickle of blood flowed quickly down her skin.

"Jennings!" Cocklyn bellowed. "Jennings, I know you can hear me. And your little girl, too." He slapped Becca's arm, right on top of the wound, and she screamed again, crying. "You want to save her any more pain, you and all your boys better come out now." Cocklyn grasped Becca's wound again and she cried out once more, unable to help herself.

"Hold up, ye bilge rat!" Otis's voice rang out from the woods nearby. "Let her be." Slowly, Otis led his small crew out of the woods, Marcus trailing behind.

"Better be all of you, old man, or she'll get more than a scratch," Cocklyn said, holding his knife close to Becca's throat.

"It's all of us. This island's too small to keep a secret on for long."

"On your knees, then," Cocklyn ordered as they drew closer. He directed his men to tie the crew of the *Dolphin*'s hands behind their backs.

"Let the boy bind up the girl's arm afore you tie them up," Otis said. At Cocklyn's reluctant nod, Marcus crossed the sand to Becca's side. He hugged her gently and pulled a bandana out of his pocket.

"I'm glad to see you, even under these circumstances," Marcus whispered to Becca as he carefully wrapped the makeshift bandage over the cut on her arm.

"I'm sorry," Becca sniffed. "I tried not to scream."

"Don't you dare apologize. Cocklyn would have made you scream sooner or later."

"All right, all right, the little princess is fine now," Cocklyn growled. He gestured both of them back into the line of men, kneeling in the sand, hands tied behind them. His men quickly tied up both Marcus and Becca and they were all allowed to sit cross-legged. More comfortable, but an even more difficult position to get up from, in the loose grit. Cocklyn left two men to guard them, muskets in hand, while he and the rest of the men with him signaled the crew on the ship to begin coming across to the island.

Otis rose from the sand, stretching his shoulders, easing the strain placed on them by having his hands tied behind his back, eliciting a shout from the pirate guard. "Pipe down, ye bilge rat. If you want me to lead you to the treasure, I'll need to walk. My stiff old bones can't stay crossed in the sand forever."

The pirate spat and growled. "Don't try anything. I'll slit your throat, make no mistake."

Otis laughed. "Aye, and have Captain Cocklyn slit yours minutes later." He nodded toward the *Dark Falcon*, anchored in the calm bay before them. "He's your only hope to get out of here and he'll not treat you kindly if you kill off his treasure hound."

The pirate glared over his shoulder at the ship, then back at Otis. His eyes narrowed. "Well, there's ways to hobble you without killing you anyway, so don't get any wise ideas about trying to escape."

Otis just shook his head at the buccaneer's idle threats and took the few steps from where he stood to where Becca sat. When she didn't look up at him, he lowered himself into the sand next to her. "Lass, are ye all right?"

"Otis, I'm sorry," Becca replied. "I've made a complete mess of this all."

"Nay, lass, nothing to be sorry for." Otis scooted closer to her and nudged her with his shoulder. "Tell me—is your arm all right? How bad was the cut?"

"Not so much. I shouldn't have screamed."

"He'd have wrenched it out of you, one way or another. I'm glad you didn't make it worse on yourself."

"But what will we do now? How can we possibly get away from him alive?"

Otis chuckled softly. "Becca, me darling, I've been in mud worse than this. I'll not be brought down this easily."

Tears sparkled in Becca's eyes. "Otis, how can you get out of this? If it's not Cocklyn, there's the soldiers after you. I've made it so you've got nowhere to go, even if you escape."

"Well, I'll not say it's not a challenge. But I've a thought or two—but I'll need to you buck up. We'll all have to pull together on this one and if you're moping, you're no good to me."

Becca sniffed and swiped her eyes against her shoulder. "I'm not moping." She kept her lips tight together, choking back her anger. "I am not moping."

Otis looked into her eyes. "Not now, you're not. That's the girl I need—that fighter. You keep your eyes and ears open, my girl, and we'll come out good." Becca looked at him skeptically, and he just smiled. "Trust me, girl. Cocklyn will get distracted, and I'll be able to get us clear." Distracted … what could distract Cocklyn? Becca listened to Otis and began to have a thought or two of her own.

Soon, nearly all of Cocklyn's men were on the beach, leaving only one man on board to keep an eye on the vessel and the *Bethany* crewmen that had been with Otis, locked in the brig—a cage made to keep prisoners in the aft hold of the *Falcon*. The pirates were ready to search for the treasure, and once they found it, to carry it back to the *Falcon*. Cocklyn himself came over to face Otis and the two children. "On your feet, Jennings. Time to take me to my treasure."

Otis struggled slowly to his feet, groaning slightly. "Oh, my old bones can't take much of this anymore." Becca and Marcus stood and did their best to help support Otis, concerned that the rough treatment they were all receiving was too much for him.

"Any trouble from you, and your precious children will pay," Cocklyn threatened. At his gesture, two pirates came up, each one taking a child by the arm.

"No, no trouble from me," Otis said. "You needn't manhandle the children any further."

"Stow it. I'm the captain here and I'm giving the orders. Let's move." Cocklyn pushed Otis ahead of him, his pistol at the ready to prod the old man if needed. The children and their keepers followed right behind them and the rest of the men strung out behind that. Otis took a few steps then looked back and forth, obviously trying to orient himself. "What's the problem?" Cocklyn asked.

"Nothing, nothing. Just give me a moment. It's been a while since I've been here and things grow, you know."

Cocklyn made a frustrated noise. "What were you doing for half the day? Didn't you find it once already today?"

"Didn't know we'd be on a deadline. Me and my boys were seeking some fresh fruit before we worked up a sweat in earnest." Otis shrugged. "It's all changed some."

Cocklyn cursed, but he knew Otis was right. The jungle on these islands was constantly growing, so that trails were covered over in a matter of days if not used regularly. Otis had stayed away from this treasure for years, so the path to riches would be well-hidden by now.

After a few minutes, Otis seemed to come to some decision, and he started decisively into the forest. It soon became clear, however, that he could not lead with his hands tied behind his back. Cocklyn called one of his men forward, and the man pulled out a huge sword and began hacking at the overgrown plants, at Otis's direction. Progress was improved, but it was still hard work. After an hour of tripping through the lush plant life—both cuttings and those still standing—Otis fell to his knees and stayed there, head bowed. The children went down next to him, grateful for the break.

"Get up, ye scurvy …" Cocklyn began.

"I can't … go on … like … the children …" Otis panted. "You've got to untie us … we need our hands …"

Cocklyn growled, "Weakling! Get up!" He kicked Otis in the leg to punctuate his command.

"Call me all the names you like," Otis said, rocking slightly under Cocklyn's boot. "But the truth is, we need our hands to get through this brush."

Cocklyn cursed and ranted, but once again, he knew the truth of what Otis was saying. He ordered his men to untie Otis first, but also retie a longer rope around his waist. Cocklyn then wrapped the free end of the rope around his own waist and tugged harshly, making Otis stumble a bit. "No funny stuff," Cocklyn growled. "I outweigh you by three stones, old man, so it won't be me who'll get pulled off his feet if you want to start to tug-o'-war."

Otis hung his head a little lower and shook it silently. Becca was beginning to worry about how elderly and feeble Otis was looking. Had he been hurt? Had all the bravery and fight they'd seen in him finally drained away through this final capture? And she worried that her bringing the soldiers into the picture may have been the last straw for Otis. But as one of the pirates untied her hands, she began to think of a way she could help. She could make that distraction that Otis said he needed. And it looked like she'd better do it sooner, rather than later.

"I … I have to … um …" Becca twisted uncomfortably, crossing her legs and looking away from the faces of the men.

Cocklyn looked at her and just shook his head. "So do what you need to."

"What?!" she gasped, her eyes widening in embarrassment. "You mean right here?!"

"Oh, my achin' back!" Cocklyn cried. "Otis, I'll kill you just for saddling me with these children."

"You could let them go," Otis said. "They can't get off the island."

Cocklyn jerked the rope, and Otis swayed, trying to keep his balance. "Shut up, you old fool." He turned to Becca. "All right, you prissy wench, you can go behind those bushes there." He grabbed Marcus and held the long dagger to his throat. "But I'll have your friend's blood on me hands if you try anything." Cocklyn pulled Marcus with him and growled at Otis. "Keep moving. Smythe, stay with the girl and catch up."

Becca pushed her way off the makeshift path on which the crew stood and as deep into the foliage as she could in just a few seconds. She prayed for Marcus and his safety but knew this was her only chance. She had to pray that God would make Cocklyn so angry that he'd come after her and not harm Marcus. She dropped to her hands and knees and began to move as quickly as she could through the underbrush. If she kept down, right up against the dirt, most of the bushes and trees had grown high enough off the ground to let her move more freely. Becca quickly began to work her way back toward the beach.

"Come on, girl," she heard Smythe say, from behind her. She quickly grabbed up a small rock and threw it back in his direction. Hopefully, he'd see the bushes move and assume it was her. She was already crawling away from Smythe when she heard the rock land, rustling the bushes.

Her plan worked because she didn't hear Smythe again until she was some distance away, his voice muffled now by the plants and trees between them. "Girl?" he called. "Girl!" Becca heard the pirate crash into the underbrush, cussing and calling for her. Now was the time to run. She jumped up, pushed back out to the path they'd made coming into the rain forest, and ran as fast as she could back toward the beach. The last she heard of Smythe was his roar of anger at missing her.

Cocklyn also heard that bellow and stopped short. "Smythe!" he cried. "You stupid swab, I'll cut your ears off!" He jerked Marcus and Otis back around, and the entire pirate crew moved back along the path they'd come, toward their furious crewmate.

Becca didn't hear any of this now, as she'd sped down the pathway toward the beach. She knew that she needed to stay hidden as long as she could, for there would be no telling what an enraged Cocklyn would do to her once he found her. She didn't know the woods well enough to avoid the pirates forever out here—besides, she wanted Marcus and Otis to have as much room to work as they could get, in making their escape. So she ran for the beach—and for the *Dark Falcon*.

Cocklyn nearly screamed himself hoarse, berating the unfortunate Smythe. He'd finally slashed at the man with his dagger, nearly cutting him, though Smythe moved quickly out of range. "All right, you lot." He pointed at four men. "Stay here with the old man and boy." He unwrapped the rope from his waist and threw it to the ground. Otis pulled Marcus down into a sitting position, bowing his head, as though to stay out of Cocklyn's way. "Do not go anywhere. I'll be back once I've fixed that girl. You just wait."

He turned to the rest of his crew. "Right. Now spread out and find her. She's mine—I want her brought back to me. But *find her!*" The men scattered and Cocklyn himself strode away, back down the path. They heard him, shouting directions to his crew, pointing them deeper and deeper into the forest in their search.

"What is Becca doing?" Marcus whispered urgently to Otis. "He's going to kill her."

Otis nodded slowly. "Aye, he might, if he catches her." He closed his eyes. "But I think she meant this as a gift to me."

"What?!"

"Never mind, never mind. Let me think a moment." Otis sat silently, his eyes still shut. Marcus stared at him disbelievingly, then he too closed his eyes. But he began to pray in earnest for his best friend, pray that she would live out the day.

CHAPTER 37

B ecca had no real desire to be back on the *Dark Falcon*, but she knew it would be the last place they'd look for her. The ship lay quite close to shore, with only one pirate on board. Becca thought she might just be able to swim out to the ship and climb up the cargo netting that hung over the side, used by the pirates to maneuver the longboats as they were being lowered and raised at the gunwale. If she could do that without being seen, she'd have a chance to hide in the hold, deep in the dark for a long time before anyone would think of looking for her there. She might even be able to free the *Bethany*'s crew to help her. She ran as fast as she could, for as long as she could, before she was forced into a trot, just to catch her breath.

After panting heavily for a few moments, she finally felt she had enough air to hold her breath for a moment. She needed to hear if there was any obvious pursuit of her as yet. Becca held for a beat, then another. Birds, cicadas buzzing, an occasional squeak or grunt that might have been a monkey. Nothing more. She whooshed out a breath and continued at a trot back toward the ship.

The woods began to thin, and Becca knew she was drawing near the beach. She slowed and approached the open area carefully. She stepped off the trail and slid into the deep brush, positioning herself to peek out at the beach and yet keep an eye on the path she expected the pirates to take to find her.

The *Dark Falcon* lay quietly in the calm bay, sun sparkling on the small waves that splashed against her hull. At first, Becca couldn't see the one crewman left on board. But as she watched, the man stood up on the aft deck, stretching as though he'd been napping. He scratched his head, yawned, and dropped back out of sight, apparently to sleep some more. Becca was glad to see that he was at the back of the ship, far from the cargo net that was her objective, near the bow of the *Falcon*. It also meant she'd better not approach the prisoners, but at least she could board the ship and hide.

Becca knew she should wait, allow him some time to fall back asleep, but she just didn't have time. She had to get across the beach, swim to the ship, and climb aboard before the pirates came through the forest behind her. She'd have to take the risk. If she got captured again as soon as this, she could only hope that she'd given Otis enough time to make his move. She broke a leafy branch off a nearby bush to brush out her footsteps as she crossed the sand and prepared to get wet.

Marcus sat huddled next to Otis for what seemed to be a very long time. When Cocklyn and the others had gone hunting for Becca, he'd told this remnant of the crew to wait here. He had no interest in his men finding Otis's treasure without him right there to oversee it all. Cocklyn's crew had been obedient, but now the time began to drag on. Marcus wondered if delay was good news or bad. He hoped it meant Becca had gotten away, that the buccaneers were having to waste more and more time and energy searching for her.

Otis stirred and stretched his arms and neck, almost casually, in the face of several pirates who drew daggers as he moved. He looked up at them and laughed lightly. "Come now, me hardies.

You can't be that afeared of an old man and young tot, can ye? Seems like your Captain Cocklyn may have run into some trouble, eh?"

The pirate they'd first seen torturing Otis—Hargest—gestured threateningly at Otis. "Belay that. You keep your mouth shut about Cap'n."

"I'm just saying you could be waiting here for a long, long time." Otis rose slowly to his feet, hands held up in front. "Just need to stretch my old bones, lads. If I sit here much longer, I won't be able to walk when the time comes." He poked Marcus in the shoulder. "Stand up here, boy, and support your old man." Marcus rose, and Otis leaned heavily on him, as though too weak to stand on his own.

Hargest stepped forward and waved his dagger close to Otis's face. "Stand fast, ye scurvy rat, or you'll never walk again."

"Cocklyn would be most unhappy if he comes back and finds me too damaged to lead him to the treasure," Otis said quietly. "I'm in no shape to outrun you, so let's not make this worse than it needs to be."

The scarred pirate glared menacingly at Otis and Marcus but stepped back slightly. "Cocklyn won't care about the boy, so you want to keep him alive, you behave yourself."

Otis nodded once, and Marcus felt him shift slightly, easing his weight off Marcus's shoulder. Marcus knew he had something in mind, so he kept his eyes on Otis to be ready to follow his lead. "So we just gonna sit here until nightfall?" Otis stretched his back, and when he leaned on Marcus again, he touched him only lightly.

"Cocklyn told us …"

"Cocklyn's got his own trouble now, lad, can't you see that? It might be time for you to be worrying about your own skin now."

The men behind Hargest murmured among themselves, casting glances at the sun overhead, moving relentlessly toward the western horizon. Cocklyn had been gone for far longer than they'd expected, and they were beginning to grow restless with the wait.

"What is it you have in mind?" Hargest said suspiciously.

Becca scuttled across the sand, dragging and swishing the branch behind her. She could only hope it would wipe out her footprints, without leaving a trail that was just as obvious. She reached the water's edge without seeing either the man on the ship or the men in the forest. Pitching the branch away from her as far as she could, Becca stepped into the clear blue water of the lagoon.

She walked as far as she could but soon had to begin swimming. Becca pulled her hands and arms from the water as slowly and quietly as possible, trying to make her movements sound no louder than the light splashing waves of the bay. Her focus firmly on the ship, she didn't allow herself to look over her shoulder, to see if the pirates had come back to the beach yet. Get to the ship, grab hold of the net, move fast and quiet. She didn't allow herself to think beyond those necessary steps.

With that concentration, Becca reached the side of the *Dark Falcon* much sooner than she'd expected. Treading water, she looked at the heavy rope net hanging above her head and wondered if she could reach it. After a couple of moments' rest, Becca kicked as hard as she could, pushing herself up out of the water. Reaching, arm outstretched, hand grasping, she went for the rope.

With Hargest's question, Otis lifted his weight fully off Marcus, though he still kept his bent posture. "I'll trade our lives for the treasure, mate. Straight up."

The murmurs broke into loud comments now.

"Treasure, Hargest."

"Ours for the taking."

"Who cares about these two?"

"Let's take what we can."

Hargest raised a hand and cut off the comments. "Why should we trust you to lead us there?"

Otis laughed. "I want to live, man! Me and the boy, that's all we want. The treasure means nothing compared to life. Cocklyn would have never let us go, but you've got nothing against me. We've got no history."

The pirate scratched the long scar that ran down his left cheek. "You make a point, Otis. I've no reason to see you bleed. And treasure … we can save ourselves a day or two, if we follow you now …" He turned to the rest of the crew who waited anxiously for his response. "What say you, men? Treasure or wait?"

"Treasure!" was the overwhelming response. The men cheered and clapped one another on the back, almost as though they already held the booty in their hands.

Otis began to move immediately, not waiting for the pirates to rethink this decisive agreement. He moved Marcus slightly ahead of him, as they pushed through a dense thicket.

This bush was even more impenetrable than the forest they had been hiking through, and Marcus had to duck very low to find his way forward. Otis pressed close behind him, urging him to move quickly. Marcus tore at the branches, trying to clear the path for Otis as well as himself. As they scrabbled ahead, the raucous voices of the pirates faded as the bush closed behind them. When their voices were barely audible, Otis gave Marcus a shove and hissed, "To the right, Marcus, and flat on the ground."

Marcus ducked down, scuttled to his right, and felt the ground slope away suddenly beneath his hands. He half fell, half rolled to the ground and was instantly covered by a thick, lush growth of ground ivy. Its leaves were about five inches across, broad and overlapping like shingles on a roof. He felt rather than saw Otis follow him in and then Otis pulled Marcus up close to him at the foot of the slope they had tumbled down. The leaves settled over them, and when Marcus looked up, he could see nothing but dark green. A quick "not a sound now, son," and they lay still and silent, hardly daring to breath.

Initially, all was quiet, but then Marcus began to hear the pirates' harsh voices again. They cursed and shouted as they struggled through the undergrowth. Marcus could hear several of them hacking at the branches with their swords. They sounded louder briefly, then their voices started to move away from where Otis and Marcus lay. Marcus took in a shallow breath, not quite ready to sigh in relief but feeling he might begin to hope.

"Old man!" Marcus nearly jumped up as Hargest's voice rang out directly above them. Otis's grip around Marcus tightened, keeping him from moving the shielding vegetation. "Where are you, you bilge rat?" Hargest roared at the others. "Find them, you buffoons! Find them now!"

Marcus lay in terror as he listened to the pirates thrash through the undergrowth, their voices becoming angrier and harsher, the longer they searched. The plants above them quivered and rustled as Hargest or one of the others pushed at the thick ivy. Suddenly, a flash of metal slashed down through the plants, slicing the air only an inch from Marcus's shoulder.

Otis clapped a hand over Marcus's mouth, muffling the gasp that had escaped him. Otis pulled him even closer, rolling back into the hillside and away from the probing broadsword blade. "Uh, it's an awful steep slope," Marcus heard Hargest say. "Nearly lost me blade in these weeds." The sword thrust into the greenery several more times, far enough out from the slope to never encounter dirt or bodies. Eventually, Hargest was satisfied that there was nothing below him but more plants, and the blade stopped piercing their leafy ceiling.

Stretching, her arm shaking with effort, Becca kicked her legs to propel herself out of the water. Her fingers brushed the hemp, scraped by the rough fibers, but she couldn't quite grasp the rope. She fell back into the water, kicking desperately to keep from slipping beneath the surface. Steadying herself against the ship's hull, she quickly readied herself to try again. Another strong kick, and she rose up the side of the ship again. Both hands up, reaching, straining, grasping for her chance now. One more kick and a wave that lifted beneath her, and she grabbed the net. She had it! Pulling hard, she got a stronger hold on the rope and began the long climb up the side of the *Dark Falcon*.

Finally, after what seemed like hours, the voices moved off, deeper into the forest, away from where Otis and Marcus lay, snuggly concealed beneath the dark green blanket of vines. As the last voice faded, Otis gave Marcus a final squeeze and then a gentle push away. "On your feet, lad. We'll need to be quick. They'll find, soon enough, that we didn't get that far ahead of them." Otis leaped to his feet, breaking up through the strong vines and pulling Marcus along with him. They scrambled back up the slope, across the path they'd been following, and ran into the woods to the east of the trail.

No sign of stiffness and weakness now, Otis charged through the underbrush, putting as much distance between themselves and the trail as he could. Marcus kept his head down and arm raised, protecting his eyes from the twigs and leaves that whipped past him as he followed gamely in Otis's wake.

Marcus wondered where they were going. Otis seemed focused on a destination. He understood they couldn't go back to the beach where they had landed and risk running directly into Cocklyn and the men he had with him. But they would need a ship to escape this island, and as far as Marcus knew, there was only one harbor where one could draw near enough to land a longboat. But he had to trust Otis in this, as he had in so much, because there was no other option.

They continued to push through the foliage, but now Marcus could hear that they were not alone. Raised voices could be heard behind them now. The pirates had doubled back, realizing they'd been fooled by the old man. Marcus knew that Otis couldn't take the time to move carefully, but that meant they were leaving a wide, easily read trail for the pirates to follow. Otis had obviously heard the voices as well, as he pushed even faster through the woods. Marcus could hear the other men crashing behind them now, and the skin of his back crawled as he imagined he felt the grasping hand of one of the buccaneers reaching out for him. "Otis," he gasped.

"Almost there, lad. Stay strong." Just then, Otis crashed through the trees into a clearing. Marcus followed hard on his heels, and they nearly tumbled onto the scrub grass that was the fringe between the trees and the edge of a high bluff they came to. Otis took a hard left and continued to run along the verge. The land they passed dropped sharply away from them to the sea below. Marcus, trying to take quick glances over his shoulder to judge where their pursuers would burst out of the trees, stumbled and caught himself before nearly tripping off the edge of the bluff. A brief look was enough to show him that a fall from here would be deadly.

CHAPTER 38

B ecca climbed quickly, but carefully, making sure she had a good grip on the thick rope before moving her feet up to the next level. Soon she reached the gunwale, the railing at the top of the side of the ship. She peeked through the rope net, trying to see where the lone sailor, left on watch, was on the deck. She didn't see him from her vantage point and knew she would just have to risk jumping over the rail and finding a place to hide on the vessel. Even if she were captured now, at least she would have given Otis and Marcus the distraction Otis had needed.

She climbed the last couple of feet and then dropped quietly to the deck. She still didn't see or hear the pirate and hoped that meant he was still napping on the aft deck. Becca looked around, wondering if she should try to release the prisoners from the *Blue Dolphin*. She knew they were somewhere below deck, but didn't know exactly where that would be. She jittered nervously for a moment, undecided. Suddenly, a gull flew over, shrieking out its loud cry. Becca jumped and ran toward the open hatch, leading into the dark hold. Becca could well imagine how awful it must be in the dark, smelly hold of the *Dark Falcon*. But it would give her plenty of corners where she could keep out of sight. She skittered across the open deck, her neck prickly with the imagined gaze of one of her enemies. But no one called out or grabbed her, and she made it to the hatch. She hesitated only briefly then slipped down the ladder into the black, unlighted hold. The prisoners would have to stay behind bars for now.

After groping her way through the dark to a spot between the hull and some crates, Becca lay hidden in the deep shadows of the bilge for what seemed like hours. There was nothing more she could do but wait in the dark, waiting for her hiding place to be found. She had no doubt she would eventually be discovered. As her mind circled around and around, trying to figure out what Cocklyn would do to her, she actually fell into an uneasy doze.

She awoke with a start, brought out of her exhaustion by a loud noise. Where was she? She couldn't see anything and wasn't even sure what had woken her. As she struggled to full wakefulness, the sound came again, and she realized she was hearing the shouts of the pirates, muffled by the deck boards above her head. Becca remembered … she was hiding in the hold of the *Dark Falcon*, having escaped Captain Cocklyn, hoping to give Otis and Marcus a chance to escape. Now, all she could do was delay her certain recapture. She trembled in the dark, listening to the angry voices above her head.

Cocklyn had finally found signs of Becca's passage through the forest and had followed her trail at top speed. When he came to the beach, he bellowed out his angry surprise. Had this wretched young girl had the impertinence to hide on his own ship? He roared out for the man he'd left on watch.

"Never a chance, Cap'n," the man shouted back to Cocklyn. "There is not any way she would have gotten past me." He quickly kicked at the nest of bedding he'd made on the aft deck, trying to hide traces of his nap. Cocklyn would kill him if he saw it.

Cocklyn quickly ordered the longboat launched from the shore. He'd seen the traces of small footprints in the sand that Becca had tried to disguise. He'd deal with the incompetence of his man later. But he knew that girl was on his ship. She had to pay for her disrespect. He and his men rowed out to the *Falcon*, and he was on board in short order. "Find her!" he shouted. "Find that miserable girl!"

Becca cowered back in the dark as she heard one of the men clatter down the ladder into the hold. His footsteps echoed hollowly, multiplying until it sounded as though the entire ship's crew had followed him below. A thud, scrape, and muffled curse sounded to her right, then as though in front of her, then overhead. She breathed shallowly, hardly daring to swallow, certain any sound would pinpoint her hidden haven for the searching pirate.

A harsh screech of wood dragged against wood, sliced through the dark, piercing Becca's heart with its sudden sharpness. "Come on, lassie," Captain Cocklyn said, his voice raspy with anger. "Don't make it worse on yourself that it already is." Becca shivered, realizing she was being sought by Cocklyn himself. He stomped another few steps and pushed another crate or barrel across the floor, seeking her in the shadows.

Becca shrunk back against the ship's hold, wishing she could become part of the *Dark Falcon*'s hull. The water barrel she crouched behind would give her scant protection, if the buccaneer persisted in his search. The darkness, which was her only real protection, began to feel heavy and cloying, like a trap itself.

Cocklyn's footsteps continued to echo loudly as his pace increased, desperation adding to his haste. "Where are you, girl? We haven't time for your games, now." Another dragging scrape, closer now, the sound distinct from the echoing boot steps. Was he at the next crate over? Becca strained her eyes against the dark, searching for an opportunity to slip past Cocklyn.

"By Jove, girl!" His anger cut the musty air of the hold. "I'm serious now. I'll kill you if you don't come out this instant." His heavy footsteps sounded, now directly in front of her barrel hiding place.

Becca slid as quickly and quietly as she could around the side of the barrel. She could hear his breathing now, ragged with his efforts, with his anger. She held her breath, afraid he'd hear her own shallow panting as she scuttled past the barrel, behind his back, and began a fast skim across the planking toward the stairs and the hatch, away from his seething rage.

Cocklyn pushed his way past the water barrel, reaching into the shadows where she had so recently hidden. Becca, darting glances over her shoulder, watched him move deeper into the dark, cursing as he went. She reached the ladder, nearly fell against them in her relief. She caught back a gasp of relief and scrambled up toward the open hatch, blinking against the bright Caribbean sunshine.

"No!" The pirate captain's shout broke from behind her, shattering their silent struggle. Becca turned and leapt up the last few steps, reached the deck, one last push to lift her other foot out, to run. One last step—

The bright sunlight dazzled as she strained to get out of the hold and after her long time in the dark, she couldn't see clearly. She flailed desperately, panic driving her movements far more than organized thoughts of escape. One moment she clutched at open air, the next a warm hand gripped hers and squeezed tight. She cried out as the hand began pulling at her, trying to drag her from the hold. As bad as Cocklyn was, she had no interest in being taken in hand by one of his men.

"Girl, be still!" commanded a man's voice, no curses or growls as she expected. She blinked, trying to focus in the brightness and finally saw Lieutenant Baker's face above her. "Let me help you this time."

At least it would not be the buccaneers, she thought as she relaxed and allowed Baker to help her up the last step. She sighed with relief—then felt the iron grasp of another hand wrap itself around her ankle and jerk her leg out from under her. She was kept from falling only by Lieutenant Baker's strong arm suddenly wrapped around her upper body, under her shoulders, and holding her fast.

Cocklyn's hard hand grasped her ankle, jerking her off balance. Becca screamed and struggled madly, her hands clutching at Lieutenant Baker's coat. "Please, don't let him get me." Becca couldn't think. Where had Lieutenant Baker come from? What was going on? How could she get away from the grip on her leg?

Her ankle burned as Cocklyn kept up his relentless pull, now shaking her to and fro to try and break Baker's grip on her. She tried to kick at his face with her free leg, feeling a connection time and again, but realized she must be hitting his less vulnerable shoulder. Cocklyn had both hands on her right ankle now and was leaning back to exert more leverage. She screamed with the pain as Baker refused to abandon her. She heard him call out, "Major Hale, here!" and another solider joined him, drawing a dagger from his belt. He reached down into the darkness and for a moment, Becca was sure he was going to cut off her foot. But then he made a sudden thrust and the hands left her ankle, accompanied by a loud bellow from Cocklyn below her. Baker quickly pulled her the rest of the way out of the hatch and away from it across the deck.

Hale stood back from the hatch, replaced his dagger in his belt, and drew out his sword. "Come out now, Cocklyn. We have your ship." Becca, leaning against her helpmate, looked around and saw that, indeed, the soldiers had taken the *Dark Falcon* crew that had followed Cocklyn in his chase of her. The pirates knelt on the deck, hands tied behind their backs and ankles strung together with stout rope. Several soldiers with muskets at the ready stood nearby, in case anyone got an idea to try and escape. But all Becca saw in their eyes was defeat. Weary, crushed defeat. She looked back to the hatch from which she had just escaped, expecting to see Cocklyn's hands emerging, raised above his head as he climbed up out of the hold.

Instead, there was a sudden crash from the smaller hatch near the ship's cabin and Cocklyn leaped out, sword held at the ready. "You'll not take me so easily as you took these scabby cowards," he shouted to Hale. He ran toward the gunwale, clearly intending to jump overboard. One of the soldiers raised his musket, taking aim, but Major Hale ran between the gunman and the pirate. He intercepted Cocklyn just before he reached the rail and stopped him dead in his tracks.

"I give you a chance to live, Cocklyn," he said quietly.

"Aye, but not for long. I come with you, I'll be dancing the hempen jig in short order." Cocklyn stood back and saluted Hale with his blade. "Let's finish it like men instead, shall we?"

Hale also stepped back and saluted. "To the death, then." He raised his sword and made a thrust at Cocklyn. Cocklyn slashed across, parrying Hale's blade and pushing the lieutenant back a step or two. Hale countered with a strong swipe of his blade, forcing Cocklyn back. Back and forth they stepped across the deck—thrusting, parrying, hacking, and slashing. Metal glinted and sparked in the sun, ringing out as the blades met, singing a destructive song. Cocklyn drew first blood with a thrust at Hale's left arm, but the lieutenant jumped nimbly aside and took only a small wound. Shortly thereafter, Hale took blood back with a strong slash across Cocklyn's momentarily unprotected side. Cocklyn hissed with pain and his legs buckled, but he kept his feet. He flung himself at Hale, trying to catch the soldier off guard with the unexpected move. But Hale knew his swordplay and danced back out of the clutching arms of the desperate scoundrel. He thrust again and Cocklyn fell back.

It was becoming clear now that the pirate was nearly at his end. His chest heaved as he tried to draw more air into his lungs. The wound in his side flowed freely, staining his shirt and pants with dark crimson life. But he kept thrusting at Hale, refusing to give up. Suddenly, he lunged and grabbed Hale's sword arm, pulling him close. Hale grabbed Cocklyn's arm and their faces were mere inches apart.

"Be done now, Cocklyn," Hale whispered harshly.

"Finish it, boy," Cocklyn's voice grated back. "Let me die a man, not like bound cargo." Cocklyn pushed away from Hale and stood again at the ready. Becca saw Hale take a deep breath and make his final thrust. She shrieked and turned her eyes into the coat front of her solider protector as Hale's sword slipped past Cocklyn's guard and slid home into the pirate's chest. She could not watch, but she heard the startled grunt from the man—his last sound on this earth—and heard the body slump to the deck with a hollow thud. Captain John Cocklyn, the scourge of the southern seas, was no more.

Becca felt Lieutenant Baker's arms move from their embrace around her shoulders. "It's over, lass." Becca looked up through tears into a kind, young face, the soldier trying to smile reassuringly. "He was a most evil man, and deserving of his punishment."

Major Hale strode back across the deck and turned Becca to face him. He knelt before her and seemed to be searching for something in her face, on her clothes. "Are you all right, young lass?" he asked, concern obvious in his eyes and voice.

"I'm … I'm fine. He didn't reach me until just at the end." She looked down and saw that her ankle had turned deep reddish-purple and swollen dramatically. She looked back into Hale's face. "Thank you. I … don't know what he would have done …" The unshed tears that had stood in her eyes sparkled and streaked down her dirty cheek. "I was so frightened."

Hale wiped her tears gently. "That's what comes of treating with pirates and not letting me and my men aid you in the first place." He smiled. "But all's well as ends well."

"How did you come to be here? How did you find me?"

Hale supported her over to the gunwale. "The *Blue Dolphin*." Becca peered out over the lagoon and saw not only the soldiers' vessel but also both the *Bethany* and the *Blue Dolphin*. "Captain Trevor left his encounter with Cocklyn and came back to get the

Bethany. We were following the *Bethany.* Once they realized we were there, Trevor enlisted us to deal with the pirates."

Becca strained to see the people on the deck of the *Bethany* but turned back to the major at that. "Captain Trevor? But he ... he betrayed Otis."

Hale said, "I'm sure that's how it seemed to you. But Trevor knew he wouldn't be able to fight Cocklyn on his own. He hated to leave you but had to get help." Hale patted her shoulder. "He told us you'd be quite indignant about him. But he did his best for you."

Becca looked back toward the *Bethany.* "And Paige? Jake?"

"They're fine, still on the *Bethany.*" As they spoke, Becca saw her friends run up to the rail on the *Bethany.* They began to wave wildly at Becca, shouting their relief at seeing her.

Becca waved back, tears running down her cheeks. "They look so good. I've missed them so much!"

"You'll be back with them soon. I'll have some of my men row you over to the *Bethany* after we find Otis and Marcus. You'll be safe enough here until then." Hale walked away, beginning to give orders to his men.

Becca tried to run after him, but her ankle made her stumble. "Ow!" Lieutenant Baker reached out a steadying hand and knelt at her feet.

"Hold on, miss, let me wrap that for you." He pulled a large handkerchief from his pocket and urged her to sit on the deck.

"Have you released the prisoners?" Becca asked anxiously, looking around to see if the *Bethany* crewmen were in sight.

Hale turned back to Becca. "We didn't know any had been captured. So who is on the island with Otis?" He made a quick gesture to one of his men to go find and release the captives.

"Just Marcus and ..." She did a quick count. "About four of the *Dark Falcon* crew."

"Direct me to where you last saw them, lass. We'll get them back for you."

"I'll show you."

"No!" Hale said sharply. "I'll not put you in further danger. There's plenty of the *Falcon* crew still out there."

"I don't know how to tell you. I just know I'll remember it as I see it." Becca's anxiety was increasing, now that the possibility of rescue was real. It was one thing to sacrifice your magical trip home when there was no other hope. But it was quite another to miss it because you were sitting, ladylike, on a ship's deck. If they found the treasure now and she wasn't with Marcus and not yet with the snow globe, she might never see home again.

Hale sighed in exasperation. "Girl, you are a trial, right enough. But I haven't got time to bicker about this. You'll come, but you must do as I tell you to stay out of trouble."

"I will, sir. I just want to find Marcus."

Hale's men quickly rallied around and soon they were launching a longboat for the island. Becca sat in the bow, keeping out of the way of the soldiers who were pulling the oars hard and strong. She prayed they would find Marcus and Otis in short order, but she worried what would happen after that. If they still hadn't found the treasure, would it count if the soldiers were with them when they did? And now she knew it was wrong to have thought she could offer Otis up to the soldiers as a way to escape. So how could she keep him out of their hands now? Or was all this just fruitless worrying? She feared most of all that Cocklyn's men had grown tired of waiting and had made good on their threat to kill Marcus if Otis did not cooperate.

Her mind continued circling around and around these depressing thoughts as several soldiers jumped into the surf to pull the boat up on the beach, out of the reach of the relentless waves. The rest of them jumped over the bow, and one reached back to lift Becca onto the fine sugary sand.

"Where to, lass?" Hale asked her, giving her a gentle push forward. "Lead on."

Becca scanned the tree line one hundred feet from where they stood. Suddenly, all the trees and bushes looked exactly the same. She'd been so sure she could pick out their trail from the beach, but now that she was faced with the wall of vegetation, she couldn't see how they'd gone earlier in the day. Her fears rose even higher, and when she tried to speak, her voice quavered, "I can't see it. It was so clear, but I can't it see it now." She turned one way then the other, trying to find the opening in the trees.

"You'll see it, Becca. Let's move closer to the trees and see if you can't tell more there." Major Hale's tone was deliberately calm and she felt her fear subsiding. She took a couple of deep breaths and led the way up the beach toward the shaded woods.

As they drew closer to the trees, Becca's vision seemed to clear and the trail they'd taken earlier seemed to magically open up before her. She pointed to the break. "There. Right there."

"Good girl. I knew you'd find it." Hale pushed ahead of her. "Now stay close and let me know if I'm going right. But we must move quietly, and if we hear voices, you need to drop back." He turned and looked back over his contingent. "You move back to Baker there and he'll take care of you. Do as I say, will you?"

"I will, sir." And she meant it then. But she knew she'd have to be willing to keep an open mind and react to whatever the situation called for to save her friends—and maybe herself.

CHAPTER 39

Otis continued to run along the edge of the high bluff, and Marcus struggled to keep up. He could hear the shouts of the pirate crew around them, and he began to wonder if Otis really did have a plan for escape.

"Ahoy there!" A sudden shout ahead of them stopped Marcus short, gasping for breath out of exertion and fear. Otis ran another few steps and swayed to a halt. Marcus looked past Otis to see soldiers stepping out of the trees ahead of them. Soldiers?! How had they gotten here? Just then, he heard an angry exclamation behind him and the pirates plunged out of the trees as well.

Otis swung around then back again to stare at the soldiers. He dropped his hands to his knees, bent over, and panted as though he'd used up all his reserves. He rocked on his heels, stumbled back a couple of steps, looked up, disoriented. "Run to the soldiers, lad," he hissed at Marcus. "Head low and *run*." Marcus hesitated but then did as he was told and took off as fast as he could toward the soldiers. He ran in a crouch as he watched the soldiers raise their rifles. He heard the roar of the pirates behind him as they charged toward Otis. And he heard Becca's scream—"Otis!"

Marcus spun midstep to see Otis at the edge of the precipice, falling backward, arms windmilling to try and keep his balance. For a moment, it looked as though Otis had caught himself and would come back from the brink. He flailed once more, and then he was gone, fallen over the edge.

Marcus fell to the ground, huddled there miserably as the soldiers ran past him to chase the pirates who had suddenly realized there was more at stake here than a treasure. Their very freedom was about to be seized. They scattered into the woods, followed closely by the red-coated soldiers.

Becca ran up to Marcus and dropped down next to him. "Marcus, Marcus, are you okay? Are you hurt?"

Marcus looked up, his eyes wide with dread. "Otis. Did he really …" Becca shook her head, and they both rose and went to the edge of the cliff where they'd last seen Otis. But there was nothing to be seen here. Bushes, vines, and small trees grew closely together, clinging tenaciously to the side of the bluff, too densely to show the soil beneath. But it was clear no one clung to the cliff, no one had saved himself in the last minute. Otis was, indeed, gone.

"Otis!" Marcus shouted, knowing it was useless but he had to do something. He crouched down and tried to see underneath the canopy of vegetation. He searched for a glimpse of the white shirt Otis had been wearing, a movement that wasn't leaves blowing in the breeze. "Otis!" Marcus was on his stomach now, easing out over the brink of the cliff, trying to see broken branches or any sign that Otis lay within the foliage.

Becca grabbed at Marcus's belt, fearing he would slide out too far and tumble over the edge himself. "Otis! Otis!" Her cries faded into the bright air, finding nowhere to land, not cliffside or human ear. There was no sound but the distant wash of the waves against the base of the island. But still they sat at the bluff top, calling for their friend, unwilling to let him go. Finally, however, the reality became clear. Marcus hung his head and wept. Becca held him close, her tears streaming down her cheeks.

For a long, silent time, they sat, lost in their thoughts. Then Becca gently took Marcus's hand. "We have to go." Marcus

SECRETS OF THE SNOW GLOBES

did not react. "Marcus, bud, we gotta go." Becca pulled on his hand slightly.

"Where do we go?" Marcus said, no emotion in his voice. "With Otis gone, where do we go?"

Becca stood and continued to pull gently, urging Marcus to stand with her. "It's not safe here," she said. "We've got to get back to the beach."

Marcus stood but continued to look out to sea. "Why? Otis isn't there."

Becca pulled harder now, finally forcing Marcus to start to move with her, leading him away from the edge of the bluff. She led him back along the way that she and the soldiers had come. "I don't know why. But nothing's going to happen here, except that one of the pirates might come back." She kept a steady pressure on Marcus now that she had him moving. "Can't you hear them?"

Marcus finally seemed to come awake and tilted his head. There were growing sounds coming from the forest that seemed to indicate the arrival of either the pirates, the soldiers, or both. They both began to trot, moving a little faster back toward what little safety there might still be for them on this island.

"Major Hale left a contingent back on the beach. At least we won't be held hostage by pirates again, if we get back there," Becca explained. "That's all I'm worried about right now." It seemed she might have a reason to worry. The noises were becoming louder, and it was increasingly clear that the pirates were running back toward the beach themselves, believing they still had a captain and a free ship to return to. They crashed noisily through the foliage, shouting and cursing as they ran.

Just as it sounded like the pirates must be right behind them, a shot rang out, and the woods fell strangely silent. Becca and Marcus fell to the ground, not sure if they might be hit by a stray shot. They lay, panting from their run, trying to hear who had fired and if they'd hit anyone. Then, as suddenly as the hush had fallen, it was broken by a shout and another crack of a pistol.

Abruptly, the air seemed filled with the sounds of battle, gunfire, grunts, and shouts of men being battled to the ground, cries of anger and pain. Marcus and Becca curled into as small a mass as they could, at the base of a large tree, and hoped they would not suddenly find themselves embroiled in the combat.

The battle seemed to rage immediately above and around them. A shot rang out and Becca cringed, certain she felt the buckshot rush by her ear. She quivered, waiting for the weight of a falling body to crush her to the ground. Instead, she heard running footsteps brush through the foliage, so close the earth vibrated beneath her. She curled herself even tighter, praying that she and Marcus would come through this seemingly endless conflict alive.

Just when she thought she'd have to give in to her terror and run, the sounds of battle faded. The shots, thudding steps, and shouts moved past them and the forest became unnaturally silent again. Still Becca lay, her head tucked under her arms, knees drawn up to her chin. She didn't move until she heard Marcus say, "Bec? Are you okay?"

She lifted her head cautiously, looking around to see if any remnants of the fight remained. She saw only some shredded leaves and mashed grass. "I … I think so. You?"

Marcus stood up and dusted himself off. "Yes, though, I'm not quite sure how we came through that unscathed." He reached down and helped Becca untuck and rise to her feet. "God had His hand covering us, I think."

Becca stretched and turned back to the pathway. "Thank you, God! Come on, let's get out of these woods so we can see what's coming at us." They took each other's hand and began to run along the path toward the beach.

When they reached the clearing that opened on to the beach, they were greeted by the welcome sight of the rest of the pirates under guard and Major Hale squarely in charge. He saw the children as they came out of the woods and gave a glad shout.

"Ah, my lass and laddie, you've survived the battle!" He shook Marcus's hand when he drew near and gave Becca a relieved pat on the back. "I was about to send some of my men to look for you. You're both all right? No damages?"

"We're fine, sir," Marcus said. "Congratulations on a well-fought campaign." He looked out into the bay and was startled to see the *Blue Dolphin* and the *Bethany* lying anchored, makeshift patch obvious on her side, along with the *Dark Falcon* and the queen's vessel. Clearly, full repairs had not yet been made on the *Bethany*. "When did they arrive?"

Hale looked out over the four vessels. "Trevor came back for the *Bethany*, which we were following. Who's that coming off the *Bethany*?" There was a longboat being lowered even as they spoke. Becca squinted against the sunlight sparkling on the waves, trying to see if Paige and Jake were among the passengers.

"There they are!" she cried. "Paige! Jake!" She jumped up and down, waving, trying to catch their attention. Jake tried to leap up from his seat in the boat to respond to her display but was jerked back unceremoniously by Captain Penner. Becca and Marcus ran to the shoreline and waited impatiently as the longboat drew near, slowly. Hale followed more sedately but was waiting all the same as the boat came ashore. Two sailors jumped out and pulled the boat up through the surf to ensure the restless waves would not drag the boat out to sea before they were ready to leave with it.

When the boat was firmly held by the white sand, Captain Penner released his grip on Jake and Paige, and they scrambled out of the boat and ran to their friends. The four adventurers hugged one another and began to try and tell their tales all at the same time. Penner and Hale waited for the loud chatter to die down, but finally Major Hale called a halt. "Enough, children, enough."

Captain Penner scanned the men on the beach then asked quietly, "Jennings?" Hale shook his head slightly.

"Yeah, where's Otis?" Jake asked, not noticing the interplay between the captain and the major. "I can't wait to see him!"

Marcus held up a hand. "Jake ... wait. Jake, Paige ... Otis isn't coming. He's ... he's ... gone."

"Gone?" Jake asked. "What do you mean? Is there another ship around here?"

Marcus put an arm around Jake's shoulders and took Paige's hand. "No, I mean he's gone for good. He ... he fell off a cliff on the far side of the island, and we ... we couldn't save him."

"No!" Paige shook off Marcus's hand and turned to Becca. "That can't be right, Becca. Tell me that's not what happened."

Becca took her friend's shoulders. "I'm sorry I can't tell you that, Paige. I saw Otis go over the cliff—I saw it with my own eyes. No matter how much I want him back, I can't make it so just by lying to you."

Paige crumpled to the ground, hands covering her face, sobbing. Jake looked to Marcus, his eyes still filled with questions, not yet with tears. "Marcus?" he asked, needing confirmation that this wasn't some cruel joke.

"Jake, man, it's true. Otis is gone." Jake's head dropped, and he quickly turned his back on the group and began walking toward the woods.

Becca started after him. "Ja—"

Marcus held her back. "Let him be a minute, Becca." He gestured to Paige, and Becca went to her side and crouched next to her, holding her as she cried.

Penner rubbed his hand roughly over his mouth. "Off a cliff, eh?"

Marcus nodded. "He'd gotten us away from Cocklyn's crew. We were making a run for it, but with the soldiers in front of us and the pirates behind us, he told me to run. I think he must have turned to hold off the pirates while I got free ... he just went over the cliff."

"We didn't see a sign of him." Becca helped Paige to her feet, as the girl's sobs finally seemed to have spent themselves. Jake also came back to the group, his nose and eyes red, but no tears in evidence now.

They all stood silently, quietly honoring the memory of their old friend or adversary. Then Captain Penner cleared his throat and addressed Major Hale. "Major, we thank you for your efforts on behalf of Otis Jennings and his children. I trust you'll bring Otis's booty to the king himself? It's what Otis would have wanted."

Hale replied, "I will certainly deliver the treasure to our king and country. Cocklyn's men will pay for their crimes when we reach London. Have you any additional information as to where specifically the treasure is stowed here?"

"Yes, if your men will press on to the center of the island, they'll find some limestone caverns. The goods are stashed in the largest of these." Penner put a hand on Becca's and Jake's shoulders. "Unless we can do something more for you, Major Hale, I'd like to take the children and head back to Nassau port. They've clearly had a terrible experience. And the *Bethany* still needs repair."

"Let me speak with them." He turned to the children.

"Of course." Penner squeezed their shoulders gently, then stepped away as Major Hale took Becca's hand.

"My dear, is this what you and the others wish? To go off with the crew of the *Bethany*?"

Becca stared blankly at him for a moment, not sure how to answer. She turned to the others. "What else can we do?"

"I will undertake to find you a good home, whether in Nassau or in London, if that is where you have relations."

Marcus laid a cautioning hand on Becca's arm. She saw the slight shake of his head and turned back to Major Hale. "Thank you, sir, but we'll stay with Captain Penner, as he's offered. They've been good to us and I believe that's what Otis would want."

Major Hale bowed his head slightly. "As you wish then, my dears. I am grateful you are all safe and will pray that our God continues to keep you so." He stepped back and then turned his men, giving orders as he went.

Penner waved the children to follow him to their longboat. "Let's be off then while our soldier friends are busy." They hurried across the sand to the longboat where *Bethany* crew members waited, hurrying toward a future they could not predict.

CHAPTER 40

Becca, Paige, Marcus, and Jake trailed after Captain Penner as he led them back to the waiting longboat. He did not hurry, but his stride was long and determined and Becca felt certain he did not want to spend any more time on this beach than absolutely necessary.

On the other hand, she and the other children dragged their feet, looking around uneasily, taking a last glance at the woods where they had lost Otis. Becca thought it must be easier for her and Marcus to accept, since they'd actually seen the last of the old man. Paige continued to wipe tears that streamed down her cheeks, and Jake looked a bit like he might bolt for the woods any second. Marcus must have gotten that same feeling, and put his arm around the younger boy's shoulders and held him close to their little band.

At the water's edge, Penner directed the children to get into the center seats on the boat. Again, without making a big show of it, it was clear he wanted to be on his way quickly and with no more delay. It seemed the second his foot lifted from the white sand, his sailors shoved the boat off and then leaped up out of the surf into the boat themselves. They grabbed oars and began to pull toward the *Bethany* with an intensity that was obvious.

"What's going on?" Becca whispered to the others. "Why the rush?"

Marcus shook his head. "There is something, isn't there? Kind of intense." Penner saw that they were perplexed and smiled a secretive smile.

"Fear not, my children. You'll be taken care of."

Paige smiled a timid smile, but her eyes told Becca that she didn't find that statement very reassuring. Becca said to the captain, "Is something going on? What don't we know?"

Penner gave her a sharp look. "There's much you don't know, miss. We'll tell you when the time is right." And she could tell by his expression that there would be no more comments or questions on that topic right now.

As the sailors pulled hard toward the *Bethany*, Becca noticed that Captain Trevor and the crew of the *Blue Dolphin* were weighing anchor as she watched. He must have been in as big a hurry as Captain Penner—and that just made her more suspicious. She poked the other kids and nodded toward the *Dolphin*, whose sails were already unfurled and billowing with the steady wind. "They look like they're in a hurry too."

"Are they scared of Major Hale?" Jake wondered.

"I don't think so," Marcus said. "The soldiers are going to be busy here for some time, tracking down that treasure. And Captain Penner certainly doesn't look afraid."

Paige said, "He looks like Jake does whenever he knows he's going to win a game. Smug."

"Not smug," Jake protested. "Happy to win."

"Self-satisfied," Becca added, peering closely at Penner's face. "He looks very happy with himself." Indeed, the mysterious little smile had not left his lips as they drew closer to the ship but had stayed firmly in place. As they pulled alongside the ship and the men on board threw the ropes over the side to them, the smile grew into a broad grin.

"Weigh anchor now, boys! Set the sails! Don't wait 'til we're aboard—move now!" His mate, Perkins, scrambled to direct the sailors as several men began to haul the longboat up to its position on the gunwale. The children clutched the seats as the boat swayed not only from the ropes that pulled them upward, but from the ship beginning to shift as the anchor left the sea floor. The chain rattled and groaned as the anchor wheel was turned by the men rushing to obey their captain. The sails snapped taut as other men clambered across the rigging and unfurled the canvas. The *Bethany* was already underway before anyone from the longboat set a foot on deck.

As Penner jumped from the boat onto his own ship's deck, his self-satisfaction was more obvious than ever. He clapped his mate on the back and laughed out loud. He strode confidently to the aft deck and took the wheel from his helmsman with a happy word of praise for his crew's efficiency springing from his lips.

Pierre reached a hand to the girls as they climbed from the longboat. Marcus and Jake jumped to the deck and Marcus asked, "What's going on, Pierre? What does the captain know that we don't?"

"Our captain has not yet shared his secret with the whole crew," the ship's cook responded. "But I know that if Captain Penner is so clearly joyous, it can only mean good things for all of us."

Paige said quietly, "I thought he and Otis were friends. I can't believe he can act this way, with Otis just gone."

Pierre started. "Otis, he is gone? Where did he go?"

"He died," Paige explained. "He fell off a cliff."

Pierre was silent for a moment, hanging his head sadly. Then he said, "The captain knows that life must go on. He has a shipload of men he is responsible for, so the loss of one friend … well, it cannot slow him down."

"But he's so *happy*," Paige said, another tear running down her cheek. "I know he has a ship to run, but how can he be so happy?"

Becca put an arm around her friend's shoulders, and Jake and Marcus moved close to comfort her.

Pierre sighed, hating to see his young friends so troubled. "Come, my dears, and let Pierre find a bite of food for you. You have had a long, hard day, and some food will lift your spirits, I think."

The children sat huddled on the deck, bowls of chicken and rice in their hands. Pierre hovered behind them, occasionally prodding one or another of them with a gentle hand. "*Mes amis*, you must eat. Otis, he would not want you to waste away." Pierre patted Jake, his favorite, on the shoulder. "*S'il vous plait*, Jake, take a bite of your food for me."

Jake tried to smile up at his friend but could not summon the will to make his lips curve upward even falsely. He hung his head and said "Pierre, I can't. I just can't."

Marcus turned to Pierre, and he had better success giving the cook a smile. "We'll all try, Pierre, I promise we will. We're just … it's hard …"

Pierre sighed and nodded. "I understand. I have lost many friends in similar ways, and it is never easy to let them go. But you must keep your strength up, *mes amis*. None of you have eaten all day, and you must be strong for your future."

Becca coughed out a short laugh. "Our future. You have no idea, Pierre." Pierre looked quizzically at her, but when she hung her head sadly again, he left them with a final reminder to try some of his "lovely *poulet et riz.*"

"What is our future?" Jake asked. "Now that Otis is gone, how do we help him find his bounty?"

Paige set her bowl of lunch on the deck and went to gaze over the gunwales at the island that they were moving swiftly past. "I think our future just may be our history."

"Huh? What's she mean?" Jake asked his buddy Marcus.

Marcus also set his bowl on the deck. "She's referring to the fact that we may have to live our lives out, here in the 1600s, rather than ever get back to our own time." At Jake's horrified look, Marcus shook his arm. "Come on, buddy. It'll be all right. We're still together."

Becca said, "But we don't even have anyone to stay with. You don't think Captain Penner will continue to keep us on the ship, do you? Even if we wanted to."

"He sounded as though he had some kind of plan, however, didn't he? When we were coming back to the ship?"

"He had some kind of secret. Probably a plan to sell us to some merchant as his shop workers."

"Oh, Becca, let's not try and think of the worst possible situation. Let's try and think this through logically."

"Logic! What has logic got to do with this? The poem says we have to help Otis find his bounty before we can go home. Now we can't help him find anything! How is logic going to help us?!"

"Well, you needn't shout. I'm just trying to be constructive here instead of making everyone feel as bad as possible." Marcus and Becca were both on their feet, their sadness and fatigue catching up with them and bringing all their frustration and anger out to the surface.

"What if bad is honest? What if we can't ever get home and that's the truth? How is your being constructive going to help in any way?"

"Guys, guys," Jake jumped up between the two shouting friends. "Don't fight, don't do this."

"You stay out of it, pipsqueak."

"Don't call my friend that name. He hates that name!"

"He's my brother, and I'll call him anything I want!"

Paige continued to gaze at the island as the battle grew louder behind her. Something seemed funny to her, and she cocked her head sideways trying to figure out what was bothering her.

"You just shut up, Becca, and stop yelling at Marcus!"

"You are just being nasty and hateful because you can't be in charge this time. And you just hate that."

"I don't care about being in charge, but we do need to be honest about the trouble we're in here. And you can't always come to the rescue with your smarty pants answers!"

Paige leaned over the gunwale and looked forward and backward. "Guys?"

"Don't call him a smarty pants! He's smarter than you'll ever be!"

"Pipe down, pipsqueak!"

"I said, don't call him that!"

"Uh … guys?"

"Pipsqueak, pipsqueak, pipsqueak, pipsq—"

"Guys!" Paige raised her voice above the bickering. It didn't slow the others down for even a second. It was as though she'd never spoken. "Knock it off!" Paige screeched, her face turning red with the effort to make herself heard.

The three battlers stopped, shocked into silence. Paige never raised her voice that way.

"We've got something odd going on here. Can you please stop your arguing long enough to check this out?" Paige turned back to the rail, and the other three joined her quietly, ashamed of their outbursts. "Notice something weird?"

"It's just the island," Jake said.

"But it's still the island," Marcus said thoughtfully.

"Huh?"

"We've been sailing quite a while already," Becca explained. "We ought to be away from the island by now. Far away."

"Unless …" Marcus started.

"Unless we're sailing around the island," Paige finished. "Why would Captain Penner be sailing around the island?"

Marcus looked up at the navigation deck, where the captain stood at the wheel, face raised to the sun, a broad smile on his face. "That just can't be right. I know buccaneers grow accustomed to losing crewmates to death, but Penner and Otis were more than just crewmates."

All the children looked at this man they'd grown to trust and respect. They'd been seeing him smile but now watched him laugh uproariously at some comment from his navigator. "What is the deal?" Jake asked.

Becca started toward the short set of steps that led up to the ship's wheel. "I don't know, but I'm going to find out. He's not going to put me off this time."

The other kids followed quickly, recognizing the stubborn set of her jaw. When she looked like this, Becca almost always got her way. She marched up to the captain and stood, hands on hips, before him. "Captain Penner!"

Penner looked down at her from his superior height, his eyes cool, the smile gone. "What is it now, persistent and annoying child?"

"You tell us what's going on. You tell us right now." Her jaw tightened and her eyes narrowed.

"If you were not such a small girl, I'd say you were trying to threaten me." Penner laughed gently as Becca's glowering expression became even more stormy. "But I will tell you what's going on despite your rudeness. We are sailing away from the island, to debate what we will do with you four children."

"That's not true, sir," Paige said, her voice quieter, but no less determined than Becca's. "We are not sailing away from the island. We're sailing around it."

Penner looked over the rails at the island that continued to be just off the starboard side of the ship. "Really? Why, look you, you're right, young miss. I thought for certain I was sailing away."

"Don't you make fun of us," Jake said, his small hands balling into tight fists. "Don't you dare …"

Marcus laid a hand on his friend's shoulder and spoke to Captain Penner. "Sir, please. It's clear there is more here than meets the eye, and we are very naturally concerned about our future. Isn't it time you tell us what this is all about?"

"Not just yet," Penner responded. Suddenly, he shouted to his men. "Furl the sails, lads. Drop anchor! Ready the longboat."

The children all ran to the gunwale, trying to see why Captain Penner was suddenly anchoring. "What is going on?!" Becca cried.

Penner laughed. "A few more moments of patience, children. Keep your eye on that bluff there."

Marcus drew in a sharp breath, and Becca clapped a hand to her mouth. "This is where ..." They were anchoring at the foot of the very cliff where they had lost Otis. "I can still see it," Becca said, her brow drawn and troubled. "Right up there, his arms windmilling. And then he fell. So quiet, not a sound. But he fell."

Marcus leaned over the rail, looking into the deep blue-green water beneath the ship. "We can't possibly hope to find his ..." His voice hitched. "His body. It's too deep here. We won't find him."

Penner laughed and pointed. "No need. He's found us."

The children all looked to where the captain was pointing, straight at the deep, lush foliage that ran down the cliff face right to the water. They saw the leaves and branches shaking, shaking as though something was pushing through the thicket. They could even hear the rustling vegetation and a grunting sound as something pushed through the thick greenery. Suddenly, a hand pushed out into the sunlight, then another. Arms followed, a foot, and then into their view popped the whole man.

"Otis!" Becca screamed.

CHAPTER 41

The children would have all thrown themselves into the longboat being lowered to pick up Otis if Captain Penner had not had them physically restrained. As it was, Jake nearly fell overboard, leaning out to be the first one to touch Otis as the boat was finally being pulled back up to its berth along the side of the *Bethany*. Otis quickly clambered over the rail but barely got his feet firmly on deck before he was overwhelmed by four laughing, entangling children, all jabbering and asking questions at once. He hugged them all once, twice, and finally pushed them away after they'd each had a third squeeze. Penner stood back, roaring with laughter, to watch their antics. He paused only to give the command to weigh anchor and run up the mainsail.

The ship lurched, knocking the children off balance, and they and Otis tumbled to the decking. The fall didn't stop the children's questions and laughter, their desire to be as close to Otis as they could be. Otis finally got himself righted and sat up. "Enough!" he roared. "Give a man some peace!"

Penner finally waded in and pulled the children off his friend, giving him room to breathe. He set them on their feet, somehow hanging on to four arms with his two hands. "Give him a space, children. Don't you want to hear his story?"

Marcus was the first to stop struggling and leaned forward, panting hard. "The story. Yes, of course. Quiet down, you lot, so Otis can explain himself." The others finally calmed down, as Otis got to his feet and took Penner's hand.

"My friend, all go as planned?" he asked.

"Just as you planned. We'll see the *Dolphin* soon."

"The *Dolphin*?" Becca asked. "What is going on here? Otis, you have to tell us what this is all about!"

"Well, pipe down a bit, can't you, so a man can hear himself speak? Such a rowdy bunch, I've never seen. This ship's life has been a bad influence on you all, I can see." Otis looked around at the crew who had gathered around. It was clear that most of them never expected to see Otis again either, though a few others had grins on their faces as large as Captain Penner. "Hello, mates. Been teaching my young 'uns some poor manners, I see."

"No more'n you yourself has done," one of the seaman called. "Seems they take after their pa."

Otis's cheeks and the tops of his ears reddened. "I ain't no pa." The men laughed.

Pierre gestured to the children gathered round Otis, who had moved close again when released from Captain Penner's grip. "Appearances to the contrary, *non*? Seems to me the proof stands before us all."

Becca said, "Close as we've got to a pa here, Otis. When we thought we'd lost you forever ..." Her voice trailed off.

"Aw, enough now," Otis said. "I'm back, and we need say no more about that." But he gave Becca an extra squeeze to bring a smile back to her face.

Marcus protested. "We need to say a lot more about that. Obviously this was some kind of plan you made. But we still don't know exactly what you were doing."

"Give a man a place to sit and a pull of grog, and I'll tell you all a story," Otis said. "Almost takes longer to tell than it did to accomplish."

The children had to keep a rein on their curiosity, for Otis truly would not say another word without a bale to sit on and a tankard in his hand. Once settled, with as much crew as could be spared from the sailing of the ship surrounding him, he took a long drink of the rum potion in his mug and wiped his mouth on the back of his hand. "Aaaahhhh! I've been dreaming of that first draw since we were first marooned this morning."

"Was that part of your plan?" Jake asked.

"Ay, lad, it was. Everything since we left the *Bethany* behind in port for repairs. It all fell into place, just like the captain and I marked it out." Otis took another draught of grog and began to tell his story.

"I knew we'd have to satisfy the soldiers somehow," he said. "Not just with the treasure but a man to punish for the stealing of the king's portion. So unless I wanted to spend long days in London prison—or a short time dancin' the hempen jig, I knew I'd have to disappear. The trick was how to do that, get Cocklyn off my neck, and get the soldiers to the king's rightful treasure."

"What about Cocklyn?" Becca asked, remembering his grisly end on the *Falcon* at the end of Major Hale's sword.

"I'm not taking this story out of order," Otis said sternly. "Wait your turn." Another pull at the mug and he started again. "So a lot to accomplish with one single day to get it all done. First off, we knew Cocklyn was already on to me. He's got spies all over the docks, so we knew they'd follow us to the *Blue Dolphin*, when the *Bethany* was out of commission." Otis paused and looked up at Captain Penner, leaning casually on the stairway railing that led to the aft deck. "Major Hale get his men all right, did he?"

Penner smirked. "No story out of order, didn't you say yourself? Press on, and I'll fill in the blanks as we reach them."

Otis laughed. "Using me own words agin me. Fair's fair, I guess. So as I says, we knew Cocklyn would follow the *Dolphin*. Captain Trevor was happy to oblige with a ride for a cut of the treasure, so off we went."

"But he's not getting a cut of the treasure," Jake protested. "Won't *he* be hunting you now?"

"He thinks Otis is dead," Paige reminded Jake. "He won't hunt a dead man."

"Out of order," Otis said warningly. "Only me and Trevor knew the locale of the treasure trove, so we had to get the *Dolphin* free of the *Black Falcon* so she could sail back and guide the *Bethany* and the soldiers who would be following her." Marcus opened his mouth to ask a question, but Otis stopped him with a squinted glare. "The navigation's a bit tricky, with hidden atolls and shallow seas, and 'twas easier to guide the *Bethany* than to try and lay out the sailing of the way for Captain Penner. That's why the *Falcon* sailed off. Answer your question?" Marcus nodded silently, and Otis bobbed his head once in return. But Becca held up her hand.

"One more question? What about the *Bethany*? I thought she needed to dry dock for repairs."

Penner responded, "Aye, and she'll need to for permanent repairs. But our Master Merrick is a wizard and helped make temporary repairs that got us under sail very quickly."

"All right now?" Otis asked. Everyone nodded, so he continued. "We planned to maroon us, just at the right moment, to get the *Dolphin* clear. We knew Cocklyn would follow me anywhere and ignore the *Dolphin* since Cocklyn didn't know about Trevor's knowledge of the treasure."

Paige shook her head in confusion. "This is kinda hard to follow."

Otis nodded solemnly. "Imagine how hard it was to think up! It's purely a miracle that it came together at all. Anyway, Cocklyn is on my tail and Trevor is off to guide the others."

"Why did you split us up?" Becca asked, risking a wrathful look from the others for interrupting the story again. "Why send us with you and keep Paige and Jake with the *Bethany*?"

Otis blushed again, and Penner laughed shortly. "Didn't plan that one, did you, old man?" he mocked.

"No, no that wasn't the plan. I'd have just as soon keep you all safe on board the *Bethany*. But Trevor still has a distrust of me and believes I do of him. So that notion of his, to keep each other honest by using you kids as hostages … well, I couldn't refuse without truly arousing his suspicions." Here Otis looked sternly at Becca. "However, Missy Becca's act of heroism, running off to split the pirate forces. That was not in the plan and no doubt nearly got her killed."

Here, Otis stopped his storytelling and Becca filled them all in on her adventure and danger on the *Falcon* with Captain Cocklyn and the major. Paige clutched her best friend's hand in terror as she heard the details of Becca's narrow escape. Jake whispered "cool" as he heard the details of the sword fight. Marcus looked proudly at his friend as he realized the depth of her concern for Otis and Marcus when she made her choice to run off.

"Whew!" Otis tried for another drink of his grog and realized his tankard was empty. Pierre stepped up and refilled the vessel and quietly poured water for the children as well. "Becca, my darlin', I never meant for you to be in such peril. You must believe that." He took her hand and looked deeply into her eyes. "It would have meant the death of me to see you hurt."

Becca's eyes filled with tears. "I know, Otis. I just … I owed you, you know."

Otis cupped her cheek gently. "Seems we're even now, doesn't it, my dearie? Never more to be spoken of between us, eh?"

"Aye, sir."

"Good girl." He patted her head and sat back straight. "Well, adventure everywhere. I thank the good Lord it came out aright. Becca's own plan changed mine up just a bit but actually made things easier for Marcus and me. That Hargest that Cocklyn left in charge of us is none too smart, and it was an easy thing to convince him to act without waiting for Cocklyn. So we were able to get freed from our bonds, get a bit ahead of them, and hide ourselves." Otis nodded at Marcus. "Boy's got a talent for silence and following along even when he doesn't know the plan. A sharp mind, young man." Marcus grinned and ducked his head with embarrassment at the praise. "There was a bit of luck in the timing here. The soldiers rounded the curve just as the pirates nearly reached us, so both halves of our audience were in place. I had planned for at least one, but this way, both of my enemies would believe me dead."

Marcus said quietly, "But your friends believed you were dead, as well."

Otis sighed and looked at his young charge, then out at the larger group of the crew. "I know, lad, and I'm sorry for that. But I needed the pirates and soldiers to believe in my death, so my friends' reactions were very important. I knew it would be hard, but I also knew it wouldn't be for long. On that island, only Captain Penner knew the truth. So Major Hale and Cocklyn, if he'd still be alive, believe I'm gone and they'll look for me no more."

Marcus sighed too. "I understand. I guess we all do. But it was very hurtful, Otis."

"Aye, lad, aye. But done now and another thing we need no more speak of between us." Otis held out his hand and Marcus took it and shook it like a man. "Well, now, story's almost done. I knew that spot on the cliff from being here before. Nearly fell over it for real when we were hiding the treasure those years ago. But that taught me that there was a sturdy wide ledge about five feet below the lip of the bluff and strong vines that lead down the face of the cliff, for a man whose nerve is strong enough to swing out over the ocean. So over I went, and then all I had to do was monkey climb my way down to the sea and wait for my ride." He sat back, took a large drink, and grinned.

"But now what?" Becca asked.

"What about Captain Trevor? He's your friend, and he thinks you're dead." Paige shook her head. "That's not right. And he thought he was getting some treasure. You never planned to give him anything?" Paige's voice rose as she became more offended for Captain Trevor and the poor treatment he received.

"Whoa, my lass, hold on …"

"Hold on nothing. You've treated him really badly, and I don't think that's fair! How could you treat a friend that way?"

"Paige, my girl …"

Paige was on her feet, and she moved closer to Otis. "A friend who didn't betray you all these years and a friend who trusted you not to betray him!" She was up in his face, her annoyance turning to anger. Otis reached out and took her by the shoulders, shaking her lightly.

"Girl! Listen now! No one's been treated falsely here. Captain Penner told Captain Trevor we had a plan, and even now, the *Dolphin* is sailing to a rendezvous with us in a couple of days." Otis patted her arm gently. "Miss Paige, did you hear me? Captain Trevor will not be misused in this."

Paige took a deep breath and stepped back from Otis. "Okay, but … all right. I just … it made me mad to think …"

"I saw that, darlin'." Otis smiled. "Your defense of your friends and rescuers does you proud. But I'd hope you'd trust me too, a little bit."

Paige smiled apologetically. "I do, really. Though you did let me think …" She bit off the last of the remark. "But we'll not speak of that again, right?"

"Just so, dear, just so." Paige sat back down, leaning against Otis's leg. "So now we come to the last of our little plan. We find our buccaneers' bounty." Paige and the others sat bolt upright, questions springing to their lips. "Calm down, calm down. We're not going back to Treasure Island."

"But Major Hale expects to find treasure there. Won't he come after Captain Trevor or even Captain Penner when he doesn't find it?" Becca voiced the concern they all had.

"Not to worry. Major Hale will find exactly the treasure he expects to find. The treasure that belongs to the king, right and true, just as I promised."

"But what bounty … ?"

Otis held up his hands, silencing their questions. "Hear me out now. I've sailed these seas for many long years and taken my share of the Spanish enemy's booty. I've never been one to throw my earnings away on wild women and the devil rum, so I've collected a tidy pile over the years. I've enough hidden away to make this voyage worth the while of every man on board the *Blue Dolphin* and the *Bethany*. I pay my debts and take care of my friends. In two days' time, we'll reach my own treasure island. Pierre, grog for everyone now!" A cheer went up from the men, and the four friends joined in wholeheartedly.

CHAPTER 42

Paige stood in the bow of the *Bethany*, her cheek leaning against the carved curls of the beautiful young woman who was the ship's bowsprit. The wind blew in her face, the refreshing scent of sea salt in her nostrils and her hair streaming back from her scalp. Dolphins raced alongside the boat, leaping and bobbing in the wake that flowed away from the ship. The children had been fortunate enough to see this dolphin dance many times as they had sailed on the *Bethany* and *Blue Dolphin*, but it still brought a smile to Paige's lips as she watched the strong muscles work and heard the chirruping sounds the dolphins used when speaking to each other. She would miss so much about this place, and her eyes misted slightly as she thought of leaving.

She had been standing here for about an hour now, glad no one had come to interrupt her thoughts. Paige knew they were just hours away from leaving Otis, the *Bethany*, and the Caribbean behind. She wanted this last time alone, to take in these last sights and sounds, to impress it all in her memory. She knew they had to go home and supposed that, in fact, she wanted to. But she felt part of a family here, not just good friends with Becca, Marcus, and Jake. They'd been a real family, with Otis as the dad Paige had never known. Back home in Minnesota, the others always included her and she'd never felt like an outsider. But here in the

Caribbean, it was as if they really were related. Living together twenty-four hours a day, relying on each other, caring about each other. Now she knew what family really felt like and she was reluctant to give that up. But Otis belonged in the seventeenth century and they must go back to the twenty-first. But she was already missing what they would have to leave behind.

"You okay, Paige?" Becca's soft question roused Paige from her thoughts. Becca joined her at the railing and smiled as she saw the frolicking dolphins. "I'm going to miss these guys."

"Me too. I'm going to miss a lot."

Becca took her hand. "Being here … it changes … everything, doesn't it?" Paige nodded, unable to speak for fear she'd begin to cry. Becca squeezed her hand. "We're different now. Kinda scary, huh?" They stood side by side for a few minutes, lost in their own thoughts but comfortable with each other's companionship.

Finally, Paige turned away from the bow and looked back over the ship's deck. "What do we tell Otis?"

"What do you mean?"

"Are we just going to disappear? Not say good-bye? That doesn't feel right to me."

Becca cocked her head to one side, thinking. "Hmmm. Hadn't thought about that. But I agree. I don't want to go without saying … something … to Otis." Becca pushed away from the railing. "Let's go find the guys and see what they think."

"Of course we're saying good-bye," Jake said, looking at his sister and Paige as though they were crazy. "Why would you even ask?" Marcus, however, did not respond immediately. His expression was somber, and he looked beyond Jake, even when the younger boy turned to him in appeal. "Marcus, tell them they're being dumb." Not a word. "Marcus?" Still nothing. Becca and Paige held their tongues, waiting for Marcus to figure out exactly how he was going to break it to Jake. "Marcus!"

Marcus finally looked Jake in the eye. "We may not be able to, bud." He put a hand on Jake's shoulder.

"No!" Jake pulled away roughly. "What is wrong with you all? Don't you remember how it felt when Otis died?" Jake shook his head, looking from face to face, confusion painting a look of anger across his features. "Think how he would feel if we just go away."

"Jake, man, listen to me for a minute."

"I can't believe you're so mean! Don't you think he'd search for us, worrying the whole time?"

"I know, but you have to listen—"

"He'd never find us and he'd just keep looking and looking—"

"Jake!" Becca raised her voice in a tone that only an older sister can produce. "Shut up for a second. Let Marcus explain."

"Fine." Jake pressed his lips tightly together and folded his arms across his chest. His brow was drawn in, and anger seemed to radiate from every inch of his skin. Marcus abandoned the smile he had tried to flash at Jake, to soothe his feelings, and his expression became solemn.

"Jake, we can't tell Otis good-bye because we'd have to tell him why we're leaving." Jake's angry look stayed in place. "We can't tell him about the snow globe." Jake did not soften. "He'd never believe us." Jake just shook his head.

Paige said, "You know, I kind of agree with Jake." Jake's eyes lit up, but he stood firm.

"Oh, please, Paige, don't you start," Becca said with a frustrated sigh.

"But I think he's right about something. We're right that we can't tell him why we're leaving. But if we don't tell him something, won't he worry? Wouldn't we kind of ruin things for him by just disappearing?"

Becca opened her mouth to respond but found she didn't know what to say. Marcus looked even more thoughtful than he had a moment before, a small frown line appearing between his eyebrows.

"I'm right, aren't I?" Jake said proudly. "We can't just leave him flat."

Marcus shook his head at Becca. "They're right. And you're right. We've got a real dilemma."

"And about twenty-four more hours to figure it out."

The four friends were silent, each lost in their own thoughts about the puzzle set before them. How could they let Otis know that it was okay when they disappeared? How would they explain the unexplainable? What could they possibly say that he would believe?

"I don't know," Becca groaned. "I don't know how it's possible."

"How can you say 'we're going to vanish, but don't worry,'" Paige wondered.

Jake shrugged. "Just like that, I guess."

Becca rolled her eyes. "Jake, don't be stupid."

"I'm not!" He reached over and punched her in the arm.

"Knock it off!" Becca shoved him back but stopped when Paige laid a hand on her other arm.

"Please don't fight! We haven't got much time to figure this out."

"I just told you," Jake said. "We tell him. That's it."

Marcus spoke up before Jake's comment or attitude could set Becca off again. "Jake, don't be a snot. But you might be right." Jake beamed and both Paige and Becca looked at Marcus with astonishment.

"What are you thinking?"

"Marcus, this is serious."

Marcus held up his hands, quieting the girls' confused remarks. "Think about it. We tell him this wild story, and he thinks we're just being goofy kids. He won't believe it, and we don't have to worry about trying to convince him. But later, when we are actually gone, he'll remember the strange tale we told him … and believe." Marcus said all this with a certainty he surely couldn't be feeling.

"Really? He'll believe? What makes you think that?" Becca said.

"Because he won't have any other explanation," Paige said. "We'll have no other way to get off the island, but we'll be gone. He won't have any other way to explain it."

They were silent again, but the mood had changed drastically. This time, they were all thinking of the surprise that Otis would be left with after they vanished. No worrying, just a wonder at the magic that brought them into his life and took them home again. It seemed a perfect solution—and really, the only option they had.

CHAPTER 43

"Land ho!"

The children ran to the gunwale and saw an island appearing on the horizon. It looked like just a slice of green on the edge of a pool of azure water when they first saw it. It quickly grew in their field of vision, as the *Bethany* flew before the wind. They would arrive at their final destination in the seventeenth century in a very short time.

Otis stepped up behind the children. "We'll have our bounty very soon, my dearies," he said. "Our quest is soon at an end." The children looked at each other, startled. Had Otis read their minds? Did he already know about the globe and its poem? "The treasure will soon be in our hands." Otis put his arms around the children's shoulders. "Where do ye say we set up housekeeping? Did you like Nassau? Or do we sail on a while longer?"

The children had decided that Marcus should be the one to tell their story. Otis always heard Marcus out, even when his ideas might have seemed strange. Marcus turned to face Otis, and the others followed his lead. "Otis, I'm afraid we won't be able to keep sailing or set up with you on land."

Otis cocked his head to one side. "Has old Otis sinned against ye somehow? Are you still angry about my little show at the cliff?"

"No, no, we understand that. And we're glad you did what you did since it saved all our lives. But it's just ... we need to tell you the story of how we came to be marooned with you on that first island."

Otis looked from face to face, seeing a serious tale in each child's eyes. "I can see I'd better be sitting down for this one." He settled on a coil of rope, and the children sat on the deck at his feet. "All right, spin me your yarn, young Marcus."

"Jake, the globe." Jake pulled his backpack off his shoulders and carefully lifted the snow globe out of the pack. It glowed gently, visible even in the bright light of the Caribbean sun. Otis gasped, taken with its beauty and the tiny ship nestled safely within.

"Otis, Becca's aunt left her this snow globe. It's magic and it sent us here to you."

Otis looked at them expectantly. When no one said anything, a more puzzled look grew across his face. "Come on now, children. Tell me the rest of the rig you're trying to run on old Otis."

"No joke, Otis. We've been sent here by magic. Look." Marcus held the globe closer to him, and Otis peered in at the small, detailed ship. "It's the *Bethany*."

"Lad, what is this?" Otis pulled back, his voice irritated. But he'd obviously seen that the small ship was, indeed, the *Bethany*.

"Magic. There's a poem that explains why we were sent here ..." Marcus pulled the small folded paper from the compartment in the base of the globe. He read:

> Weigh anchor, ye lubbers and unfurl the mainsail.
> Brace up your heartstrings; put your courage to the test.
> Hands to your cutlass and look sharp at the gunwale,
> Prick up your ears now and hear the tale of your quest.

> 'Tis booty you're after, a buccaneer's bounty.
> A treasure's been lost and your home is behind you.

Show yourself fearless; worry not for your safety.
Accomplish your task and your history renew.

"We were sent here to help you find your bounty, Otis. We've
done that." Marcus carefully refolded the paper and placed it
back in the base. He wanted to give Otis some time to react to
what he was hearing. The other children watched anxiously to
see how Otis would take their story.

He looked steadily at the children, and Becca couldn't decide
if it was a glare of anger or a stare of disbelief. The moment
stretched, seemed to grow into minutes and even hours as
they waited.

Suddenly, Otis burst into a loud peal of laughter. "Oh my
stars, you children are the clever ones, aren't you?" He bent
forward, laughter shaking him to his very core. "I wonder where
you found that globe. Lovely work that. Did ye all work on that
poem together?" He pointed to Jake. "*Booty* was your word, wasn't
it, lad?" Glee shook him again.

Marcus tried once more, wanting to be sure Otis was left with
the complete message he had to deliver. "Otis, it's true. And it
means, once we've actually gotten you to the treasure, we'll go
back home."

"Oh, and that would be Trafalgar Square in London, I imagine."

"No, a town called Ramsey in Minnesota," Jake offered.

Otis produced another guffaw, louder than any before. "Mini-
so-dah! Oh, Jake, you'll burst my poor heart, making up Red
Indian words like that." Otis stood, still quaking with merriment.
"My dears, you will keep me young with your hijinks, I'm sure."
He turned to head down to the main deck. "Be ready, we'll take
the first longboat ashore as soon as we anchor in the bay." He
walked away, down the stairs, laughing as he went.

"We didn't get to say good-bye," Jake said quietly.

It seemed like only moments before the *Bethany* was closing in on a spot to anchor in the quiet bay of the real treasure island. The children had tried several times to pull Otis aside to tell him good-bye in a meaningful way. But each time he saw them, he broke into peals of laughter, and they couldn't speak to him at all. They resigned themselves to the fact that they might not be able to tell him what was in their hearts before they left this time.

"We did accomplish our goal, however," Marcus reminded them. "When we disappear, at least he'll know we're safe."

Jake was trying to be brave, but it was clear that his heart was broken at the thought of never saying a true farewell to his friend. For once, Becca seemed to understand and didn't tease or prod him to toughen up. She sat next to him on the coil of rope, her arm around his shoulder, letting him know he wasn't alone in his regret.

Paige suddenly looked up from the bale of straw she'd been seated on and picking at. "Hey, why don't we leave him a note?" Jake's eyes light up. "No reason not to, is there? If we don't say anything about being from another time. Just a note saying how much we love him."

Becca jumped to her feet. "That's a great idea! Jake, you've got a pencil in that backpack, don't you? And you must have some paper."

Jake was already pawing through the contents of his bag. "Course I do!" He pulled the pencil out triumphantly. "Me first!"

Marcus grabbed the backpack. "Paper as well, Jake." He dug through the pack, careful not to jar the snow globe. "Come on, man, you must have paper." He dug a bit more. "Here we go ..." He pulled out a folded page from a lined notebook. "Looks like just one piece. So we all have to write on this. Just a couple of lines each."

"Yeah, yeah." Jake flung himself on his stomach in front of the paper and stuck the eraser end of the pencil in his mouth. "Just gotta think."

"We don't have a lot of time," Becca told him, looking toward the gunwale where the seamen were beginning to ready the longboats for launch. "Keep it simple."

"All right, all right." Jake began to write, carefully forming his letters clearly.

> Dear Otis, you never acted like I was a little kid. It was great having adventures with you. I don't think I've ever had more fun. Thank you. Love, Jake.

He pushed himself off the deck and handed the pencil to Paige, who was waiting eagerly. She too plopped on her stomach, but she began to write immediately.

> Otis, you were like a father to all of us. You took care of us and loved us and kept us safe. I will never forget you and will always pray for you. I love you. Paige

Paige sat up, tears sparkling in her eyes as she handed the pencil to Marcus. "Getting very close now," Becca said as they all heard the captain call the order to prepare the anchor.

Marcus didn't answer but sat down and began to write.

> My friend Otis, you are the most unforgettable person I have ever met. You have changed my life for the better, and I will always be grateful. I pray that God will guide you safely always. With my love, Marcus

Marcus handed the pencil to Becca then stood and stepped aside. Becca sat, but almost felt like she couldn't write anything. Her embarrassment over her own behavior toward Otis was almost overwhelming. But she knew she couldn't leave without a word for him. She sat down and began to write.

> Otis, I hope you have forgiven my stubborn behavior and know that I only meant to do good. You taught me a lot,

and I will always be better because of that. Thank you for everything. God loves you, and so do I! Becca

She handed the pencil back to Jake, with a sigh and a lighter heart. "We did it."

"Now we just have to get the note into his pocket."

Paige picked up the note and folded it carefully. "I'll do it. Next time I hug him." The others smiled. Otis wouldn't think anything of a hug from Paige. She'd hugged him regularly almost from the moment they'd arrived.

They all grinned like fools at each other, relieved to have accomplished their good-byes—even if it had to be in this slightly impersonal way. Jake pushed the pencil and globe back into his pack, just as Otis called to them to join him at the longboat. The last leg of their adventure was about to begin.

CHAPTER 44

The longboats were pulled high up into the sand, out of reach of the incoming tide. Otis, the children, and the other crewmen from the *Bethany* were out and preparing to trek inland to the treasure site. The children had all been greatly relieved when Paige had managed to give Otis a hug as they sat next to one another in the boat. She'd slipped the note into his pocket. Now, at least, when the snow globe did its magic, they could be sure Otis would have some kind of explanation, would not worry about them, and would see their good-bye thoughts.

Captain Penner directed most of his men to accompany Otis and the kids. "I'll wait here for Captain Trevor," he said. "He'll be less suspicious of a double-cross that way."

"Aye, he'll take the respect kindly," Otis agreed. Just then, they heard the faint cry of "Sail ho!" from the watchman out on the *Bethany*. Sure enough, the *Blue Dolphin* was coming into view, approaching the island from a different direction than the *Bethany*.

"Get moving, old man," Penner said fondly. "Let's have that treasure back in our hands before nightfall." The treasure hunters slung empty sacks on to their shoulders and marched up the beach toward the forest.

Otis led the way, and initially, the children kept close on his heels. But as the men began to outstride them, they allowed themselves to drift toward the back of the band. They weren't sure how the globe would take them home, if there would be another snowstorm or if they would quietly wink out of this time period. But they had agreed that it might be best if they weren't in the midst of a larger group, if they could help it. So they dropped back and intended to stay there until Otis came to his treasure.

Jake said quietly, "He was planning to keep us with him."

"Of course he was," Paige said. "He's like our dad."

Marcus smiled. "We'll be home with our first families soon. But we'll always have our buccaneer family to remember." He took Paige's hand and squeezed, understanding that she had the least reason to return home to her own family. "And we're really a family now."

Becca said, with a laugh, "Good, you guys can help me keep Jake in line." Her laugh and quick hug made sure that Jake knew this was just a small joke between brother and sister, and he grinned rather than getting angry.

"And you guys can keep her off my back!" He hugged her back. "Some, anyway."

By now, the rest of the group had moved ahead of them, and Otis was out of sight beyond a thicket of overgrown ferns. The children heard a shout, and the other men began running toward the sound. "Treasure!" was the call and the privateers were drawn to it like moths to a flame. The children trotted a few steps as their friends called for them to hurry, but slowed and stopped just as they reached the thicket.

"Can't we look through?" Jake asked. "I'd really like to see a treasure just once."

"We'll never get another chance," Becca said. They pushed through the ferns and saw the treasure cavern.

It wasn't a very deep cave, actually, more like a hollow in the limestone cliff face. Otis and a few of the men had partially pulled aside a thick patch of thornbush limbs that had been stuffed in amongst a growing thicket of the strong, prickly plant. It had thoroughly covered the opening of the shallow cave and the sharp, strong thorns would have kept anyone from looking too closely. The treasure had lain safely behind its protective barrier for years and no one had suspected. Of course, this island was so remote there likely hadn't been many visitors to hide from.

Otis had told the children in the longboat that this island was not known to many, as it was so small and off the regular shipping routes. He and Captain Trevor had been careful not to visit or even go too near the area over the years. The kids had come to realize that, in this time, there were not even maps of everywhere in the world. In a way that would never be possible in their own time, a small corner of the world like this could stay hidden.

As the men continued to pull and tug at the thorny barricade, the kids could see past them to the treasure. Small wooden chests were stacked against the back of the cave. In front of those lay rotting burlap bags, which spilled their contents out on to the ground. "Gold!" Jake said.

Coins were heaped on the bottom of the cave, shining brightly even through the dusting of sand that had blown through the thick barrier of thorns over the years. Becca saw golden cups and plates. Marcus had told them all the Spanish had stolen the golden ware from the Aztecs, who had used it in their worship of their gods. Much of it, they had melted down into bars and coins, but some was still intact. The Spanish corsairs had also raided British ships, just as they had been raided by pirates. It would have been almost impossible to tell who should receive this bounty back, as it was sure to have passed through too many hands to count.

Their friends in the *Bethany* crew were, as expected, going crazy with excitement. They laughed loudly and ran their hands through the piles of coins. They clapped each other on the back, congratulating themselves on their good fortune. A few even danced some jig steps in the dirt.

Otis stood back, a huge grin on his face. Becca could see his pleasure in sharing with his friends. His crewmates would haul this all back to the beach, split the booty with Trevor and his men, and put this whole dangerous episode behind them. A perfect ending.

Except for one thing. The kids were still here.

"He's found his bounty," Becca said. "Why haven't we gone?"

Marcus reached into Jake's backpack and pulled out the globe. It was still glowing, but nothing else was happening. "I don't know. It seems we've finished our quest."

Jake said nervously, "Aren't we going home? What about Mom and Dad? We have to go home." Becca patted his shoulder.

Paige said, "It's still glowing. We're still on the right track. There's just something missing."

They all looked around the clearing, trying to figure out what was out of place. But it seemed like they'd done all they were supposed to do.

"We were brave. We went on, even when it wasn't safe." Paige shook her head. "What could it be?"

Becca felt her shoulders droop. It was too much. They'd gotten Otis to his treasure and still they hadn't gone home. She let her legs follow the lead of her shoulders and dropped slowly to the ground. "I just want to go home!" she moaned.

Paige sat beside her. "Don't worry, Becca. We'll think of something. It'll be okay."

"I … I just can't anymore. I've tried and I've tried. We've traveled through time, landed with pirates, had our ship blown up from under us. I've been chased and almost caught by a cutthroat. I just want my mom and dad and my own bed and my backyard. What else can I do?" Becca covered her face with her hands.

The boys knelt beside her as well, forming a small circle. Marcus set the glowing globe in the center. Their attention was all on their tired, upset sister and none of them noticed that the glow had grown stronger. Marcus reached over to touch Becca's arm and Jake leaned forward, his hands on Paige's and Marcus's shoulders. The snow globe glowed, flared, and the wind suddenly grew stronger. The children huddled close to comfort their friend, hoping to dry her tears, and the wind howled. White flakes flew around them, as though the snow globe had suddenly reached out and pulled them inside.

"Becca!" Jake was the first to notice. "The snow! It's working!"

All the children looked up to see the wind-swirled flakes surrounding them. The snow grew thick, so dense now that they could no longer see their friends on the island. They were enfolded in the flakes and wind, louder and whiter, blowing them closer to one another and to the globe. They tried to keep their eyes open to see the trip this time, but the sharp gusts forced them to squint and then, suddenly, they were gone.

CHAPTER 45

A cardinal's call trilled sweetly, bringing Becca back to the world. She felt grass, lush and soft, beneath her cheek. Grass? Not sand? Becca opened her eyes and sat up. Home? She quickly looked for her family—Jake, Paige, and Marcus. They were sprawled on the grass right with her, opening their eyes. Good, they were all safe. Looking around, she spied the back of their house—home! They'd made it home!

Becca stood slowly, grabbing Paige's hand and helping her up. Marcus and Jake jumped up, looking around the Kincaid backyard as though they'd never seen it before.

"We made it!"Jake shouted, laughter in his voice. "We're home!"

Paige put her arms out and spun slowly. "It's beautiful. Minnesota is beautiful!"

They listened to the birds singing, felt the gentle June breeze caress their cheeks, and dropped back into the soft, sweet smelling grass beneath their feet. "The Caribbean was gorgeous," Becca said, pulling a handful of grass up to her nose, sniffing deeply. "But Minnesota summers ... I was afraid we'd miss it all."

"How long do you think we've been gone?" Jake asked. "What're we going to tell Dad?"

Marcus squinted up into the sunny sky. "Well, whatever day it is, it's not even noon yet."

Just then, the back door to the house was thrown open, and Becca and Jake's dad stepped out on to the steps. "Hey, you all are staying for lunch, right?"

Becca ran to her father and wrapped her arms around his waist. "Dad ..."

Laughing, he leaned forward and hugged Becca back. "What brings this on, my darling daughter?" He pushed her bangs off her forehead and gave her a quick kiss. "Worried that I'm still mad about this morning?"

"This morning ... what ... oh, yeah. It was a stupid fight. I'm ... I'm just sorry to be so stubborn sometimes."

Mr. Kincaid hugged her to his chest again. "Baby girl. I know." He straightened and saw Jake standing near. "You come to apologize too?"

"Yes, sir." Jake reached up for a hug and his dad gave him one. He looked up at the two sheds in the yard.

"I see you've made a good start. Working together," he said.

"It's been fun," Becca said. "We ... uh ... had a good morning."

Mr. Kincaid waved to Marcus and Paige, who had stepped closer. "Kids, you'll have lunch with us, won't you? Paige, I'm making your favorite grilled cheese."

"Yes, we'll stay," Marcus said. "Thanks!"

"Thanks, Mr. Kincaid."

"All righty—just a bit longer then. I'll call when it's time to wash up." With a final squeeze to Becca's shoulder and a pat on Jake's head, Mr. Kincaid headed back into the kitchen.

Becca looked disbelievingly at her friends. "It's the same day, the same morning."

"Well, it's magic," Paige said. "I guess the globe can do whatever it wants."

"The globe!" Jake said. "Where is it?" They all turned and ran back across the yard to where they'd awoken just a few minutes before. The globe lay on its side, in the grass, and they all sat down around it.

Marcus pulled the snow globe toward him. "It got us home, just like the poem said."

"It's different, though, isn't it?" Paige questioned. "Doesn't it look different?"

Becca looked closely. "It does … It's not glowing."

Marcus held it up, turning it to catch the sun. "You're right. Just regular glass shining normally in the sunshine."

Jake reached out, took the globe from Marcus, and shook it gently. The snow lifted off the bottom of the globe, swirled gently, and settled back down. "Just a snow globe."

Paige said, "We must have used up the magic—at least for now." She took the globe from Jake and cradled it gently in her arms. "We'll never see Otis again." She gazed sadly at the tiny ship, with its tiny bowsprit leaning into the wind. "The *Bethany* is just a memory." She looked up. "Or was it all just some kind of dream?"

"All of us, having the same dream?" Becca shook her head. "Don't think so."

"Still," Paige said sadly. "I wish we'd been able to bring something back with us. Something to prove we were really there, that we really helped Otis."

"Yeah," Jake said. "We don't know if we really helped Otis. We didn't get to see if he got the treasure to the king—and got the soldiers off his back."

Marcus took the globe and gazed deeply into the interior. "It would be nice to have some closure, wouldn't it? To know we really made a difference."

Becca sighed. "We're just going to have to live with the fact that this dull, non-sparkly globe is all we've got left of our adventure." She frowned. "That kind of takes the joy out it, doesn't it?"

Marcus was squinting at the globe, turning it to one side, then the other. "There's something else different about the globe … it's not just that it's no longer glowing. Something else has changed. What is it?"

Becca peered into the globe as well, staring at the ship. Then she shouted "The flag! Look at the flag!"

Marcus laughed happily. "Yes, that's it! We did it."

"What are you talking about?" Paige asked.

"Here, let me set it in the light." Marcus set the globe on the top of the box it once nestled inside. "Look carefully at the flag on the main mast of the *Bethany*. Do you see it? See the difference?"

Paige and Jake examined the flag intently. Then they saw it. On the main mast, at the very tip, waved the flag of the good ship *Bethany*. When they'd first seen the snow globe, a bloodred flag with a skull and crossbones had flown on this mast. But now ... now there flew a festive red, white, and blue banner.

"That's not our flag," Jake said, puzzled.

Marcus nodded. "That's right. It's not the flag of the United States. It's the flag of Great Britain—England."

Becca grinned. "The flag of the king!"

"The king?" Jake looked up at his friend, Marcus. "I don't get it ..."

Marcus clapped Jake on the shoulder. "A pirate ship doesn't fly the flag of the king. A pirate ship might fly some random flag, trying to fool a victim vessel. But this flag is preserved here through the ages—from Otis's time to ours. The ship isn't running a rig—she's a king's vessel now."

Jake's eyes lit up. "Oh! I get it. The *Bethany* isn't pirating anymore!"

Paige clapped her hands and danced a jig step she'd learned on the *Bethany*. "We did change something! We helped! They're back in the good graces of the king and country, just like Otis wanted. Oh, I'm so glad. It wasn't just a dream."

"We made a difference, despite everything." Becca sighed happily. "When I think of all that could have gone wrong."

"But it didn't," Paige laughed. She grabbed Jake's hands and pulled him into an impromtu dance with her.

Marcus bowed deeply to Becca, and they joined Paige and Jake, dancing to the sound of the concertina tune they could all still hear, ringing in their memories. They danced for the joy of a quest completed, for the delight of the friends they'd made, for the happy memories they would always hold close. They danced and then collapsed, laughing, to the lush grass in the Kincaid backyard.

They talked excitedly of their recent adventure, of all the obstacles they'd overcome, the dangers they'd come through. They spoke of their friends from centuries ago, friends whom they would never see again, but whose lessons they would never forget. Their excitement settled into contentedness, happy with their memories and happy to be home.

Finally, Becca stood and walked over to the globe and the box that waited to contain it once again. She lifted the globe once more and stroked it gently before opening the box.

Jake gasped quietly. "Look at the other globes." Indeed, all of the other snow globes in the box glowed gently, their magic alive and awaiting their time to shine out.

Becca carefully set the *Bethany* globe back into its protective wrapping. The dimness of its glass stood out, a gray mate to the other sparkling adventures that awaited the children.

"Looks a little sad," Paige said.

"Sure, but look at all the other places we'll have to go."

"New quests," Marcus said, touching a glowing globe.

Jake grinned. "New adventures. Where will we go next?"

Just then, their father appeared at the back door. "Kids, come wash up!" he called.

"Lunch," Becca said. "Looks like the next place we go is lunch!"